ALSO BY DOUGLAS SKELTON

FICTION

The Janus Run
Tag – You're Dead
Open Wounds
Devil's Knock
Crow Bait
Blood City

NON-FICTION

Glasgow's Black Heart: A City's Life of Crime
Dark Heart: Tales from Edinburgh's Town Jail
*Indian Peter: The Extraordinary Life and Adventures
of Peter Williamson*
Bloody Valentine: Scotland's Crimes of Passion
Deadlier Than the Male: Scotland's Most Wicked Women
Scotland's Most Wanted
Devil's Gallop
A Time to Kill
No Final Solution
Frightener (with Lisa Brownlie)
Blood on the Thistle

THE DEAD DON'T BOOGIE

A case for Dominic Queste

Douglas Skelton

CONTRABAND

Contraband is an imprint of Saraband
Published by Saraband,
Digital World Centre
1 Lowry Plaza
The Quays, Salford, M50 3UB
www.saraband.net

ISBN: 9781910192443
ebook: 9781910192450

Printed in the EU on sustainably sourced paper.

10 9 8 7 6 5 4 3

Prologue

The scene was pure film noir. Robert Mitchum or Dick Powell or Alan Ladd should have been sitting where I was. The cop should've been some bit player.

But this wasn't an old black and white crime movie. This was all real.

The room was dark apart from the single spot casting an inverted V of light onto the small wooden table, the empty chair opposite and the man on his feet, leaning towards me. I knew there were two other people in the room because I'd seen them come in. If I strained I could make out dim shapes in the darkness, but I didn't feel like straining. I was tired. I was worried. Truth be told, I was downright freaked out.

The man giving me his best hard stare had been up all night, by the looks of it. His chin was roughened by stubble, his breath smelled of too much coffee. He had taken his jacket off about an hour before and it dangled on the back of his chair like Igor the hunchback. I could see he was exhausted, could see it in the redness in his eyes and the deep lines on his face, hear it in the rawness of his voice, but he still kept at me, probing, questioning, trying to trip me up. But I fooled him, I fooled them all. I told him the truth. Mostly.

'Let's go over it again, Queste,' he said.

'We've already been over it three times,' I said. My voice seemed distant, alien somehow, the words slightly slurred even though I hadn't touched a drop. I needed a drink, though. I needed a few.

'And we'll keep going over it until I get it straight in my head,' he said. 'Why were they after the girl?'

'I don't know.'

'Who is this guy Sykes?'

1

'I don't know.'

'You made him up, didn't you?'

'No. Check the CCTV tape from the car park. He'll be on it.'

He had nothing to say to that and I wondered why. He sighed and straightened, running his hand through his thinning hair. I saw him glance into the gloom, as if taking instruction from one of the others who had sat quietly throughout the interrogation. Maybe he had a clearer view, I don't know. Certainly neither of them said a word that I could hear.

He looked back at me and his face was tight, his voice hoarse. 'Seven dead, Queste.'

It was my turn to have nothing to say. I knew how many were dead and it wasn't seven. There were more. And something told me it wasn't over yet.

He sighed, his tone as patient as he could make it. 'So let's hear it again, Queste.'

'Where do you want me to begin this time?'

'Let's go back to the beginning. From when you found the girl.'

It wasn't a film noir and I wasn't Bob or Dick or Al.

But that didn't mean there couldn't be flashbacks...

Chapter One

I found Jenny Deavers in one of those old-fashioned seaside cafés that I didn't think existed these days.

It hadn't been that difficult to track her down, but I wouldn't tell the client that. We're in a recession and Jenny's Aunt Jessica looked as if she had a bob or two to spare, so I fully intended inflating the cost of the search. Not too much, just enough to make her think that I'd worked my backside off tracing her niece.

The thing about kids like Jenny is that they know their rights, they know what they're due, so even if they decide to vanish into the night – as Jenny had done four years before – they still want their benefits. I've got a guy in the Department of Works and Pensions who, for a small consideration, can slip me a few details now and then. He doesn't give me their addresses, but he will tell me the office where they sign on. He's got principles, my guy, and I can understand that. I used to have a few of them myself.

It doesn't always work – hell, what does? – but this time he came up trumps. He told me that a Jennifer Deavers, aged 20, was registered at the Saltcoats JobCentre, so armed with that information and a photo supplied by Aunt Jessica, I climbed onto my trusty steed – more accurately, a rusty Ford – and made my way to the Ayrshire coast. I hadn't been in Saltcoats since I was a boy, back when towns like this were holiday centres for thousands of Glaswegians. It was the mid-sixties when I'd been there last, and the package holiday boom had not yet introduced the common man to the lure of paella, cheap wine and bullfighting. My only hazy recollection of one holiday to Saltcoats was of walking to the harbour at night with my father and my sister. Memories can play funny tricks and I always visualised a lighthouse at the harbour, a big white thing, but there isn't one, I discovered. The lighthouse must be a remnant of another part of my childhood, but God knows what. Also, for some reason, that stroll down memory lane to Saltcoats harbour is sound-tracked by the song Michael, Row the Boat Ashore. Don't ask me why, because I really don't know. My mother doesn't appear in that memory. But then, she never does appear in the good ones.

The grey sea rolled against the solid stone of the harbour and the tang of salt water hung in the moist air. If it had been a clear day, I might not've seen forever, but I would've seen the jagged profile of the Isle of Arran rising out of the Firth of Clyde. But the sky was dark and low and merged with the surface of the water. Nothing else of the town sparked any further happy recollections. Not that I have many of my childhood right enough, happy or otherwise. Some people recall things from their formative years, but not me. There are shadows, fragments of the past that play out in my mind now and then, like out-of-focus scenes from a movie, but they're just clips with no context, no subplot, and I really don't know what it's all about. But not knowing what it's all about is the story of my life.

I hit all the places you might expect to find a teenage girl on the cusp of womanhood. I called in at bars and clubs and amusement arcades and chippies and kebab shops. I stopped by the library and asked them to haul out copies of the electoral register and went through it laboriously street by street, name by name, but that was a non-starter, not only because I knew she hadn't been in the town long enough to register, but also because youngsters like Jenny don't vote. But I did it to be thorough. I am nothing if not dedicated.

I tried not to ask too many people about her, or show her picture too often, because you never can tell what could get back to my quarry and scare her off. So I sipped fresh orange and soda and coffee and shot at aliens on screens and even found a pinball machine, which took me back to Butlin's Holiday Camp down the coast near Ayr, another clip from the past. I walked the streets of the town and I studied faces, trying to pick out the one among the many, until finally I ended up at a café wedged on a side street between a tattoo parlour and that bastion of the modern-day high street, a charity shop. It was around seven on a damp April night and I'd been schlepping round the town all afternoon, so I was tired and I was hungry and my mouth was shaped for a greasy burger and fries. My body may well be a temple, but I wasn't above desecrating it.

Joe's Cafe, it was called. Not particularly original, but it suited the place. It had a hackneyed look about it, as if it had been transported from the early 1960s into the 21st century. It boasted Formica-covered tables with plastic chairs and a few alcoves along the tiled wall with faux leather benches. The counter ran the entire length, with a row of bar stools in front and a hatch in the wall behind revealing the small kitchen. The décor was yellow and green and it probably hadn't changed since the days of vinyl and the hit parade. It was cheap and it was tacky and it was down-at-heel. I felt right at home.

The young girl behind the counter listlessly flicking through her mobile phone didn't look like a Joe to me, but I couldn't resist sliding into one of the high chairs in front of her, giving her my best grin and saying, 'How's it going, Joe?'

She looked up from the fascinating world of Twitter and frowned. 'Whit?' she said, and that one word carried with it all the cosmopolitan promise of the establishment.

'Sorry,' I said, picking up a plastic-covered menu from the counter top, 'thought you were somebody else.'

My eyes ran down the list of tasty treats on offer, mostly fried, although there was a salad roll on offer to appease the health conscious. 'So,' I said, 'what do you recommend?'

'Wouldnae know,' she said, her attention having returned to her screen to find out who had washed their hair that morning, her thumb jerking like a hitch-hiker with a twitch. 'I don't eat here.'

'Good to know,' I replied and laid the menu back down. 'Just gimme a cheeseburger and chips, then. Mug of tea would be nice too.'

She grudgingly thrust her phone into the pocket of her remarkably clean apron and headed towards the kitchen. That's what I like about the country of my birth – service with a sigh. VisitScotland must love this place.

I swivelled round on the stool and studied the rest of the customers. It's something I did when I was writing for a living, and it's stayed with me. The joint was not exactly jumping. An old man with a face like a stained and wrinkled bedsheet sat in the corner, nursing a cup of tea. Three young guys were in one of the alcoves, hunched over cups of coffee, talking about nothing and really knowing what they were talking about. But it was the final customer who caught my attention. She had her back to me but as I surveyed the room she glanced round, giving me a glimpse of her profile, and right away I was sure it was Jenny. Sometimes it happens like that - you waste a lot of shoe leather and then you trip right over them. It's a funny old world.

I heard the cheap meat of the frozen burger spitting on the grill and the hiss of the frozen chips being immolated in the deep fat, so I knew I had time. Standing against the wall near the girl was an old Rock-Ola jukebox – it was that kind of place – so I slid off the stool and sauntered over, my hand digging in my pocket for some pound coins. I wanted to have a better look at her, and I knew I could sneak a few glances as I made my selections.

I surmised the owner was a child of the sixties, hence the jukebox. They're not too popular in these days of iPods and MP3 players. When I studied the playlist, I knew he was around my age, as there wasn't a track beyond 1975. I silently blessed a kindred spirit and fed in some coins – I was surprised it didn't take shillings – then punched a few buttons and waited until the machine found the first track. It was The Shadows twanging through Apache.

A casual peek at the girl confirmed she was who I thought she was. I didn't need to take the picture out to look at it, I'd seen it so often that afternoon that it was burned into my mind, like an image that's been too long on a computer screen. She'd lost a bit of weight since the photo had been taken and there were lines around the eyes that told me she'd lived a little since she ran away from her auntie. Seen things, done things that a young woman of 20 shouldn't be seeing or doing. She still bore the freckles across her nose that I'd noticed in the snap. Her light brown hair was longer and tied back away from her face. In other girls from the west of Scotland this might have appeared severe, but it worked for her. Her eyes looked brown, but her Aunt Jessica had told me they were hazel and sometimes took on a greenish tinge. So did mine, but it was a while since a woman had looked into them long enough to notice.

She caught me looking at her and there was a silent challenge as she held my gaze. I could've looked away, but I didn't. She could've looked away, but she didn't. Plucky kid, not about to let some old man creep her out. Yes, Jenny Deavers had been around a bit since she left the comfort of her Glasgow West End home.

'Seen plenty?' she asked. Question number one in the Mastermind challenge, specialist subject Glasgow. She had a tough exterior, all housing scheme and rent arrears, but I knew it was an act, for her Aunt Jessica was as West End as fondue parties.

I smiled. 'You're Jenny, right? Jenny Deavers?'

The hardness in her eyes turned to mush and she shifted slightly in her seat. I saw her body tense as she flicked a glance at the door, no doubt gauging the distance.

'Your Aunt Jessica sent me,' I said, trying to sound as reassuring as I could.

'I've no got an Aunt Jessica,' she said, her eyes growing hard again.

I'd been expecting that. Aunt Jessica had told me she would probably deny her existence. My mind flashed back to the meeting I'd had with her the week before. Jessica Oldfield was an uptown, up-tempo woman and had looked out of place in the old-fashioned Glasgow bar on Woodlands Road, but I didn't have an office, my clientele being mainly referrals. It was a downtown, downbeat kind of place, and I was a downtown, downbeat guy – thank you Randy Edelman – but the owner knew me and didn't mind me meeting all kinds of folk in his lounge bar. Just by walking in, she gave the place a boot up the class and I was sure the owner was already inflating the price of his drinks and digging out the cocktail umbrellas for the pints of real ale.

Her ash-blonde hair was cut short, her blue eyes were confident and her make-up so skilfully applied it would've made Max Factor applaud. She wore a powder-blue trouser suit that accentuated her figure. She was in her forties, but could pass for 30. I could've fallen in love with her right then and there, but decided to be professional. It wasn't easy, because I'm a pushover for blondes. And brunettes. And redheads. I've even fantasised about that bald woman in the first Star Trek movie.

'I understand you find people,' Aunt Jessica had said in her cut-glass voice.

'Sometimes,' I said.

'Eamonn O'Connor tells me you're the best.'

Good old Eamonn, always steering something my way. He was a decent guy, for a lawyer.

'Eamonn's very kind – although I do pay him a lot of money to say nice things.'

She gave me a small smile, which was more than I deserved. 'I'd like you to find my niece.'

She pushed the photograph across the small table towards me and that was the first time I clapped eyes on Jenny Deavers.

'She's only 15 in this,' Jessica said, almost apologetically, 'but it's the most recent I've got. She ran away a few months after this was taken, just as she turned 16.'

Smart girl, I thought. Smart enough to know the age of majority in Scotland was 16, so if the police ever approached her, she could tell them where to go.

I looked at the photo without picking it up, because in my mind to handle it would be tantamount to accepting the job. I didn't do contracts, I didn't do formal minutes of agreement. I knew that as soon as I touched the snapshot I would be in, and I'm never certain I'm going to take a job until I actually take it. I've lost a lot of money through indecision. Or maybe it's just laziness. Really can't make up my mind which way.

So I eyed the photo on the table top and asked, 'Why'd she run off?'

Aunt Jessica's blue eyes looked pained. 'Jenny could be difficult and I...well, I resented my life being turned upside down when she came to live with me. She's my sister's child. When she died, I took her in. I'd been divorced for two years by then, happily divorced, and I'd organised my life very nicely, thank you. I really did not need a stroppy child coming in and messing up my little nest. I'm afraid I was not as warm as I should have been. Jenny was only eight when Bernie – my sister, Bernice – was killed.'

'Killed?'

'A fire in her home. Luckily, Jenny was staying with friends that night or she would've died too. My sister had...issues, I suppose you'd say. She was never the most stable person and had a habit of getting in with the wrong people. The wrong *kind* of people, if you know what I mean?'

I nodded, knowing exactly what she meant. There were those who said I was the wrong kind of people.

'Anyway,' Jessica went on with a sigh, 'it seems Bernie was drunk or drugged or whatever and she set fire to the place somehow. A lit cigarette, probably. She was never a particularly caring mother and I'm afraid I didn't make up for that during the time Jenny was with me.'

'And what about her father?'

Aunt Jessica's eyes clouded. 'Long gone. Dead, perhaps. Certainly not in the picture, anyway.'

I nodded and stared at the smiling face in the photograph, seeing a young girl who should have had everything to live for but who clearly felt she had nothing worth staying around for.

'I want to make it up to her,' said Jessica. 'I want her back home where she belongs. I know she was in London for a time because I hired a private detective who managed to trace her to some dingy flat in Fulham. But she denied she even had an Aunt Jessica and in the time he took to check back with me she'd moved on.'

'What makes you think she's back here?'

Jessica slid an envelope across the table top. 'This arrived last week.'

I picked up the envelope, studied the handwriting. Nice script, clear, confident, and I was impressed because I didn't think young folk knew how to write letters these days. Emails could be traced, though. It had a Kilmarnock postmark but that didn't mean anything, although it did suggest the girl was in Ayrshire. At least it would be a starting point for my DWP guy. The letter itself was short, to the point, the gist being she was a big girl now and wished to be left alone. She had a new life and she was happy.

'Sounds like she wants to stay missing,' I said.

'I don't think she knows what she wants, Mister Queste. And that's not the letter of someone who is happy. She would've expanded more, talked of a job, friends, of a boyfriend, a husband even. She needs to be home, she needs me. I'm all she's got. She's a lost soul and Eamonn tells me that's what you do, you find lost souls.'

I stared into her eyes and saw in them a plea for help, which doesn't come easily to people like Aunt Jessica. I also saw guilt, knew she was only a moment's hesitation on my part from getting down and begging, and I couldn't have that. She would've got the knees of her designer trousers dirty.

That was when I picked up the photograph from the table top.

Now here I was, face to face with Jenny Deavers. Eamonn was right – I found lost souls. It's what I did occasionally. But sometimes, it's better if those souls stayed lost.

Chapter Two

Jenny Deavers had managed to regain her tough composure but I knew she was rattled. I had to be careful how I played this, because she could easily bolt and I was in no condition to pursue a 20-year-old through the streets. Anyway, I could see the girl whose name wasn't Joe coming out of the kitchen with my burger and chips and I was hungry enough to eat it without wondering what was in it. She dropped the plate in front of the bar stool I'd been sitting in, then frowned when she saw me chatting to Jenny. I practically saw the words *dirty old man* form on her lips as she gave me a look that would require considerable dry-cleaning before being introduced to polite society.

That did not concern me now, though. I turned my attention to Jenny again.

'Your auntie really wants you back, Jenny,' I said.

'Told you, don't have an auntie,' she said, looking down at the empty plate in front of her. 'So why don't you just piss off before I call the police.'

The girl who still wasn't Joe had moved round the counter to the three young men. She leaned over the table and whispered something. I saw her head jerk once towards me and three cropped heads swivelled in unison.

'Jenny,' I said, 'I've a feeling I've not much time here, but let me tell you that your auntie is sorry, really sorry, for everything. She's worried about you and she wants to take care of you.'

She gave a small, humourless laugh and shook her head slightly. 'Don't need no looking after, do I?'

'We all need looking after, hen.'

A scrape of a chair leg drew my attention back to the young men. The largest of the three was on his feet and on his way towards me. I sighed inwardly. It always had to be the big one. He was wearing a grey-coloured hoodie, dark tracksuit bottoms and white trainers. He was a picture in monochrome. His hair was blonde and cropped so tightly he looked bald. There was a sparse crop of darker bristles on his chin, but none on his upper lip. Maybe he was keeping it clear for the tough guy sneer he was showing me.

'Haw, mate – you botherin' this lassie?' Sir Galahad proving the age of chivalry is not dead. If she'd dropped her handkerchief, he'd be sure to kick it back over to her.

I kept my voice light. 'Just having a word. That right, eh, Jenny?'

Jenny looked up at me first, then at the youth. I saw something approaching amusement in her eye as she realised this was an opportunity to get rid of me. 'He's chattin' me up, Ryan. Wantin' me to go back to his place. He's a perv, so he is.'

'That right?' Ryan drew himself up to his not-inconsiderable full height and his sneer seemed set in stone. I wondered if he'd had it tattooed on next door. 'Maybe you should just bugger off, mate, know what I mean?'

I sighed. 'Listen – Ryan, is it?' He nodded. 'Listen, Ryan – despite what she says, I'm here on business...'

'Aye, funny business,' laughed Ryan, and glanced back at his mates for approval. They dutifully sniggered. The girl who would always be Joe to me didn't laugh, she simply stood there with her arms folded, treating me to a stern expression.

She shouted, 'You gonnae have a giggle or you gonnae throw the old letch out, Ryan?

I was getting pretty tired of being called old by this time, even if to them I must appear ancient. I glanced at the other man in the café, giving him a look that said us middle-aged blokes needed to stick together, though he had at least twenty years on me. Either that or he had a hard paper round. However, he shook his head to tell me I was on my own. So much for brotherhood.

Ryan waved an appeasing hand at Joe and turned back to me. 'Think you'd better leave, mate,'

I gave him my best Clint Eastwood glare, but I guess he'd never seen Dirty Harry, because it didn't scare him one bit. His two pals edged forward, the notion of giving an old geezer a hiding clearly being the ideal way to liven up a dull Tuesday night. I turned my attention back to Jenny, who smiled back, proud of herself.

'Your auntie's not giving up on you, Jenny. And she's paying me not to give up too. You can move on, but I'll find you.'

She wrinkled up her nose. 'How can you be so sure?'

'Because it's what I do.'

Ryan grew impatient with our conversation and placed a hand on my shoulder. I'm sure he meant to be gentle, but it was such a big hand it felt like someone had a laid a brick on me. I thought about making an issue of it. Mossad, the Israeli security service, developed a form of self-defence called Krav Maga and as payment for helping him find his runaway daughter, an Edinburgh martial arts instructor gave me a few lessons that he said would help keep me safe. The idea is to hit fast, hit hard and hit where it hurts. It sounds easy, but it's not that simple. Man is built for fight or flight, with flight almost always taking the upper hand. We want to pull away from trouble, but with Krav Maga, my instructor told me, you move in closer. I probably could've brought Ryan down, but there were his pals to consider. I was far from an expert and had no desire to spend the night in some Ayrshire nick.

'Okay, Ryan,' I said, hands raised in a placating manner, 'no need to get physical here. I'm going.'

I nodded once to Jenny, who shrugged in return, before picking my way between the tables back to the counter. I shoved a couple of chips into my mouth then plucked a handful of paper napkins from a metal holder and used them to wrap up my cheeseburger. I was still hungry and there was no way I was leaving that place without my dinner. I fished around in my trouser pocket and dropped a fiver on the counter. I was overpaying and I knew it, but sometimes you just have to make a grand gesture. Then, with a breezy wave to Joe, who was still glaring at me with such intensity I feared it would burn my burger, I walked out as quickly as my machismo would allow.

A light rain wafted through the air as I crossed the road to where

I'd parked my car. I settled myself into the driver's seat and took a bite of the burger, mentally berating myself for not squirting some ketchup on before I left. As I chewed, I reached into the pocket of my brown leather jacket and hauled out my mobile phone. It was a good few years old, but was small and compact, which I liked. It didn't access the internet, it didn't send emails and it didn't let me update my Facebook status – as if I had one – but it made calls and it sent texts and it took photographs, which was a handy tool in my business. I rifled around in the other pocket as I took another bite of the burger, which wasn't that bad even without ketchup. My pal Joe might've been a hard-faced wee bitch, but she knew how to singe beef. I'd scribbled Aunt Jessica's number in the margin of a copy of *The Sun* that had been lying on the table in the pub. If I'd been organised, I'd have programmed it into my phone, but no-one ever accused me of being organised where technology was concerned. I wedged the torn sliver of newsprint between two fingers of the hand holding my burger and raised it to the side window to catch the orange glow of the street light while I punched the number in with the other. It rang three times before Jessica answered it.

'It's Dominic Queste,' I said. 'I've found her.'

There was a pause then, which surprised me. I thought she would've been delighted, but when she spoke there was little animation in her voice. 'Very well, Mister…em…'

Her voice trailed off and I waited, expecting her to request details, but she said nothing. I decided to fill the void. 'I'm not with her right now and as you expected, she doesn't want to come back. I need to know what you want me to do.'

There was another gap in the conversation then and I began to get a bad feeling about this, as they said in all the *Star Wars* movies. I said, 'Mrs Oldfield?'

'Yes, I'm here. I'm thinking.'

'She's in Saltcoats and I know where she is right now, but that may not be the case shortly…'

'I understand.' Her voice sounded hurried and I felt she didn't want me to say anything further. I also had the strong impression that she was not alone. Don't ask me why, just a gut feeling. I get them sometimes. And occasionally they're right.

'May I call you back, Mister…em, perhaps later this evening? It's not convenient to talk at the moment.'

It was my turn to fall silent, just for a second, while I processed this. Not convenient? She's been searching for this girl, so why was Aunt Jessica not jumping up and down with glee? Why did she not want details of where Jenny was? And why didn't she say my name? I didn't believe she'd forgotten it, it's not easily forgotten, she just didn't want to use it again. I was now totally convinced my gut was right, that someone was listening and she did not want that person learning anything further. I wondered who this person was. I wondered why Jessica wanted them kept out of it. I wondered a lot of things, but all I said was, 'Sure. I'll await your call.' Jessica was paying the piper and it was my job to keep the chanter between my teeth and squeeze the sheep's bladder.

I pressed the red button with my thumb to end the call and dropped the phone onto the passenger's seat. I settled back to finish my burger, all the while watching the door to Joe's Café through the rain-speckled windscreen. I was still hungry and I wished I'd grabbed more of the chips too. I clicked the radio on just in time to hear the final couple of minutes of Tobacco Road by the Nashville Teens, one of my favourites from the sixties, and then the beginning of a commercial break, which are never my favourites. The first ad had a shouty man selling double glazing at the top of his voice, as if yelling at me would make me believe every claim he made, while the second was about the impending visit of Ritt Bobak, an American evangelist, to the Exhibition Centre in Glasgow. Ritt Bobak, what the hell kind of name was that? Not that I was one to talk, right enough, for you won't find many Dominic Questes in the Glasgow phone book. I recalled his face from the newspapers – a big American, handsome and as slick as an oil leak off Florida. He was on a mission to save Britain from the dangers of socialism, liberality and, judging by his toothpaste-ad smile, poor oral hygiene. I didn't like him on principle. I hit the button to find another station, finally settling on Classic FM, which would be fine until they played opera. Or plinky-plonky piano music. Or the first commercial break. I'm very easily put off.

The old man came out of the café first, produced a telescopic umbrella from a plastic Asda bag he was carrying, and walked down the road, the brolly tipped against the rain. Half an hour later, Ryan and his buddies came out. They pulled up their hoodies, but apart from that they ignored the weather, because they were tough guys and tough guys don't care about getting wet. They slouched away, their hands buried deep in their pockets, probably still talking about nothing but by now well on their way to a PhD in the subject.

Jenny came out shortly after. From where I sat I could see right into the café and when I spotted her heading for the door, I slid down in the seat. It was dark and I was confident she wouldn't see me. She hesitated in the doorway, peering up and down the street, no doubt looking for me. Her eyes settled on my car for so long I thought I'd blown it, but eventually she pulled the collar of her coat up against her neck and stepped into the gentle rain. She was still cautious, kept looking around her as she walked quickly along the street, arms crossed over her chest, head ducked against the weather. I watched her go, waited until she turned a corner and then unfolded myself from the car. I closed the door very gently and locked it. I tutted as I realised I was about to get wet. Clearly, I was not a tough guy.

I trotted in the direction she had walked, reached the corner, flattened myself against the brickwork and peeped round the building. There she was, still making a brisk pace. I ducked back as I saw her head begin to turn, waited, then risked another look. She was moving faster now, but I was confident she hadn't seen me. When I saw her cross this road and then vanish round another corner, I slid out and followed her.

I saw the big black guy before she did. She had crossed another street, her head down apart from the occasional glance over her shoulder, and he came out of a tenement entrance halfway up the street, stopped to take in his surroundings, spotted her.

His mouth tightened into something that wasn't a smile of pleasure. Then his hand slid into the pocket of his expensive-looking Burberry. I didn't like that. I had nothing against the coat, but I wasn't too keen on what he may have been about to pull out, so I quickened my pace.

He was almost on her before she raised her head and saw him. She froze as he broke into a steady lope. His hand came out of his pocket and I saw the knife. I shouted her name and began to run, and she glanced back at me with genuine terror on her face. But she seemed rooted to the spot, like a rabbit in the headlights.

'Run, Jenny, for God's sake!' I shouted, and this gave her a jump-start. She leaped off the pavement and sprinted towards me, but the guy veered off too, and he was big and he was fast and he would have caught up with her had I not reached her first and pulled her behind me.

He came to halt, the knife held loosely in his hand like it belonged there. It was a big knife, a hefty knife, the kind of knife that made me think of Sylvester Stallone sewing up his own wounds, and I really did not like the look of it at all. I also didn't like the look of this bloke. He was handsome, even I had to admit that, with coal-black skin and expensively shorn hair and designer clothes. He looked, I realised, like a younger Idris Elba. But there was a glint of nastiness in his eye that told me he would not hesitate to use his weapon. The prospect did not appeal.

'Stay out of this, man,' he said. He even sounded like Idris Elba. He was a Londoner, although my ear wasn't attuned to whether he was from north or south of the river. I'm a Scot, and all southerners sound the same to me.

'Look, I don't know who you are, mate,' I said, pleased that my voice came out low and even, which was quite a feat because I could feel every muscle trembling and I really needed to go to the toilet. I spread my arms out slightly, as if trying to block him from passing, and took a step back, as did Jenny, just to put a bit of distance between us. The guy stepped forward to narrow the gap again, which was disconcerting. 'But let's just put the blade away and we'll talk.'

He shook his head. 'Not gonna happen,' he said, and aimed the point of the knife at Jenny, who was cowering behind me. 'Her and me got business.'

'I didn't take it, Jerome,' Jenny whined, 'honest, I didn't.'

I wanted to turn and face her, but there was no way I was giving this bloke my back, so I just said, 'You know him?'

Jerome smiled, showing a double line of gleaming teeth that must have had his dentist puffed with pride. But there was very little humour in the smile. 'Me and Jenny, we're old friends. Ain't we, darlin?'

I wanted to know more about this, but this was not the time to start a question and answer session. I took another step back. He took another forward. I didn't like this dance. I thrust out my hand in the ancient gesture of peace and harmony. 'Pleased to meet you, Jerome – I'm Dominic.'

He ignored my proffered hand. Obviously observing the proprieties of gentlemanly conduct were not top of his agenda right now. 'Keep out of this, *Dominic.*' I don't know how he did it, but his inflection made my Christian name sound like a punch-line. And that from a guy named Jerome. However, he was the one with the knife, so I let it slide.

'Can't do that, Jerome. I've been looking for Jenny here for a while and I saw her first. Finders keepers.'

My reasoning seemed to confuse him a bit, because he lowered the knife and gave me a look that suggested I needed professional help. That was the opening I was waiting for, and I made my move.

Move in closer, that's what I was taught, so that's exactly what I did with Jerome, who was already on the wrong foot thanks to my wickedly funny patter and the fact that I had been backing away slowly during the entire conversation. The last thing he expected was for me to get up close and personal. Even so, he reacted quickly and swung the knife up, but I blocked the movement with the wrist of my left hand, swept his knife hand away and at the same time jabbed my right fist into his windpipe. That's a basic with Krav Maga – go for the soft tissue first, if you can. And I'm a very basic kind of guy.

He reeled back, his breath catching in his throat, but I continued to move. My right leg came up and my foot connected with his groin. He went down like a demolished tower block, the knife sliding from his fingers. He needed both hands now – one to clutch his throat, the other to clasp his injured manhood.

I heard Jenny's footsteps beating a hasty retreat, and I did not plan to hang around and wait for him to regain his strength. I took off after her. I'd lost the element of surprise, and you know what they say about discretion and valour.

Chapter Three

Jenny had transformed from a rabbit in headlights into the Duracell bunny hooked up to the national grid. Adrenalin still surged through my body, so I was making good time myself. The quick look I threw over my shoulder to see Jerome dragging himself to his feet helped spur me on.

We followed the route back to Joe's Café, but it was dark now and offered no sanctuary. I groped in my jacket pocket for my car key and pressed the button on the fob. Jenny was still up ahead as the sidelights lights flashed twice and I yelled, 'Jenny – get in the car!'

She ran beyond the car then stopped and looked back at me – then past me. I cast another wild glance over my shoulder to see Jerome was closing in at a steady jog. He must have had cast-iron testicles, because I'd delivered a kick hard enough to win accolades at Murrayfield. Not to mention the punch to the throat, which should have been enough to disable any ordinary man. But Jerome clearly was not ordinary, because there he was, pounding after us, coat tails flapping behind him, knife held in his hand like an additional finger. An extra large additional finger.

I picked up my own pace, a feat which I found impressive if no-one else did, and screamed again, 'In the car!'

Jenny had already thrown open the passenger door. She climbed in, slammed the door behind her and punched the lock down before I got there. I didn't even bother to see where Jerome was, I knew he wasn't far behind, I just leaped into the driver's seat and rammed the key into the ignition. The engine roared and I jerked it into gear before jamming my foot down hard on the gas. The Ford jumped forward just as Jerome reached us, stretching his knife hand out as if he could bury the blade into the bodywork to stop us from leaving. I heard the edge scrape the paint as we slid past him. It didn't bother me – there were so many scratches on the car I was thinking of exhibiting it at the Tate Modern.

In the rear-view mirror I saw him standing in the middle of the road, watching us speed away. He did not look pleased. Had he been a character in *The Dandy*, he would've shaken his fist. We didn't say a word until we were well on the way out of the town, although there was a lot of panting and gasping, mostly from me.

Finally, it was Jenny who spoke first. 'Where we going?'

'Where do you think?'

She saw a road sign for Glasgow and fell silent again.

'So who is Jerome?' I asked.

She didn't answer at first and I expected a smart comment in reply. When it didn't come, I was disappointed.

'Guy I knew in London,' she said.

'And does this guy you knew in London have a last name?'

'Kingsley, Jerome Kingsley. You want his shoe size too?'

That's my girl, I thought. 'Why's he looking for you?'

She paused again and I sensed she was struggling to decide whether or not to tell me.

'Come on, Jenny,' I said, unable to keep the irritation from my voice. 'I've just tackled a guy with a knife that makes Rambo's look like a toothpick. I think I deserve some answers, eh?'

She exhaled through her nose and said, 'I lived with him for a while.'

'Lived with him as in you shared a flat, or lived with him as in you knew what side of the bed he slept on?'

'None of your business.'

I didn't press it. I can show restraint sometimes. She turned her face towards the side window, out of shame or anger, I didn't know. She was right, it wasn't any of my business, but asking questions gets to be a bad habit.

'So,' I said, 'I'm guessing you didn't part on the best of terms? Or does he always greet old friends with a knife?'

Her face was still turned away when she said, 'He thinks I ripped him off.'

'Ripped him off how?'

She turned back and her old defiant face was back. 'Drugs, okay? He thinks I nicked some of his drugs.'

Aha, I thought. I didn't reckon many pharmacists went out armed to the teeth, so that made Jerome a drug dealer. I'm quick that way.

'And did you rip him off?'

'If I had a suitcase full of coke, do you think I'd be living in a crappy wee flat in Saltcoats? I'd be off punting it in Glasgow or Edinburgh.'

Cocaine. I sighed inwardly, feeling like Indiana Jones being confronted by snakes. Why did it have to be cocaine? Charlie and I were old friends, but I was never glad to see him again.

'So if you didn't take the drugs, who did?'

She shrugged and went back to her window. 'Beats the hell out of me.'

I decided that she wasn't going to give me anything more, so it was my turn to go quiet. She squirmed and thrust her hand under her backside to produce my phone. I'd left it on the seat when I started to follow her. She handed it to me without a word and I drove with one hand while I held it up to the light with the other. She hadn't damaged it. There was a missed call message on the small screen so I flipped the phone open and dialled my voice mail. I know I shouldn't have been driving and using the phone, sets a very bad example, but I figured what the hell – I'd just come to a knife fight with nothing more than a cheery smile and a merry quip. I was getting used to living dangerously.

The message was from Aunt Jessica. Her voice was hushed, hurried, as if she was trying to finish before she hit some sort of deadline – like someone else coming into the room.

'Mister Queste, I haven't much time – things have taken a very strange turn. There are people looking for Jenny, bad people.'

No kidding, I thought.

'I should never have asked you to find her. You must get her to safety. I can't explain, but please – get her to safety. If she...'

And then she stopped. I heard another voice in the background, indistinct but obviously male, and the connection was cut.

I closed the phone and drove on in silence. My first thought was that Jerome had paid Aunt Jessica a visit, but the voicemail had been left only a few minutes before, while I was doing my Chuck Norris in the street. Jerome had obviously tracked Jenny down himself. If he was as successful a dealer as his expensive coat suggested, he'd have his own methods of finding her. So why would he need to see her aunt?

I decided not to mention any of this to Jenny just yet. I don't trust easily, especially someone who may or may not have nicked a case full of happy dust from a dealer. I gave her a quick glance as we sped along the dark country roads between Saltcoats and Dalry. I'd plumped for the back roads to the city, deciding that a southerner like Jerome would stick to the main routes. My way had more curves than Kim Kardashian and was unlit, but unless Jerome knew his way around, he wouldn't tackle it. I was reasonably certain he wouldn't be steaming up behind us, but I kept my eye on the rear-view anyway.

Jenny reached down to the alcove beneath my radio and its defunct CD player to see what discs I had. She leafed through the plastic cases and I saw her frown when she saw names like John Williams, Jerry Goldsmith and Best of the West.

Without looking up, she asked, 'What kind of music is this?'

'Soundtracks, film music.'

'What? Like the stuff that goes on in the background?'

'That's right.'

'You listen to this?' There was a note of disbelief in her voice, as if I'd told her I liked to thrust hot needles into my privates.

'No, the CDs are just there for decoration.'

I was used to this reaction. People did not understand my fondness for film scores. It didn't annoy me as much as it used to.

She smiled when she came to the last disc. 'Really? Disney songs?'

'Hey,' I said, 'Hakuna Matata – words to live by.'

She was still smiling as she pushed the CDs back into the slot.

'So,' she said, settling back again, 'as we're obviously going to

23

spend some time together, you'd better tell me your name. You already know mine.'

I noticed the hard Glasgow accent she'd spoken with in the café was gone now, replaced by the more refined West End tones she'd grown up with. Something of a chameleon, this girl, I decided. I answered her question. 'Dominic Queste.'

She looked surprised. 'You're kidding me!'

I'm also used to people being surprised at my name. 'Why would I kid about something like that?'

'And what are you? Some kind of private detective?'

'Not officially. Think of me as an odd job man.'

'Dominic Queste, Dominic Queste...' She leaned over to the side and surveyed me through narrowed eyes. I know what she was seeing – a thin-faced bloke in his early fifties, long thick hair down to his collar, still brown but greying at the sides. Not terribly good-looking, but not so bad he could model for gargoyles. 'Yeah, I suppose it suits you...'

'Thank you.'

'I mean, that's what you do, isn't it? Go on quests, find people and that.'

'Well, there's an extra 'e' in my name.'

She thought about this. 'That would make it Queest, wouldn't it?'

'Not when it's at the end.'

'Oh – still, it fits.'

'Some people do live up to their name, I suppose. I know a cop called Nick.'

She gave me a look that I'm certain mothers teach all their daughters. It's the combination of patience, pity and dismissal with which most women greet my attempts at humour. I do know a police officer called Nick, although when I called Detective Chief Inspector Nicholas Cornwell that to his face, he looked like he'd give me a going over with a phone book. Granted, that wasn't as much a threat as it used to be, given the lack of heft provided by modern-day phone books, but I wouldn't put it past him to have a few vintage copies in his drawer.

Jenny asked, 'How did you get into this odd job game, then?'

What could I tell her?

Could I tell her about the strange little boy who grew up with no clear idea what he wanted to do, but who loved movies so much he thought he could make them? Who lacked the talent or the push to do anything about it, so he thought if he couldn't make them he could write about them? Who drifted into journalism, got a job in a weekly and then an evening paper on the features desk, never did write about movies but did become what they used to call an investigative reporter, now an endangered species in the industry?

Should I tell her he started doing crime exposes and probes, won a couple of awards for a series on gun crime and another on human trafficking, back before it was trendy?

Would she then want to know how it all went wrong, how the dodgy characters he needed to feed him a line of news started to feed him lines of coke, good old Charlie? And to keep in with them, he took it, powdering his nose from the inside as often as he could? And as his money evaporated, turned to less expensive ways of getting high? Should I tell her that, I wondered?

Does she want to hear about how his work suffered and the editors lost faith while the police looked at him askance because they believe that if you lie down with dogs, you get up scratching and sniffing butts?

And after that, the downward spiral of unemployment and, worse, unemployability? Of the things he did to get enough money to eat, pay rent and keep snorting and smoking? Does she really want to know?

I decided she didn't really want to hear any of that, so all I said was, 'Just lucky, I suppose.'

I don't know whether she sensed I was evading the question, but she didn't pursue it. We lapsed into silence again and I thought about the message from her aunt. Naturally, it had bothered me. She'd mentioned 'bad people'. I didn't know what the hell was going on, but my nose was twitching, and it had nothing to do with my ingrained yen for the all-time high. Although once a cokehead, always a cokehead, I suppose.

I needed to find somewhere to stash Jenny while I made a few more inquiries.

Take her to safety, Aunt Jessica had said.

And there was only one really safe place I could think of.

About thirty minutes later we crossed the Kingston Bridge and Jenny noticed that I was not pointing the nose of the car towards the West End. I kept the wheels firmly on the M8, heading east.

'I thought you were taking me to Aunt Jessica,' she said.

I shook my head. 'Change of plan,' I said. 'We're going to see some pals of mine...'

Chapter Four

Back in the '70s, the Sutherland Brothers – Gavin and Iain – had a hit called Lying in the Arms of Mary along with a band called Quiver. The first time I met *my* Sutherland brothers – Duncan and Hamish – I asked them how Mary was and they understood right away. I guess they must have got that a lot over the years. It's always good to be on the same wavelength as your mates.

Despite their Highland-sounding names, Duncan and Hamish were not even Scottish. Born and raised in Newcastle, they pitched up as young men in Glasgow in the mid-1980s to take part in the city's boom industry – drug dealing. However, the day-to-day business of supply and demand was not their field of expertise. They had a more basic skill.

They could break bones.

They could inflict pain.

They could put the fear of death into anyone – a rival, a tardy payer, a witness.

Their reputation in Glasgow and Edinburgh was such that they could command relatively high fees. They were admired for their professionalism – no civilians were ever hurt, although there were some who had to be convinced that whatever it was they thought they'd witnessed was an hallucination. A few even found they could not properly explain why they had ever told the police they were in one street on a certain date at a specific time when in actual fact they were on the other side of the city.

But something strange happened after Hamish was convicted of giving a particularly loathsome little dealer called Shuggie Booth a slap or two. Shuggie had been trying to punt his gear to young teens at a private school up the West End. What he didn't know was that one of the pupils at the school was the daughter of Bill 'The Bull' Nolan, one of the city's dominant godfathers. The Bull was none-too-chuffed at Booth's enterprising spirit, a somewhat hypocritical stance given how he made his millions, but nevertheless he hired Hamish to express his displeasure in a physical manner. Shuggie, unusually, ran to the law and told a tale. Unfortunately for Hamish, there was also a snatch of CCTV footage which showed him leaving the alley in which Shuggie had received said slap or two. Hamish was inside for three years, having been convicted of Assault to Serious Injury – okay, maybe it was more than a slap or two, given the fact that Shuggie was never able to walk again without the aid of two sticks.

The strange thing was that Hamish came out of Barlinnie Prison a changed man. He didn't get religion, even though it was a priest who had helped him see the error of his ways, but he did develop a conscience. On his release, the priest took him to see the damage caused by the drug trade. Both Hamish and his brother had been insulated from the end users, out of sight being very much out of mind. On some level they had known about the misery and destruction of lives and families, but they tended not to let it concern them too much. This old priest – Father Francis Verne – opened Hamish's eyes, convinced him to renounce his former ways and start helping addicts back on the straight and narrow. Amazingly, he also convinced his brother Duncan to do the same. I say amazingly because Duncan had always been the more vicious of the two. But then, Father Verne could be very persuasive.

Now they both helped with his mission to save the lost and addicted in the city. That was how I met them, after the old priest had found me lying in the street, barely conscious following a fight with a man I'd tried to rob at knife-point. That's what happens when Charlie gets under your skin – all you think about is getting him in your hands again. I'd chosen the wrong mark this time, because he gave me the hiding of my life and left me there to bleed. I don't hold any hard feelings against the bloke, because in the long run he did me a favour. And it was a long run. But Father Verne, Hamish and Duncan were with me all the way.

The Sutherland brothers had salted away a bit of money during their strong arm days, but lived in an unostentatious second-floor flat in a red sandstone building on Alexandra Parade in Dennistoun, or Merchant City East, as the estate agents would have you believe. It was almost eleven when I brought the car to a halt outside their closemouth, but I knew they would still be up. I'd phoned them from the road, telling them I was on my way and I needed a favour. They didn't ask what the favour was, they just said *sure thing, come on by.* That was the Sutherland brothers for you. I'd trust them with my life. In fact, I already had, many times.

Duncan opened the door to us clad in a long apron with the outline of a naked woman on the front. He was small and thin, his head shaved totally bare. He had begun to go bald in his early twenties and decided that an extra wide parting was not for him, so scraped the rest off. According to legend, he did this every morning with a knife blade. He told me that this was totally untrue, that he used soap and a razor like everyone else, but such legends are handy to have in the underworld.

'Come away in,' he said, his strong Geordie accent filled with warmth. 'Hamish and me are just experimenting in the kitchen.'

Jenny threw me a quizzical glance as she stepped over the threshold and I nodded in what I hoped was a reassuring manner. Duncan was already halfway down the hallway as I closed and locked the door behind me – three locks and a chain, because old habits die hard. It was a sturdy door and the only way anyone could force their way in was if they had a tank, and they're difficult to get up the stairs of a Glasgow tenement. We followed him as he turned right into the large kitchen. In the old days this would have been a kitchen-cum-living room with an alcove behind the door carrying a recess bed. But over the years, the brothers had turned it into a modern, hi-tech kitchen. Hamish was standing at the large six-ring range, stirring a pot of something with a wooden spoon. When you meet the Sutherlands for the first time, you would not take them as brothers, as they looked so different. Where Duncan was small and thin, Hamish was big and powerful. Where Duncan had a fine head of skin, Hamish had enough hair on his head, his face and, presumably, on his chest to choke many a shower drain.

He looked up from his pot as we entered and smiled. 'Come away, man,' he said, his voice rumbling from the depths of his belly. He nodded at Jenny and said, 'Lass.' I was glad he didn't say 'bonny lass.' Sometimes the guys had a tendency to over-emphasise the whole *Auf Wiedersehen, Pet* thing.

I made the introductions and we sat down at the large wooden table Duncan had found at an auction. Word was it was once owned by an old gangster who wound up dead in his own home. It was old and deeply scored, but was always spotlessly clean. When they weren't working for Father Verne, they tended to spend a lot of their time in this room, working on the assumption that anything the Hairy Bikers could do, so could they. Unfortunately, their success rate was patchy, to say the least.

'We're making smoked sausage and prawn jambalaya,' said Hamish. 'You won't like it, Dom.'

Duncan smiled. 'Dom doesn't like seafood, do you, Dom?'

'Not unless it's fried in batter and wrapped in yesterday's paper,' said Hamish.

Duncan looked at Jenny. 'Very unsophisticated palate, has our Dom. Puts ketchup on everything.'

I shrugged. 'I don't like foods that sit on my plate and look back at me.'

Hamish lifted a plate from where they were piled on a shelf near the range and said, 'You hungry, bonny lass?' Bonny lass. I knew he wouldn't be able to resist.

'Starving,' said Jenny.

'That's what we like to hear.'

He scooped a mess of red, green and yellow food from the frying pan simmering on the stove. 'This has got onions and peppers mixed with rice. There's smoked pork sausages, peeled king prawns, some pistachio nuts – you're not allergic, are you?'

Jenny shook her head.

'Good. It's garnished with some thyme and lemon wedges and this...' Hamish dripped some sauce from the pot he'd been stirring when we arrived, 'this is a Creole sauce. Nothing to worry about, just some tomatoes, peppers and spices.'

He brought the plate over and laid it in front of her as Duncan fetched a knife and fork. Hamish poured a tall glass of mineral water from a bottle out of the fridge and placed it beside her plate. I knew their cooking, so she would need that glass of water. Sometimes the boys were a touch heavy-handed with the peppers and spices. They once made a curry that could've given napalm a run for its money. I watched with interest as Jenny hooked a forkful and popped it into her mouth. She smiled and said, 'This is delicious.'

I couldn't tell if she was being polite, but the fact that she didn't immediately reach out for the cooling water suggested that this was one of their successes.

'We'll make you some beans on toast, philistine,' Duncan said to me. *Lovely*, I thought.

Hamish dished out a further two platefuls while Duncan threw a plastic pot of beans into the microwave and dropped two slices of bread into the toaster. He then joined us at the table and began to eat. I watched them, waiting patiently for my beans and toast.

'So,' said Hamish through a mouthful of rice, 'what's the favour?'

'I need you to look after Jenny for a while,' I said.

Duncan nodded, smiling at Jenny. 'You're welcome for as long as you like, lass. Any friend of Dom's and all that.'

'Thank you,' said Jenny but her focus was still on the plate. She was either very hungry and could eat anything, or the boys had surpassed themselves.

Duncan smiled with satisfaction as he watched her eat. 'So how did you come to be in tow with this low-life, Jenny? You're a cut above the usual young ladies he sees.'

Hamish chimed in, 'Mind, we don't often see our Dom with a young lady, do we, Duncan?'

'Old slappers, mostly.'

'Jenny's a *subject*,' I said, just as the microwave dinged. Duncan made to get up but I told him to stay where he was, I'd see to myself. I'd been here often enough, had lived here during a particularly bad patch when the old cravings came back with a vengeance, so I knew my way around.

'Bet you didn't know that, eh, lass?' Hamish said, with a wink in his voice, if not in his eye. 'You're a *subject*. Got a way with words, has our Dom.'

'Comes from being a writer once,' said Duncan. 'Knows how to make a girl feel special, like.'

I looked up from buttering my toast to see Jenny was smiling. Hamish and Duncan had the ability to make people smile, to feel at home. I wonder how long her smile would last if I told them how the Chuckle Brothers used to make a living.

'I need you to look after her, just for a night, maybe,' I said as I carried my plate back to the table.

Hamish nodded and chewed on his food as he thought about this. 'So who's after you, lass?'

Jenny glanced at me, her eyes wide. Of course, I knew they would suss the situation immediately.

'An old boyfriend,' I said, and felt Jenny's eyes flash with anger. I glanced at the brothers and saw Duncan watching both Jenny and I through narrowed eyes.

'More than that, I think,' he said. No-one ever accused them of being stupid.

'He's a candyman from the Smoke,' I said, and that prompted a smile from Hamish.

'Oh yes, a real way with words, has our Dom. Sometimes likes to sound like a Scottish Mickey Spillane. A candyman from the Smoke, eh? And has this candyman got a name?'

'Jerome Kingsley,' I said and felt, rather than heard, Jenny sigh with some exasperation. Hamish noticed it too because he reached out and patted her hand.

'Now, love, don't get yourself all worked up. We've got to know these things, okay? Believe me, we don't judge. Has Dom told you anything about us?'

'Just that I'd be safe with you,' said Jenny.

Hamish nodded. 'Well, that's all you need to know for now. You'll stay here tonight, maybe longer?' He raised an eyebrow at me and I shrugged. I had no idea how long I needed her to hide out here. For the second time that night I mentally quoted Indiana

Jones: *I'm making this up as I go.*

Once the food was eaten and the coffee was drunk – percolated, no instant stuff for the Sutherland brothers, even though I would have much preferred a Nescafé– they showed Jenny her room. The flat was a deceptive size, with three well-proportioned bedrooms. The guest room had been mine during my dark periods and I knew it well. Jenny apologised, explaining that she had nothing of a personal nature with her. Duncan smiled, vanished into his own room and then reappeared with a loose-fitting t-shirt and some tracksuit bottoms. He also had a fresh toothbrush and some towels.

'You'll be fine here, Jenny,' I said. 'Wait till you see the breakfast they'll cook you.' I was standing in the hallway and started to zip up my jacket before I turned to the front door.

'Where are you going?' She asked.

'To see your Aunt Jessica.'

'Why am I not coming? I thought she wanted me found?'

I didn't want to tell her that I felt it was unsafe. 'You've had a tough night, so you get some sleep and then we'll see what tomorrow brings.'

I caught looks from both Hamish and Duncan. They knew I was avoiding telling her something. They could read me like a pulp novel.

'Maybe you should wait until tomorrow, Dom,' said Duncan. 'You can doss here, on the couch.'

'No,' I said. 'I really want to see her tonight.' I gave them a look that told them it was important. They understood. Another chapter read.

I'd regret that decision.

Chapter Five

The two detectives looked at me with blank expressions. I swear they practice for hours, making a poker face seem like Jim Carrey having a fit of histrionics. I couldn't tell whether they believed me or not. They probably didn't. Couldn't blame them really.

Tell us again, Mister Queste, they'd said in patient tones. *Tell us again how you came to be here.*

And so I sat in the spacious kitchen of the Hyndland townhouse, the machinery of a murder investigation whirring upstairs, and I told them everything again. Well, maybe not everything. I told them why Aunt Jessica had hired me in the first place, but I didn't tell them I'd found Jenny. I don't know why. Sometimes I never know why I do things.

I told them I'd come over at Jessica Oldfield's request to give her a situation report on the search for her niece. After all, when they checked my phone records they'd see that I both made and received calls from her earlier that night.

The streets of Hyndand are quiet even during the day, but after midnight they are truly deserted. Glasgow's reputation is one of tenements and poverty, but there's a lot of money in the city, and if you listen carefully, in parts of it you can actually hear property values rising. I reached Aunt Jessica's street from Byres Road, arguably the heart of the West End, by driving up Huntly Gardens and turning right at the top. It is an attractive area, filled with Edwardian terraces and townhouses, some of which had remained intact over the years, the rest having been converted into flats. Expensive flats, it has to be said. I always feel like I'm an interloper in these areas, out of place. Downtown, downbeat guy, remember?

Aunt Jessica lived in one of the intact townhouses in a crescent-shaped street that looked down on a leafy glade. The West

End is filled with leafy glades, probably left over from when all this was farmland. I parked my car in the shadow of one of the bigger trees, its branches stretching out across the road towards the houses. *Someone would have to come and neaten that up,* I thought. I'd been lucky to find the space because the street was lined with vehicles. I heard the soft rumble of an engine turning over and saw a dark-coloured four wheel drive parked a few cars from mine. I could just make out the figure of a man in the driver's seat. I thought nothing more about it. High-end vehicles like that are common across the city, as if the cost of petrol wasn't a concern. A cat skittered out from the darkness and shot past me. I think it had something in its mouth, but it was moving so fast, and the glow from the tungsten street lights was so dim, that I couldn't be sure.

I could see there were lights on two floors of Aunt Jessica's three-storey terrace. The properties on either side were in complete darkness. One of them had that empty house feel about it, even though curtains hung at each window. Don't ask me what gave me that impression. I always feel there's something listless about a house that's unoccupied, as if it's not living up to its destiny. And that, at least, was something I knew all about.

I started to feel uneasy as I climbed the steps towards the front door of Aunt Jessica's home. My queasy feeling wasn't caused by the sound of the music drifting from inside: it was Neil Diamond, and he's not that bad. It wasn't even the sign that said 'No Salespeople or Mormons', even though that was a bit harsh on the followers of the Latter Day Saints. I'm sure they mean well. No, what made my guts tighten was the fact that the door was slightly ajar. Aunt Jessica did not know I was visiting so late, I'd purposely not phoned because I wanted to catch unawares whoever was with her, so it wasn't as if she'd left the door open for me. I know in decades past they say you could've left your front door open without fear of a passing ned or junkie seeing it as an invitation to rip you off, but those days had gone the way of black and white TV and Betamax video.

I hesitated on the doorstep, listening to the track change to

Don't Think, Feel. It was from the album Beautiful Noise, an album I'd bought myself, years ago. I don't just listen to film music, you know. The music was not too loud, you wouldn't hear it until you were actually at the door, but despite its jaunty beat, there was an ominous feel in the air. I decided not to walk in unannounced. There was a brass bell push set in a plate to my right, so I pressed my thumb to it. I heard something jingle inside, but no-one came to the door. I gave it another push, but still the only thing I could hear other than the tinkle of the bell was Neil singing his heart out.

Okay, I thought, *here goes.*

I pushed the door open with the back of my hand and stepped into the hallway. It was tastefully decorated, all pastel shades and polished wooden floors. A staircase curved slightly upwards to my left, its dark wooden banisters buffed to a high gleam. I'd only been in a matter of seconds, only taken an initial look, but I'd bet my bank book that the entire house would be just as spotless. Not that my bank book was much of a bet. I didn't see Aunt Jessica as the type to get the Mister Sheen out on a regular basis, so I presumed she had a very efficient cleaner.

'Mrs Oldfield?' I didn't shout too loud, just enough for anyone nearby to hear. 'Mrs Oldfield, it's Dominic Queste.'

The music was coming from a room to my right, which I presumed was some kind of sitting room. I moved towards it and, again using the back of my hand, swung the door open. Unsurprisingly, the room was tastefully furnished and decorated, the cream three-piece suite alone probably costing more than I could raise if I sold everything I owned and threw my body in as an added extra. There was a pricey-looking, if old-fashioned, hi-fi system in the corner, from which Neil was now giving us Surviving the Life, on original vinyl too, which pleased me for some twisted reason. The arm of the record deck was pulled back so that it would continue to replay once it reached the end of that side of the album. I could smell something in the air, the after-stench of a cigar. There was an ashtray on the low coffee table where the remains of its source still smouldered.

I took another look around the room, studied the framed photographs on the mantelpiece. They all seemed to be of Jessica with various people. I'd noticed that she was a handsome woman when I met her, but when she was younger she was what The Super Soaraway Sun used to call a stunner. Two of the pictures were of her and another woman who I decided was her dead sister, Jenny's mother, even though Jessica was blonde and Bernie was dark. They both had the same look about them, the same cold attractiveness. It was as if they knew they were beautiful and they knew how to use it. But Jenny's mother had another look around her eyes. Something unpleasant, something that said this was a woman who needed to be watched. I thought I even saw a hint of madness there, but perhaps I was just being fanciful, imprinting what Jessica had told me about her sister on the two-dimensional print. It's like studying the photo of someone who has subsequently died tragically, looking into their eyes, and seeing past the smile to a sadness, as if they knew they were destined to never grow much older. In reality, that sadness isn't there, it's simply a transference of knowledge, the mind making the eyes see what it feels they should see. Or something like that.

I stepped back out to the hallway and peeped down what I would call the lobby, but no doubt Aunt Jessica and her cronies called a vestibule. I called out her name again because I am nothing if not optimistic, though I was really beginning to wish I'd never come. My gut had tied itself into a knot that would take Alexander and his sword to cut through, because I knew this was not going to end well. The logical part of my brain told me I should walk right out that front door now, get in my car and get as far away from the leafy West End as I could. But I don't listen much to the logical part of my brain, which is why I get myself into so much trouble.

I heard, or thought I heard, something creak upstairs. I placed a foot onto the first step and looked up, calling out again. I heard it again, as if someone was moving on the next floor, taking each step stealthily, carefully, slowly.

Get out – get out now, my logical brain screamed, but I climbed the stairs anyway. It seemed like a long way. Sherpa Tensing would have thought it too dangerous a climb, but I did it.

The first-floor landing was empty. There were three doors, presumably to bedrooms or bathrooms, or maybe even a full-size ballroom for all I knew. Maybe Aunt Jessica held cotillions where the belles of Hyndland, dressed in long flowing gowns, flirted with their young beaux and sipped punch. I shook my head slightly to clear the image of Vivien Leigh flouncing around Leslie Howard while Clark Gable watched and concentrated on the matter at hand. Two of the doors were closed, one was open, and that was the one I headed for. After all, there was a light on inside the room. Sometimes I can be pretty logical.

Aunt Jessica was lying on the bed, her arms outstretched as if she was making a snow angel. Her face was bloody and already discoloured, her tongue bulged from between her lips. Her eyes stared sightlessly up at the carefully painted plaster cornicing. I didn't need to examine them to know that I'd find them blotched red with burst blood vessels. Someone had strangled Aunt Jessica. I didn't touch the body, I knew my way around a crime scene well enough. After all, it wasn't my first.

I was reaching for the phone in my pocket to call the police when I heard the footfalls on the landing outside. I spun and rushed out of the room to see a man about my size but far more powerfully built beginning to dart down the stairs. He looked up at me as I burst onto the landing and I saw the face of a street fighter. One ear seemed thicker than the other, his bullet-head had a thin covering of razored hair and scar tissue above his eyes. He looked familiar. He also looked mean and he looked nasty, but despite that I leapt after him and caught him at the bottom step. I barrelled into him, slammed his body against the wall. The air burst from his lungs, but it didn't stop him swinging his right hand at my head in a powerful roundhouse which I think would have broken my jaw had it connected. I ducked under it, grabbed his arm as it flew past and gave him a push, using his own impetus to spin him round. I rammed my fist into his kidneys, putting my whole shoulder behind it, and was rewarded with a satisfying grunt. But he wasn't down yet. He jerked his left elbow back and smashed it into my nose. Tears stung at my eyes and as I staggered, my heels caught the lip of a step and I toppled backwards. He whirled round, lifted his right leg and gave me a flat-footed kick to the chest. I'm sure he was aiming at my face, but we were on an uneven surface and I think he simply misjudged. I felt the agony right through to my spine as my lungs spat out air.

Then he was off and out the front door. I heard him pound down the front steps as I struggled to my feet and stumbled after him. By the time I reached the street he had jumped into the large black four-wheel drive I'd noticed earlier. I tried to make out the license plate as the gas guzzler sped away, but my eyes aren't what they once were. Even without them watering from that blow to the nose.

I contemplated giving chase in my car, but knew it would be a worthless exercise. Hyndland and Dowanhill is a warren of streets and lanes and roads and by the time I fired up my old Ford, they could have made two or three different turns and I'd never know.

I flipped open my phone and punched in 999. It was time to call the cavalry.

The two detectives listened to the story again and gave me their impassive stares. I gave them one back. I was tired, I was sore and I'd been doing all this on a plate of beans on toast and a greasy cheeseburger, the memory of which was now burning its way from my gut to my gullet. I was telling the truth and I had nothing to worry about. Well, I was telling some of the truth but I still felt I had nothing to worry about. I wondered if Aunt Jessica had any antacids in her medicine cabinet.

A uniformed officer came in and whispered something to one of the detectives. They both glanced at me in a pointed way that I didn't like and then the uniform left. The detective nodded.

'Okay, Mister Queste,' he said. 'We'd like you to come down to the station now.'

I didn't like the sound of that. I asked, 'Why? Am I under arrest?'

'No. Not yet.'

Not yet. I didn't like that either. 'So why...?' I began.

'Our boss would like a word with you, if you don't mind.'

'Your boss?'

I knew what he was going to say next but even so, it made my heartburn flare up even further.

'Detective Chief Inspector Cornwell.'

I *really* needed to find a packet of Rennies, because now I had something to worry about.

Chapter Six

Partick police station used to be situated near to the River Clyde, hence its old name Partick Marine, and actually looked like a police station. It was dark, forbidding, almost Gothic, and when you walked through the large, heavy doors, you knew you were walking into a cop shop. All it needed was a sign that said 'Abandon Hope All Ye Who Enter Here.' But that was then and this is now and as a wise man once said, shit happens. The old, grey building did not fit into the world of modern policing and was replaced with a modern office on Dumbarton Road and renamed Glasgow West End. Take away the blue and white Police sign at the front and it could be anything – an office, a care home, the headquarters of a charity. I'd been in the musty old station on the riverside many times when I was a cub reporter on the local weekly and made a number of friends on the force there, and in other stations across the west of the city. However, once I made the move to the evening paper, I wrote a series of articles on a miscarriage of justice which suggested that certain admissions of guilt made by a guy convicted of a nasty sex murder may actually have been coerced or – heaven forbid – perhaps even fabricated. Many of those former friends subsequently scored me off their Christmas card list. There is a strong brotherhood in the police and they don't like people like me coming along and impugning their good name. Even if they knew that what I was saying was probably true. There are still a few who stop and say hello when I meet them. There are even a couple I could turn to if I was in trouble and they would help me.

Detective Chief Inspector Nicholas Cornwell was not one of them.

When I first met him, he was a Detective Sergeant on a bank robbery case in Maryhill. Even then, he was a stickler for protocol and viewed members of Her Majesty's loyal press as a pest, an inconvenience, and at times a downright bloody menace. Even so, he was polite and occasionally even helpful. That changed when I wrote my articles about Clive Merchant, the man wrongly convicted for the sex murder. Well, I say wrongly convicted, but his appeal never did stand up and he completed his sentence. Cornwell took my aspersions on the probity of the police evidence in the case personally, even though he had not been part of the investigation. Whenever we met he was cold, distant and, when he felt the occasion demanded it, rude. Later, when my habit of snorting up anything but the white line in the middle of the road precipitated my fall from grace, he took great pleasure in watching me flail around in the gutter. He didn't like what I did for a living, he didn't like my friends, he didn't like those who employed me. In short, he just didn't like me, which is puzzling, as animals and children adore me. But then, Nick Cornwell was no cute puppy and I doubt he was ever a child. I think he came into the world a grown man with a broom shoved up his back passage.

He kept me waiting for 45 minutes, an old police trick designed to show who held the power. I took the opportunity to grab a cat nap as I sat in a bare little interview room. It wasn't easy in the uncomfortable plastic chair with my head resting on my arms on top of the table, but it was quiet and peaceful and I hadn't closed my eyes for twenty hours. My stomach still burned, though. I'd mentioned it to the two cops who had brought me in and they'd promised they'd find something at the station for it, but it was slow in coming.

I woke with a start as the door behind me opened and DCI Cornwell strode in, accompanied by the great smell of Brut. Or maybe it wasn't Brut. I don't even know if you can still buy Brut after shave anymore, but there was something about Cornwell that always reminded me of Henry Cooper, who used to splash the stuff all over in the telly commercials. He was a powerful man, his hair thinning and his face looking as if it had gone a few rounds with Mohammed Ali. I knew Cornwell used to box, probably still did even in his fifties, and I for one would not like to face up to him. I don't think my smattering of Krav Maga would do me a damn bit of good.

'I'm sorry,' he said, not sounding sorry at all, 'did I wake you?'

'Just grabbing forty winks,' I said.

He grunted as he sat down in the chair opposite me and dropped a manila folder on the table. He flicked the cover open and started to read the handful of typed reports inside. I had the impression he'd read them before and this was merely an example of his interrogation technique. Maybe he was hoping I'd suddenly blurt out a confession to save him the bother of beating it out of me. Then I realised he wasn't recording this so it wasn't an official interview.

I asked, 'Don't suppose you've got an antacid on you, have you?'

He didn't grace me with a response, just kept scanning the words on the sheets. It was a shot in the dark, but I decided not to give in. 'A slice of bread, then? Glass of milk?' Seriously, the heart-burn was raging through my chest like a prairie fire in August. Not that Nick cared, for he still didn't even register my presence.

Finally he sat back in his chair, looked at me with those steady, clear, brown eyes of his and said, 'So, what have you got to tell me?'

'I've got heartburn that could melt the polar ice cap.'

His eyes were hooded and his voice tight when he said, 'About tonight's events, Queste.'

Obviously there was no relief coming my way soon, so I shrugged and replied, 'Nothing that you've not read in those reports.'

'I want to hear you say it.'

'Like my voice, do you, Nick?' I saw him react to my calling him 'Nick'. He hated his name being shortened. It was Nicholas, or DCI Cornwell or even just Cornwell, but never Nick. However, I was in extreme discomfort here and I really didn't care.

'It's DCI Cornwell to you, Queste,' he said.

I smiled through my pain. 'Then it's *Mister* Queste to you, DCI Cornwell.' Poking the bear is the only extreme sport I ever do. He looked at me as if he wanted to rip my head off, which he probably did. To his credit, though, he controlled himself. Maybe he'd achieved his head-ripping quota for the week.

'Fair enough,' he said. 'So, *Mister* Queste, suppose you talk me through the events of last night? Leave nothing out.'

'Do I need a lawyer?'

'Why? Have you done something wrong?'

'Plenty of things, but I'm talking about last night. Am I suspected of being involved somehow in the death of Mrs Oldfield?'

'But you *are* involved somehow in the death of Mrs Oldfield. Otherwise you wouldn't be here.'

I sighed. I hate it when people use logic to prove a point. 'Do you think I did it?'

I saw something that bore a close resemblance to a smile tickle his lips, but he brought it under control just in time. 'No,' he said, almost ruefully, 'I don't think you killed her. If I did we wouldn't be having this nice wee chat. We'd be videoing it, I'd have a Detective Sergeant in here with me and you'd have that scumbag Eamonn O'Connor in here with you.'

I nodded. That's what I thought, 'So I can go if I want?'

He exhaled deeply. 'Yes, you can. But I've got a woman strangled in her own home, a nice house in Hyndland, where such things should not happen. I've got the killer out there somewhere and the only witness I have is a smart-arsed little loser who could be telling me all about it but is wasting time in meaningless conversation.'

I was about to ask who the smart-arsed little loser was and if he was in another room but I decided it would be more of that meaningless conversation he was talking about. I nodded, conceding his point because, after all, when a man's right, he's right. Anyway, the sooner I got out, the sooner I could douse the flames licking at my chest. 'Okay, where do you want me to start?'

'Why did Jessica Oldfield hire you?'

'She wanted me to find her niece, Jennifer Deavers.'

'The one who ran away a few years ago?'

'You know about that?'

'We're the police, Queste – we know lots of things.'

We'd already dispensed with the 'Mister', I noticed, but let it pass. 'So, I was dropping by last night to give her an update on how it was going.'

'Bit late for that, wasn't it?'

'She wanted me to tell her right away. I'd just got back from Saltcoats, where I'd been making inquiries.'

He nodded. 'So you got to the house and then what?'

'The door was lying open, music playing inside. I went in, had a poke around. I didn't steal anything.'

He grunted again, as if to say *remains to be seen*. 'What made you go upstairs?' He asked.

'Heard a noise.'

'What sort of noise?'

'I don't know, a couple of creaks, like someone was up there trying to move quietly.'

His head bobbed. 'Go on.'

'I went up the stairs, looked in the bedroom, found Mrs Oldfield, then I heard someone running down the stairs and I went after him. Caught up with him at the bottom of the stairs.'

'You were trying to stop him?'

'No, I wanted to ask him if he'd read any good books lately.'

He blinked and I saw a look that suggested exceeding his head ripping quota might not be a bad thing. When he spoke, his voice was low and even, maybe a bit too low and even. 'But he got away?'

'Yes.'

'Did you recognise him?'

'Kind of. Can't place him, though. But I've met him somewhere.'

Nick growled a little, as if to say that did not surprise him one bit. 'Would you know him again if you saw him?'

'I'd know him.'

He nodded, satisfied with that at least. 'So what then?'

I shrugged. 'He got into a large black four-wheel drive and drove off.'

'Was he driving?'

'No, it must've been waiting for him.'

'And you didn't get the licence plate?'

'No.'

He clucked his tongue and I knew this was another black mark. It didn't matter a great deal, in his eyes my copy book was well blotted. 'Did you touch anything in the house?'

'A door or two maybe, with the back of my hand, nothing else. Not my first rodeo, DCI Cornwell.'

He grunted as he looked down at the folder again. He knew I'd been around and didn't like it. He said, 'You don't smoke, do you?'

'That's one bad habit I don't have.'

'Very commendable, I'm sure.' I know what he was thinking about – the cigar in the ashtray. I'd been thinking about that, too. It looked expensive to me, the kind that are hand-rolled on the silken thighs of Cuban peasant girls. Not that I knew much about expensive smokes, right enough. Or Cuban peasant girls, come to that, but I'm always open to possibilities.

He said, 'And the girl, Jennifer Deavers. Did you find her?'

I'd been dreading this question. Until he asked I still did not know what I would say – the truth or a lie. I felt I should tell the truth and get myself away from this mess as fast as I could. The smart thing would be to tell Cornwell that I had Jenny in safe-keeping, tell him about Jerome Kingsley and the drugs and the knife. Tell him it all and let him take Jenny away and then I'd be out of it. Yes, that would be the smart thing to do.

'No,' I said. No-one ever accused me of being smart. I was rewarded with a puff of brimstone wafting its way to the back of my throat.

He took a deep breath and for a second I thought he was going to call me a liar, but he simply nodded and stared thoughtfully down at the file. 'What do you know of the family?'

'Only what Aunt Jessica...Mrs Oldfield told me. The girl's mother died in a fire, father not in the picture.'

He nodded slowly. Maybe he was warming to me. More likely my hot breath was defrosting his icy exterior. 'I don't like amateurs like you meddling in this sort of thing, Queste.' So much for warming to me, I thought. 'Mrs Oldfield should have left finding her niece to us.'

'Yeah, because you'd made such a neat job of it over the years.'

His eyes flashed. 'I want you out of this from now on.'

'Mrs Oldfield paid me in advance for two weeks,' I said. 'I've only been on it four days.'

'Treat it as a bonus. She's hardly likely to take you to the small claims court.'

I shook my head. 'Can't do that,' I said, but really I was just being awkward.

He leaned on the table top, clasped his hands in front of him. 'Have you got a line on her?'

'You mean what you police call "a positive line of inquiry"?'

'Something like that.'

'Maybe...'

'I could arrest you right now for impeding my investigation.'

'You could, but you know and I know that Eamonn would have me out on the streets faster than you can say "wrongful arrest".'

His jaw was working as he glared at me. 'If you know something, you must tell me.'

'Do you think she's in some kind of danger?'

There was a pause, a very slight pause, but it told me that there was something he wasn't telling me. 'I didn't say that.'

I leaned forward in my chair, suddenly alert and curious. 'What are you not saying, Nicholas?' I thought by using his full Christian name it might help us bond. Guess what? I was wrong.

His lip curled as he said, 'I don't remember ever giving you permission to call me by my first name. And if there is something I'm not telling you, then either I've got a damn good reason or it's none of your business.'

I sat back again, glad that I hadn't told him about Jenny. 'Fair enough. We finished here?'

He was considering this when there was a knock at the door. 'Stay there,' he said and got up to open it. I twisted round in my chair and saw a red-haired plainclothes officer framed in the doorway. She wasn't small, but she only came up to Cornwell's shoulder.

'Sorry to disturb you, boss,' she said, and I detected a pleasing

Irish lilt to her voice. I find the accent sexy, don't know why. I once interviewed the singer Dana over the phone, fell in love with her right there and then. Mind you, I'm a pushover.

'What?' Cornwell snapped. He always did have a way with women.

She flicked her eyes at me and lowered her voice, but I could still hear her. It wasn't a very big room. 'There's been a development, sir.'

Cornwell glanced at me and stepped out into the hallway, closing the door behind him. I turned back around in my seat and wondered what the development was. Then I wondered about the red-haired female cop and what her name was and if she was married and if she'd ever go for a washed out ex-hack with a sad story and a latent coke habit. Then I wondered why I was even wondering about it – she was about 25 and I was twice her age. Still, hope springs eternal. Or, in my case, limps.

Cornwell came back in and stood by the open door. He threw me a packet of Rennies, the chewy kind, bastard probably had them with him all the time. I eagerly popped a couple into my mouth and then noticed he looked even more grim than usual – and that's quite a feat. 'I think you'd better come with me, Queste,' he said. 'Something I want you to see.'

Whatever this something was, I knew it wasn't going to be good, and thought I might be needing the entire pack of antacids.

Chapter Seven

As a boy I visited the old Transport Museum when it was based on Albert Drive on the south side of the city and later in the Kelvin Hall up west, but I've never been to the serrated-roofed Riverside Museum which was helping turn the long-derelict banks of the Clyde into a tourist hub. It was pulling in thousands, maybe millions, of visitors every year, but I'd not been one of them.

Standing on the quay beside the museum is the SV Glenlee, an honest-to-God Tall Ship built on the Clyde over one hundred years ago. I'd read somewhere though that only the hull was original, and that the rest had to be replaced or restored after years of neglect. Visitors love stepping aboard a vessel that plied its trade on the tough Atlantic trade routes back when air travel was little more than a gleam in the eye of Thomas and Orville Wright. Needless to say, I'd never set foot on it.

Bobbing along on the briny beside it was the SV Sprite, a visitor to these shores. It was another historic vessel, had at one time plied the sea routes between Liverpool and New York, but was now used as a training camp for troublesome inner-city youths. The idea was to teach them something about discipline and teamwork by taking them on fairly lengthy voyages. It had berthed in Glasgow as part of a round-Britain voyage in order to carry out some minor repairs, and during the daytime it permitted visitors. Guess what – I hadn't found the time to climb aboard.

That was until Cornwell took me down there early one morning, just as the sun was rising. But I didn't hear any young maids singing in the valley below. You don't get many young maids singing in Glasgow streets at that time of the morning, not unless they're still out from the night before and believe me, if that was the case, you would not want to hear them sing.

Cornwell didn't tell me what it was he wanted me to see and I didn't ask. I didn't want to give him the satisfaction. The Rennies had worked their magic and drenched the broiling acid in my gut with chemicals. I was a lot more comfortable when we left the police office and turned left onto Dumbarton Road to take the Expressway. We even passed by the site of the old station and I remembered that they used to film scenes for *Taggart* out the back. Taggart and his team were supposedly based at Maryhill, but the office there was a 1960s monstrosity that no doubt did not impress the art directors. The rough-hewn charm of the old Partick Marine was visually more appealing.

We pulled into the car park at the museum and walked round the building towards the Tall Ships, which were bathed in dawn's early light. The smirr of the day before had gone and it looked as if it was shaping up to be a beautiful, crisp spring morning. A red glow crept over the city from the east, and the soft rays made the two sailing ships look even more spectacular. I wished I'd brought a camera.

'We going for a wee sail doon the watter?' I asked. Cornwell glowered at me.

As we approached I could see there was a lot of activity on board the Sprite. The Glenlee, snugly inaccessible behind its fences and barricaded gangplank, was deserted. We reached the Sprite gangplank and Cornwell showed his ID card to a uniform standing sentinel with a clipboard in his hand.

'DCI Cornwell, son,' he said and the young copper nodded as he scribbled the name down on the log sheet. Cornwell jerked a thumb at the red-haired officer. 'This is DC Theresa Cohan and *that...*' I didn't merit a thumb jerk, merely a twitch of the head in my direction, 'is Dominic Queste. He's with us.'

The uniformed cop looked at me, his eyes narrowing. He was young but he was already suspicious of me. I must have a sign hanging over me.

The young cop asked, 'How are you spelling that?'

'Two Es, a Q-U, an S and a T,' I said, leaving him to work out the correct order. If he was any sort of policeman he'd get there.

As we stepped off the gangplank onto the deck another three detectives, who had been lounging around gossiping and generally making the place look untidy, caught sight of Cornwell and straightened themselves so they were ship-shape and Bristol fashion. For a minute I thought they were going to pipe him aboard.

Cornwell snapped. 'Where is it?'

'Over here, sir,' said one of the detectives, walking across to the right-hand side of the ship, which I presumed was starboard, given that we had just stepped off what would be the port side. I knew reading those CS Forrester books when I was a boy would come in handy one day.

Cornwell asked, 'Has it been touched?'

'No, sir, we waited for you.'

Cornwell grunted. He did a lot of that and I think this one signified satisfaction. It certainly sounded very different from the grunts I'd heard in the interview room.

We reached the far side of the ship and a crowd of cops and scenes of crime officers. At first I was a bit puzzled as to why we were all gathered here, until I realised that some of them were squinting upwards. I followed their gaze and saw the body of a man dangling from a spar above our heads. He swung gently, as if caught by a breeze, his head twisted down to reveal his face, which was blackened and bloated, his tongue lolling through his teeth, his eyes bulging. He wasn't a pretty sight dead, but he hadn't been an oil painting when alive.

'You recognise him?' Cornwell asked.

'It's him,' I said, 'the guy I saw at Aunt Jessica's last night.'

Cornwell nodded as if I was merely confirming what he already knew. Which I probably was.

'Snaps taken? Tests done?' Cornwell was talking to the detective again, who nodded. 'Then get him down from there, careful as you can.'

Two men I presumed were experienced sailors clambered up the rigging and worked to bring the body down. It took a bit of doing, because they really didn't want to touch the corpse too much, and I can't say I blamed them, but finally it was lowered gingerly to the deck. Cornwell, Cohan and I stepped a bit closer. The young officer's face was filled with professional interest. She'd seen some pretty horrible things, I suppose. Me? I've seen some sights, sure, but I've never got used to being this close to violent death and this made two corpses in a matter of hours. If I'd had any breakfast I'd've been losing it.

'Remember him yet, Queste?' Cornwell asked me.

I leaned over, careful not to get too close and holding my breath. There was a hell of a smell coming from the corpse and I recalled that in hanging cases, the body tends to void itself of all waste. In the hanging shed at Barlinnie they used to have a sand pit under the drop to catch the fluids and solids that burst from the executed felon.

The rope looked like the type that would commonly be used on a sailing ship and it had bitten quite deeply into his neck. His lips and tongue appeared slightly blue. But the blackening on the face was nothing to do with the cause of death. This guy had been beaten first.

'I know I've seen him somewhere before, but still can't place him,' I said. 'I see a lot of guys like him in the course of my work, I can't be expected to remember every one of them.'

Nick looked as if he was going to take issue with me but he obviously thought better of it. 'You give him that doing?'

I shook my head. 'I hit him a couple of times, but not enough to leave that kind of bruising. Truth is, he hurt me more than I hurt him.' That was true – my nose still throbbed.

Cornwell bobbed his head towards the male detective, who snapped on two pairs of rubber gloves and stooped to go through the man's pockets. He came up with a wallet from the inside breast pocket of the dead man's jacket and probed the various slots, pulling out a driver's licence.

'He's a Walter Reilly,' read the cop, 'lives out in Ruchazie.'

I squinted at the bruised face again. He didn't look like a Walter to me and I'd bet the farm he used another name on the street. Cornwell confirmed it for me.

'There was a Tiger Reilly, used to do a bit of boxing, low-end stuff. I'd heard he went bad.' He looked pointedly at me. 'Too much booze and drugs.'

Cohan said, 'You think it's him then, boss?'

Cornwell shrugged. 'Could be, never met him myself so can't say for certain. Name mean anything to you, Queste?'

I shook my head, but I was lying. I'd met Tiger Reilly years before, just the once. He was strong arming for Fast Freddie Fraser, a nasty bit of goods from the East End schemes. It was during my love affair with Uncle Charlie and I'd found myself owing some cash to Fast Freddie, a debt I was proving slow to repay. Tiger was sent out to make me more fiscally responsible. He didn't break any bones, but I couldn't smile properly for a month. Needless to say, I found the necessary funds to reimburse Fast Freddie. I won't tell you how, because I'm not terribly proud of it. It wasn't something I wished to share with Nick, either.

'So what do you think, sir?' Asked the male detective, still looking through the wallet. 'Killed himself out of despair? Guilt for having murdered the Oldfield woman too much for him?'

Cornwell looked up at the spar above us then across the river, as if looking for divine guidance in Govan. Then he looked back and treated the cop to one of his trademarked glares. 'So first he battered himself black and blue then strung himself up there? Tiger was murdered, man!'

The detective withered under the heat of Nick's glare and tried to escape by taking a closer look at the body. One of his colleagues decided to garner some brownie points. He tried to hide his smirk as he spoke but wasn't wholly successful. I decided I didn't like him. 'Seems there was some kind of party going on below decks, sir,' he said. *Ooh, below decks*, I thought, *he's well up with his nautical.* 'They'd left the gangplank down because some of the young people crewing the vessel come back quite late. No-one heard anything, but then, they admitted they were quite loud.'

Nick gave him a congratulatory grunt and the detective visibly preened.

'Even so, bit public, isn't it?' Cohan was frowning. 'I mean, why not just dump his body somewhere more secluded?'

'I don't know, DC Cohan,' said Cornwell, but he was looking at me. 'Maybe it was meant as a message for someone else. A warning to keep his nose out of their business.'

I held his gaze as steadily as I could. 'Or maybe they like boats.'

He grunted and turned away. 'DC Cohan, take Mister Queste back to his car, will you?'

A look of annoyance flashed across Cohan's face but she nodded and I followed her off the ship. I was grateful to Nick Cornwell, not just for the lift back to my car, which was still parked outside Jessica Oldfield's house, but also the opportunity to get away from Tiger's body. To see someone who just a few hours before had been alive and literally kicking was disturbing. It proved that our hold onto life can be tenuous. I wondered if Tiger had any regrets, any unfinished business, any unfulfilled dreams. I knew I did. As the man said, regrets, I've had a few.

As we walked back to the car park from the ship, I kept thinking about Cornwell's words regarding this being a warning. He may be a right sod, but he was a good cop and his gut feelings were generally correct. The question on my mind was now that I'd received the message, was I going to listen?

My own gut knew the answer to that.

* * *

DC Theresa Cohan drove fast. She drove very fast. Thankfully, the rush hour was an hour or two away, otherwise I'm certain we would've come a cropper. I suspected she had a nippy wee sports car as her personal vehicle, judging by the way she handled the gears on the police issue banger. I got the feeling she did not like being treated as a glorified taxi for a down-at-heel old man like me and was unhappy at being away from the action. Still, the drive wouldn't take long – Hyndland wasn't too far from the riverside.

'So, how long you been in the Job?' I asked. As a conversation opener it was right up there with 'do you come here often?' but I was dog-tired, so cut me some slack.

'Five years,' she said.

'Like it?'

'Love it – always wanted to be a police officer.'

We were approaching the bottom of Byres Road by then and the streets were just beginning to come to life. Even so, it was spooky just how quiet this normally busy road was.

'I get the impression the boss really doesn't like you,' she said.

I smiled. 'Yeah, we've got a history, old Nick and I.'

She stifled a grin. 'He'd kill you for calling him that.'

'He'd kill me for breathing if he thought he could get away with it.'

'He says you're a scumbag who's not to be trusted. He says you hate the police and would do anything to do us down. He says you're a crook who's just not been caught yet, but one day he'll get you.'

'Right talkative, isn't he?'

She smiled then. Up until then she'd been all business, the professional cop, straight of face and severe of demeanour. Now she was human. Red hair, green eyes, freckles, button nose, she couldn't be more Irish if she pinned a shamrock on her lapel and started singing 'Too-ra-loora-loora.'

'Well,' I said, trying to sound fair-minded, 'he's not all wrong, I suppose. I'm no angel, certainly, but I'm not quite the demon he seems to think I am. As for hating the police, that's not true. I just don't believe you lot should be allowed to have free rein, that's all.'

'But we don't. You know that the laws are heavily weighted towards the scumbags...'

'No, I don't know that. I do know that the police force and the politicians who smell votes in it will certainly give that impression.'

'Our hands are tied wherever we look. You bleeding heart liberals have got us so wrapped up in rules and regulations that we can barely function.'

'Those rules and regulations have been brought in because of strokes you lot have pulled in the past. If you hadn't broken the rules back then, you wouldn't be restricted by tighter controls now. Now, you can blame people like me all you like, but really, you brought it on yourself.'

We fell silent then as she turned left into Huntly Gardens to head up the hill towards Hyndland and Jessica's house. I felt she was angry with me and she had every right to be. However, I hate it when people paint a picture of our legal system as biased in favour of the accused, because it really isn't. Eamonn O'Connor always calls it the Scottish Legal Industry, but I see it as the Justice Game, with the lawyers and judges being the players and the rest of us the pieces they move around.

Cohan stopped the car outside Jessica's house, where a uniform stood at the front door. Across the road a couple of press photographers waited for something to happen, unaware as yet that the focus had moved to the riverside. They had a good look at us but decided we weren't interesting enough to snap. Then, as if by magic, a phone rang and one of the snappers answered. He listened, broke the connection and ran towards his car. Then the other received a similar call and soon he was legging it to his vehicle. The word was out and they were being sent down to the Tall Ship. In the good old days the newspapers would have sent another snapper, but austerity hit the industry long before it was fashionable in Westminster. Now it was make and mend.

I thanked Cohan and started to climb out of the car. It took some time and I think there was some groaning as my body protested at the amount of time it had been on its feet. I'd just straightened again when she spoke. 'You're wrong, you know. You think all cops are just out to get an arrest, to get a result. We're not all like that. In fact, I don't know any who are. We want to put the scumbags away, the right scumbags, and people like you just want to stop us doing it. So we break a few rules here and there, but as long as the right person gets banged up, so what?'

I leaned back in. 'That's the problem though, Theresa…can I call you Theresa?' She nodded. 'If you're breaking the rules, how can you be certain that you're getting the right person? And breaking the rules can become a bad habit. Believe me, I know.'

'Sometimes we just know that we've got the right person.'

The tip of my tongue was heavy with a comeback about Bush and Blair *just knowing* there were WMDs in Iraq, but I was too exhausted to carry on, all I wanted to do was get home, so I simply nodded and said, 'Okay. Good luck with that.'

I closed the car door and turned towards my battered old Ford. I climbed into the driver's seat and twisted the ignition, praying that the engine would fire and not shame me in front of Theresa Cohan, who still watched me from her car. Thankfully the engine turned and I drove away.

The traffic was still light, so I crossed the Kingston Bridge to the south side of the river in record time, which was just as well because my eyes drooped most of the way and I had to struggle to keep them open. I longed to slip some really loud and boisterous film music in the CD player, but there had been no miracle and it still refused to play, so I settled for Good Morning Scotland on BBC Radio Scotland and caught up with the day's events. Aunt Jessica's murder was in there, along with Ritt Bobak's impending visit and the Beeb's latest health exclusive. I shuffled into my flat near the site of the old Victoria Infirmary like an old man who'd lost his zimmer frame. I contemplated having a cup of tea and a shower, but decided I was too beat even for that. I fell onto my bed fully-clothed and must have conked out immediately.

I woke up four hours later and dragged myself into a sitting position. I felt hungover but I'd not touched a drop. I hadn't felt this bad since my snorting days, in fact. Long nights were not for me anymore, I decided. It wasn't that I was too old, it was just that I'd subjected my body to far too much punishment. As Indiana Jones said, it's not the years, it's the mileage.

It was just after ten and even though every muscle and nerve in my body was screaming at me to lie down again and go back to sleep, I decided I had to get back over to the East End to see Jenny and the Sutherland boys. First though, I had to bathe and anoint my body. I was still wearing the same clothes I'd had on since yesterday morning and my days of wearing underpants two days in a row were long gone. I clicked the kettle on in the small kitchen, dropped a couple of slices of bread into the toaster, then went into the bathroom to give myself a scrub.

The shower felt good and I let the hot water sting my flesh

for quite some time. I wrapped myself in a large bath towel and padded through to the kitchen to make my brew and ignore the full-fat butter to scrape some low fat spread onto my toast. My brush with death that morning had made me more aware of my mortality. Then I thought, bugger it, and smeared some strawberry jam on too. One slice was devoured in almost one bite as I realised just how hungry I was. I chewed on the second while I carried the mug of tea into the living room and switched on the telly to catch up with any further news on the BBC News channel. It was as I was standing sipping my tea, crunching the toast and manipulating the remote that I heard Jerome Kingsley's voice from behind me.

'Morning, Dominic,' he said. 'Hope you had a nice kip.'

Chapter Eight

I don't like guns, especially when they're pointed at me. I also don't like it when I only have a bath towel standing between me and my dignity. It made me feel doubly vulnerable. I tried not to let my nervousness show as I swallowed the mouthful of toast and jam, but I'm afraid my voice did tremble a bit when I said, 'How did you get in?'

He gave me a modest shrug, but the gun's muzzle never wavered, which was troubling. It looked as comfortable in his hand as the knife had the previous evening. 'No big problem. Used to do a bit of housebreaking, back in the day. You really need to get better locks, my son. That one couldn't keep my old gran out, and she's crippled with arthritis.'

'I'll keep that in mind. How did you find me?'

He smiled, his teeth really white against his flawless black skin. He really was a good-looking fellow and it seemed a friendly grin, like we could be mates talking here. Chewing the fat. Only mates don't wave guns around.

'Wasn't that hard, really,' he said. 'I've got business associates up here and they've got friends in certain places, if you know what I mean, so once I got the licence plate of your motor, Bob was your proverbial. And here I am.'

'Yes, here you are,' I said, holding the towel tight to my body. I should have known Kingsley would have contacts in Glasgow, criminals who in turn would have a friendly copper or two on the payroll. It would be a simple thing to get my address from the computer, as long as they were smart enough to cover their tracks. It could have been even simpler than that. One or more of Kingsley's contacts might be mutual acquaintances.

I looked down at myself. 'Don't suppose you'd let me get some clothes on? I feel kind of naked here...'

He raised the gun slightly and shook his head. 'No, I like you just the way you are. And do me a favour, keep over that side of the room. I'm not falling for that stuff you pulled last night.'

Okay, so he had a new-found respect for my Krav Maga skills and I found that heartening. There was no way I was going to tell him that I'd only had three lessons and I'd pretty much shown him my entire arsenal of moves. At any rate, it would be damned difficult to do anything while wrapped in a bloody towel and I was not about to drop it and rush him like a scene from *Women in Love*. There might be inadvertent cupping.

He asked, 'So where's Jenny?'

'Not here.'

His eyes flicked around the room. It didn't take him long. My flat is far from spacious. There's the living room, the small kitchen, the bathroom and the bedroom, and that's it. 'I can see that. Where is she?'

I forced a smile. 'You don't honestly expect me to tell you, do you?'

'I could shoot you, somewhere unimportant but extremely painful, that would loosen your tongue.'

Yes, it would, it certainly would, but any form of shooting was out of the question – and I could not think of anywhere on my body that I deemed unimportant. I shrugged, 'She got away from me, I'm afraid.'

'Where?'

'Dalry,' I said, it being the first place that came into my head, not to mention I was fairly confident he wouldn't know where I was talking about. 'I stopped for petrol and she ran off. She's a slippery one.'

He gave me a long, hard look as he tried to decide whether or not I was telling the truth. I endeavoured to look as innocent as I could, but it's not something I can pull off very easily.

'I know a thing or two about you,' he said finally. 'My mates up here told me. You were a cokehead, weren't you?'

I didn't answer. I don't think he really expected me to say anything.

'See, that makes me think, doesn't it? Jenny ripped off a sports bag full of cocaine – my cocaine – and the next thing I know she's hooked up with a former snorthound up here. Now, I'm sure you can see what way my mind's going.'

'I've not seen your drugs, Jerome. And if your mates up here know me at all, they would've told you that I won't have anything to do with that stuff anymore.'

'Yeah, they did,' he conceded, 'but see, here's what I think – guys like you, users, you never change, you know? And you lie to everyone, even yourselves. Once a user, always a user. So maybe you and Jenny have teamed up to move my product up here, make yourself a bit of green.' He looked around my room, at the second-hand furniture, at the rug in serious need of an industrial-strength vacuuming. His eyes took in my TV and DVD player, easily the most expensive items in the flat, and then the open recess cupboard filled with discs, both DVD and CD. You may have noticed I like my movies. Despite that, he knew I was no millionaire. 'And I've gotta say, my son, you look as if you need it.'

I sighed wearily. My four hours sleep had done little more than take the edge off and I was still tired. 'Jerome, the first time I saw Jenny Deavers was last night, just before you showed up. I don't know anything about your drugs and she told me she didn't even take them.'

His eyes flashed. 'Jenny's a lying bitch.'

I held up a hand, the other one still clasping my towel tightly. 'Okay, you know her better than I do. But believe me when I say I don't know where she is. If I did, I'd tell you. I've got nothing to gain from protecting her. I was hired by her aunt to find her but now her aunt's dead.'

His eyes narrowed. 'She said she had an aunt in Glasgow. When'd she die?'

'Last night.'

'Sudden?'

'Very.'

There was a pause then as he processed this information. He wasn't faking it, he really didn't know anything about Jessica Oldfield's death. 'Who did it?'

'A guy who was found this morning hanging from the yardarm.'

He looked puzzled but he didn't probe further. There was something else on his mind. 'There were these men what came to see me, just after Jenny ran off. They was looking for her.'

'Who were they?'

He shook his head, he didn't know. 'I was angry at her, you know? I told them she'd probably come back here, to Glasgow. To her aunt. Then I made my own inquiries, you know? Tracked her down to that other place...'

'Saltcoats.'

'Yeah. My mates here had contacts, they found her for me. Didn't need to go nowhere near the aunt.'

'What can you tell me about these men?'

'Two of them, well-dressed, big. Got the feel they could handle themselves, you know? Looked like ex-military, SAS types.'

'Why were they looking for her?'

'They didn't say and I didn't ask. Got the feel they wouldn't tell me, you know?'

And I got the feel that Jerome was beginning to relax a bit. The gun had lowered a touch and the tension seemed to be dissipating. Maybe I'd come out of this without any extraneous holes after all.

I decided to keep him talking. 'They leave you a contact number or anything?'

He nodded. 'A mobile, said if I heard anything about her to give them a call.'

'And did you tell them she was in Saltcoats?' When he shook his head, I went on, 'You still care for her, don't you?'

He gave me a big smile again. 'No, man – I want to get my gear back. Wasn't sure why they wanted the bitch, but I didn't think I'd get my stuff back if they got to her first. I was gonna grab her, get my product then give them a bell, hand her over. Might be some green in it for me.'

And then the gun came up again, proving I didn't know the

first thing about the situation. 'So that brings us back to the beginning, don't it? Where's she at, mate?'

'I told you, I don't know. She got away. She could be anywhere by now.'

He stared at me, still not sure whether I was telling the truth. Then he shrugged and the gun dropped. 'No problem, my son. My mates told me that you wouldn't cough but I wanted to give it a try anyhow. They said you'd probably stash her somewhere and that there was only a couple of people you would trust. Two brothers.'

I cursed myself for being so predictable that even cheap Glasgow neds knew what I would do. 'There's some blokes heading over there now,' said Jerome, still smiling. 'If she's there, they'll get her for me.' I glanced at the phone in the corner and he followed my gaze. 'Go ahead – phone. You're already too late.'

I moved quickly and snatched up the receiver. I had the Sutherland brothers' number on speed dial and I punched the button. Jerome watched me as he languidly put the gun into his coat pocket. The ringing on the other end of the line seemed to mock me.

'No answer?' said Jerome. 'Maybe they're too busy.' He took a mobile from his pocket. 'Maybe you should see this text I got while you was in the shower...' He turned the phone towards me, so I hung up my landline and stepped closer to him. He took a step back. 'That's far enough, don't want no more of your *Bourne Identity* stuff. This is from those lads I'm working with. They're outside a flat in, what's the name of the street? Alexander's Parade?'

I didn't correct him. I screwed up my eyes to see the print on the screen – luckily it was a Blackberry and it was fairly large . WERE HERE is all it said, and taking into account the inability of texters to use apostrophes, it meant whoever Jerome was teamed up with had been at the Sutherland brothers' flat for over five minutes. A lot can happen in five minutes.

'She's not there,' I said, feeling my voice constrict in my throat.

'Ah, see – I don't think that's the truth, my son. Judging by the way you ran to that phone you knew exactly who I was talking about.' He thumbed a brief message into the phone. Telling them to move in, presumably. 'It looks like my mates were right about you. So, although it's been really nice chatting to you, I have to go now.'

'You don't know who you're up against over there, do you?'

'Me personally, no. But my mates do and they went prepared, if you know what I mean. I think they looked forward to it. Old scores to settle and all that.'

Though they were out of it, the brothers had made enemies during their years in the Life. One or two would relish the chance for some payback. My only thought now was getting over to the East End as fast as I could.

Then I had another thought. 'So if you thought she was there, what are you doing here?'

'I wanted to see you again. To confirm we was on the right track – and you did that, ta very much. And to give you this.'

By the time I realised his fist was swinging towards me it had connected with my jaw and rocked me back on my heels before I hit the floor. Thankfully, I managed to retain my grip on the towel. Being sprawled on my own rug was undignified enough without giving him the chance to ridicule my manhood.

'That's us even, I think,' he said, and sauntered from the room. I waited until I heard the front door closing behind him – truthfully, it took me that long to stop my head from spinning – before I hauled myself to my feet and moved groggily to the bedroom for some fresh clothes. Within minutes I was out, in the car and heading over Prospecthill Road towards the East End.

As I drove I kept punching the redial on my mobile phone, hoping that Hamish and Duncan would pick up. I think I even screamed 'pick up, pick up' a few times, but that didn't do any good at all. The journey from south of the river to Dennistoun went by in a blur. All I could think of was how I would never forgive myself if anything happened to either the brothers or Jenny. I cursed myself for being so easy to predict, I should've known Jerome would have friends who would, in turn, know of my connection to the Sutherland boys. I knew The Geordie lads had lost nothing of their old skills – but Jerome had said the men he'd sent had gone prepared. That might mean guns. And it didn't matter how tough you are, you can't beat a bullet.

I pressed my foot on the accelerator and prayed that I wasn't stopped by a traffic cop.

I didn't see the dark four-wheel drive that kept a steady three car lengths behind me all the way.

Chapter Nine

When they kicked the door in, Duncan was in the process of crossing the hallway from the kitchen to the front room because the phone was ringing, no doubt one of my calls. It had rung a number of times earlier but he and Hamish had been busy so they had ignored it.

There were four big bruisers, two with guns, one with a machete, but the last one armed only with a mean look. There was a smaller man with them and he sidled in behind them like an afterthought, having let the muscles do their thing. They had been sitting in a white Ford Transit outside for over twenty minutes, perhaps plucking up the courage to do what they had been sent to do. It happens like that sometimes. They would have been filled with bravado on the way over but once they reached their destination it took a while to screw their guts in place – especially as they knew who they were going up against.

When the door flew open – it didn't take much for them to break it down as it was secured only by the Yale – Duncan darted back into the kitchen and over to the stove, just as the first man barged into the room and moved towards him, a gun outstretched in his right hand. Duncan hefted a pot that had been heating on a gas ring, sending boiling water flying, his aim perfect. The man screamed as the liquid seared his flesh and he dropped the gun, his hands darting to his already livid face to wipe the stinging water away. Duncan jumped closer and thudded the pot against the man's temple. He went down with a groan just as his pals piled in behind him, fanning out into the room.

Duncan snatched the gun from the floor with his right hand, took a couple of steps back. He held the weapon like a professional, the fingers of his left wrapped round his wrist to steady his aim, his feet firmly placed on the floor one in front of the other, right elbow slightly bent, his left shoulder turned inwards to turn his body slightly side-on, offering a smaller target. This was not the first time he had held a gun and he prayed it would not be the last.

He kept his sights squarely on the only man now armed with a firearm. The rest he could deal with as and when the need arose, but this one had to be watched, though he was obviously no pro. He stood square-on, the weapon held at arm's length, elbow locked straight. He even held the pistol slightly to the side, as he'd probably seen gangstas do in the movies. It was amateur hour at the Palladium, but Duncan knew the guy could still do damage in the small shooting space between them.

The small guy held up his hands to calm things down. His grey hair was thinning on top and his face was weathered. Duncan knew him. He'd been a jockey and his skin was burnished with many hours of galloping in the open air. He'd been forcibly retired from the sport of kings some years before under suspicion of involvement in race rigging. No-one could prove it, but muck like that sticks and he was now a firm part of the Glasgow underworld, where he was known as Wee Willie, because he was small and his name was Willie. Simples.

'Easy, pal,' he said, his voice bearing a trace of an Irish accent. 'We're not looking for trouble here.'

'Yeah?' said Duncan, still not taking his eyes off the guy with the gun. He didn't watch the barrel pointed in his direction, he watched the eyes. Duncan knew he would see the trigger being tightened there before the man's finger even tensed. 'That why you battered the door down?'

Wee Willie shrugged, raising his hands slightly in an apologetic gesture. 'We only want the girl.'

'What girl?'

The man smiled. 'Come on now, we know she's here. Just hand her over and we'll be out of here.'

Duncan knew it was useless to maintain the pretence. Still, he had to play for as much time as possible. 'What do you want with her?'

'We don't want anything with her, we're just here to collect her. It's Mister Fraser that wants her.'

So Fast Freddie's behind this, Duncan thought. *Interesting.*

'What does Freddie want with her, then?'

Wee Willie smiled, revealing startlingly white, even teeth. 'Ours is not to reason why, as they say.'

Duncan knew two of the men. Sammy Simpson, brandishing a machete, and Lennie Watson, seemingly with no weapon at all, but somewhere on his person he would have an open razor. He was old-fashioned that way, was Lennie. If he had anything he would wield it with his left hand, his right hand being all but useless thanks to Duncan having once worked on it with a hammer. Sammy and Lennie were nasty little shits and Duncan had given them both hidings in the past, so he knew they had reasons to be here other than grabbing the girl. Without looking, he knew their eyes had flicked towards Wee Willie when he said they would simply leave. He knew they wouldn't go until they got what they came for. And it was not the girl.

Duncan's mouth stretched into a mirthless smile. 'I don't think Sammy and Lennie here like the idea of just going, do you, lads?'

The Irishman looked over his shoulder at the two men, then back at Duncan. 'I give you my word.'

Duncan's smile stretched. 'Your word? And I just accept that, right?'

'There are five of us.'

'Four. Lobster boy on the floor there is out of it. And I've got a gun.'

The Irishman gave a wry laugh. 'And so have we.'

Duncan thought about this. 'That's true.' He dropped his aim slightly and squeezed the trigger. The gunshot was very loud in the small room but not as loud as the screams of the gunman opposite when his knee erupted in a shower of blood and gristle. His weapon flew from his fist as he toppled over, both hands clasping his shattered leg.

'Jesus!' exclaimed the Irishman.

'That bastard shot me!' screamed the man, blood streaming

through his fingers.

'Yeah, and I'll do it again if you don't shut up,' warned Duncan as he trained his barrel on Lennie, who had leaned forward, his hand stretched for the fallen weapon. 'I'd leave it where it is, Lennie,' said Duncan, his aim now fixed firmly on the man's face. 'And then there were three. And I've still got the gun.'

Lennie froze for a second, calculating the odds against him grabbing the gun on the floor before Duncan fired. He decided it was not a bet he wanted to place and slowly straightened. Sammy pushed forward slightly and said, 'We can just rush the bastard.' Say what you like about Sammy Simpson, he didn't lack courage. Brains maybe, but not courage. He bore the scars of Duncan's handiwork on his face. Sammy liked to think that he was a hard man. Duncan showed him there is always someone harder.

'You could do that, Sammy,' said Duncan, reasonably. 'You could rush me and you might even get me. But one, maybe two of you will go down first. Now, the question is, who's it going to be?'

There was a moment of uneasy shuffling of feet and glances between the three of them, accompanied by groans from the guy bleeding on the floor. Then Duncan's phone started to ring again. They all stood there, listening to the sound from the front room, Duncan keeping the gun trained on Sammy, who glared back at him with such a ferocity it could've been the source of global warming. Lennie was still eyeing the gun on the floor and Wee Willie simply stood there, as if wondering what the hell to do next. Duncan knew Fast Freddie would not be chuffed if they returned empty-handed. In fact, there might be chastisement.

'You're a bastard, Sutherland,' said Sammy, his teeth gritted.

Duncan was forced to admit the truth in that statement. 'That I am, Sammy, that I am. And you'd be best never to forget it.'

A mobile phone rang then, a loud shrill tone that made the Irishman jerk in fright. His hand moved towards his jacket pocket and Duncan swung the gun in his direction.

'You bring anything else out of that pocket other than a phone, Willie, I'll put a hole in you,' warned Duncan. The Irishman froze for a second, then slowly put his hand into his jacket pocket and very deliberately brought out a small mobile phone. He held the phone to his ear.

'Okay,' he said, and cut the connection. 'Right, lads, we're out of here.'

'Leaving so soon?' said Duncan. 'And I didn't even offer you a cup of tea and a home-made scone.'

Sammy and Lennie exchanged looks, each one expecting the other to do something. When neither of them did, it was left to Sammy to fill the machismo void. 'We'll get you one day, Sutherland, so we will.'

'Sure you will, Sammy, sure you will,' said Duncan, gently. Then he jerked the gun towards the two men on the floor. 'Don't forget to take your rubbish with you, lads.'

Wee Willie stooped to haul the still unconscious man to his feet, snapping at Lennie to give him a hand, while Sammy helped their wounded mate onto his one good leg. His groans grew louder as he hopped towards the door.

'That bastard shot me,' he said again, as if they had not noticed the shooting in the first place or his previous comments on the matter. No-one said anything as they manhandled their wounded out of the flat, followed by Duncan, still holding the gun in the classic shooter's stance. He shadowed them up the hall like a sheep dog with some particularly untrustworthy sheep, and once he had herded them out the door, slammed it shut and rammed the remaining locks in place, the Yale now useless.

He let out a long, slow breath as he moved swiftly back down the hall, into the front room and on to the large bay windows overlooking Alexandra Parade. It took a minute or two, but he saw the men leave the building and climb into the white transit van parked at the closemouth. They piled their wounded into the back and then took off at speed eastwards.

Duncan took out his mobile and thumbed his brother's number in speed dial. When Hamish answered, he said, 'Where are you?'

'Heading towards the park,' said Hamish, breathlessly. 'I think we were spotted as we left. I think one of them's been following me.'

Duncan nodded. There would've been at least another two in the van, watching the street, one to drive, one to keep an eye out for Hamish and the girl slipping out. Wee Willie wasn't stupid, he would've tried to cover all eventualities, even the possibility that the brothers knew they were coming, which they had. They certainly did come team-handed, which in a perverse way pleased Duncan, as it's nice to know you're still a force to be reckoned with. He said, 'They're coming after you. I've taken two of them out but there's still plenty of them.'

'Shit!'

'Get to the park, stay in the open. I'll be right there. How's the girl?'

'Scared.'

'Okay. How are you?'

'Kind of enjoying it. It's like old times...'

Duncan smiled. He knew what his brother meant. They had sworn off crime and that had been relatively easy. And yet the violence was in them and always would be. Sometimes it had to come out.

* * *

I was only a few minutes away, but I tried phoning them again. This time Duncan answered. Before I could say a word he said, 'I know, Dom, they've already been.'

'You okay?'

'I'm okay but a couple of their boys will need a kiss and a cuddle.'

'Where's Jenny?'

'Safe for now. She's with Hamish on the streets, but they're after them. They're on their way to Alexandra Park.'

I was heading down the hill from the Duke Street direction and I could see the expanse of green ahead of me. 'I'm almost there now. I'll find them, pick them up.'

'I'm just leaving too,' said Duncan. 'Dom, watch yourself – these boys were sent by Fast Freddie and they don't want to go

71

back home without the lass.'

Fast Freddie Fraser again. Tiger Reilly had also worked for the East-End gangster, now he was getting his boys to do Jerome's dirty work. Maybe I'd been wrong – maybe Kingsley did know more about Aunt Jessica's death than he was letting on.

'Okay,' I said and hung up. I was almost at the park now and I had to find somewhere to dump the car.

Chapter Ten

Although I drove by it God knows how many times in a week, I'd not set foot in Alexandra Park since I was a boy, during a day trip from school. I lived in Springburn on the north side, and being brought to the East End was strangely exotic for us tenement kids. The park is not the size of its counterparts at Queen's Park or Kelvingrove, but it was still a sizeable chunk of real estate to comb, so I hit Hamish's number on my mobile and told him to meet me at the boating lake, a narrow strip of water near the Edinburgh Road end.

I parked the car on the Carntyne side, near where the Parade becomes Cumbernauld Road and juts north or continues east as Edinburgh Road. The early morning promise had been fulfilled and it was a bright spring day: warm if you were from Glasgow, but nippy if you were used to greater temperatures. I took my life in my hands and darted across the busy junction, received a few horn blasts for my trouble, and entered the park at a small side entrance on Provan Road. I ran down the slight incline and emerged at the end of the long boating lake. A fenced-off football field sat to my left, where an elderly man in a cowboy hat walked a Husky dog. I startled two young mums pushing prams as I sprinted past them. I had spotted Hamish and Jenny sitting on a bench beside the lake, in full view of any passers-by and what looked like a class of nursery school kids and their two attentive teachers at the water's edge. *Good*, I thought, *less chance of any unpleasantness when there are people around.* I was certain Fast Freddie's boys would not wish to try anything violent with so many eyes on them. Glasgow crooks prefer to operate outside public scrutiny if they can. A pair of swans swam in their usual haughty manner on the surface of the pond, their long necks and tilted heads like question marks poking from fluffy white clouds, and I was confident we would get out of this without giving them a scare.

Which just goes to show you how wrong I could be.

I slowed down as I neared Hamish and Jenny, not wishing to attract too much attention. There was a hint of a blue sky above, but not strong enough to reflect on the water, which was grey and murky and choked with weeds, telling me that not much boating had taken place here recently. They sat on the bench like a father and daughter taking the opportunity to catch the rays. On the opposite side of the lake I could see the bulky figure of Sammy Simpson, his pal Lennie beside him. Wee Willie I knew, but the fourth man was new to me. They were all watching Hamish and Jenny the way a pride of lions watches the impala, just waiting for their chance.

I sauntered over to the bench as casually as I could, given my sphincter was tighter than a movie star's facelift, and sat down beside them. Jenny looked at me with large frightened eyes and I gave her what I hoped was a reassuring smile.

'Nice day,' I said and Hamish squinted at the sky.

'Probably rain later,' he said.

'Course it will – it's Scotland,' I said. 'Two things you can always depend on – we'll never win the World Cup and it's going to rain.'

Hamish smiled, but there wasn't much humour in it. 'How do you want to play this?'

I glanced at the four men and gave them a little wave. Sammy, Lennie and Wee Willie glared at me, but the fourth man almost waved back. He dropped his hand sharply and shot his companions a shamed look. 'We're safe for now, I think. Duncan's on his way. How the hell did you get away from them in the first place?'

'They made the mistake of sitting outside the flat for too long. We've got friends in the street, they still keep an eye out for us.'

God bless the nosey neighbours, I thought. 'The guys have their own early warning system,' I explained to Jenny. 'Their neighbours watch out for them, let them know if there's anything dodgy going on. It's like NORAD, without the planes and the satellites.'

I could see the girl was terrified and it was important to keep her as calm as possible. If she panicked and bolted, things would only get worse, a lot worse.

'We knew they were there for the lass so we hid in the bedroom until they forced their way in,' said Hamish. 'We made it easy for them – just one lock. Duncan kept them busy in the kitchen while we slipped out the door. But there was another two in the van and one followed us here.'

I nodded. That's the problem with bastards, they're everywhere.

'Who are they?' Jenny asked.

'They work for a Glasgow crook called Freddie Fraser,' I said.

'Fast Freddie? What's he got to do with it?' Hamish asked.

'He's in cahoots with Jerome Kingsley,' I said, then pointedly to Jenny, 'You remember Jerome, don't you, Jenny?'

'Ah, yes – the candyman from the smoke,' said Hamish, smiling again at my terminology. 'He must really want you something bad, lass.'

'He thinks Jenny ripped off some of his product,' I explained.

Hamish raised his eyebrows. 'And did you?'

Jenny's eyes turned away from us, as if she was looking at the kids playing at the water's edge. 'I've not got his drugs,' she said, her tone flat. Hamish turned those eyebrows to me and I shrugged, as if to say *leave it*. He nodded and looked back at Freddie's men. The nursery teachers had gathered their charges together now and it was obvious they were planning to leave. Hamish saw that too and said, 'Looks like we're losing our protection.'

'We'll follow them, stay as close as we can,' I said. 'They won't try anything, not with kids around. Freddie's an arsehole, but he'd have their balls for clackers if they pulled anything like that. Nice and easy, Jenny, don't let them know you're scared.'

'I'm not scared,' she said. It wasn't true but even if it was, that was okay. I was scared enough for both of us.

Hoping we looked like a family out for a stroll, although what kind of family would lay claim to Hamish I don't know, we walked a few feet behind the gaggle of noisy children, who were doing their level best to prevent the two patient teachers from keeping them together as they headed along the edge of the boating lake towards the duck pond. I glanced across the water and saw that the four men had split up, with Wee Willie and the one who almost waved keeping pace with us while Sammy and Lennie loped off and were making their way through a swing park, presumably to catch us in a pincer movement.

'They're splitting up,' said Hamish.

'Saw that,' I said.

'Maybe we should do the same,' he said.

'And that will help how?'

He shrugged. 'Make them think. If you carry on with Jenny, I'll veer off up along the path here, somewhere they can't see us. They won't know what I'm up to.'

I followed his thinking. They would keep us in sight, but the fact that they could not see Hamish might keep them wrong-footed. They would also know that Duncan was not far away – and to have both Sutherland brothers as unseen entities would be enough to unsettle the strongest disposition. To put it in movie terms, Wee Willie and the others were the crew of the *Nostromo* while Hamish and Duncan were a pair of aliens. There might not be any chest-bursting, but there would certainly be terror.

We were at the far end of the boating pond and walking through the children's play park, the school party fragmenting, with some of them being drawn by the allure of the swings. Their teachers sounded very weary as they called them back into line. Sammy and Lennie lurked at the edge of the duck pond ahead of us. They saw us making for the left-hand path towards the main entrance to the park, with our young bodyguards still just ahead of us, and set off along the right hand side. *Okay*, I thought, *they're looking for a place to jump us that's not quite so public.* That meant we had the duck pond between us and them, which was good, but we still had the other two behind to deal with, which was not good. We were surrounded by mature trees and bushes, the water to our right, a high metal fence and the back yards of tenements to our left. I felt my skin tingle as my nerves stretched and my senses heightened. The children's laughter, the birds in the trees, the tinkle of the fountain in the centre of the duck pond all seemed extremely loud. Even the air seemed warmer. Or maybe I was just having a hot flush. Hamish, I sensed, was looking for the opportunity to peel off and hide without the guys behind us spotting us.

'We could just keep right on, get to the main exit. They won't try anything there,' I said to Hamish.

Hamish's phone bleeped that he had a text and he read it quickly. I saw a smile tease at his lips.

'No,' he said. 'We teach them a lesson.' I guessed the text was from Duncan. *That'll even things up a bit*, I thought, but didn't like the idea of any lessons being taught. I liked the idea of running away and living to teach lessons another day.

We reached the end of the duck pond and Hamish steered us to the right, taking us out of sight of our followers as well as Sammy and Lennie. The trees and bushes converged slightly to shield the area from the tenements and Hamish darted to his left into the foliage. Despite his size, Hamish could move fast and was out of sight in a split second.

'Is this a good idea?' Jenny asked.

'Hamish and Duncan know what they're doing,' I said, hoping I sounded more confident than I felt. 'We'll be fine.'

The nursery class had carried on along the path and we were alone now. Over to our left stood a huge ornamental fountain which was not working. Had it been a warmer day, or even a weekend, there might have been people lounging on the benches, but there was no-one. The only person I could see was a tall, fit-looking bloke with brown hair and a brown moustache sitting on a bench reading a newspaper, but I doubt he would be much help if things turned nasty. Bystanders tend to look to themselves when the fists – or bullets – start flying no matter how buff they look. Anyway, I wouldn't want some punter out for some air getting hurt because of us.

And then Sammy and Lennie loomed into view from the shadows of some large trees. We were caught between them and the two behind, which is probably what Hamish wanted. I cursed him for using us as bait.

Jenny had seen Sammy and Lennie now and she also put the plan together for she said, 'Dom.'

'I know,' I said, irritation creeping into my voice. I was pissed off with her for getting me into this and I was pissed off at the brothers for treating me like a Judas Goat. Most of all I was pissed off with myself for continually getting embroiled in situations that really had bugger all to do with me. But some people attract trouble the way a TV screen attracts dust.

Sammy and Lennie were on the move now, heading into our path. My mind raced through the possibilities. I was confident I could take one of them, probably Lennie as I knew he wasn't quite as handy since Duncan had taken that hammer to him, but Sammy would bring me down pretty quickly. Now, if I could take Sammy first then maybe – just maybe – I'd have a chance to tackle Lennie too. But hope, as they say, is the thing with feathers, and it flew away pretty damn smartish as the simple truth dawned on me that Sammy Simpson could snap me like a twig. Even if I could deal with them, there were the others to consider – and there was no way on God's green earth that I was capable of handling them all and getting clean away with Jenny. Not unless there was a miracle.

And then there was a miracle. Rather, two Geordie miracles, one big, one small, bursting out of the foliage behind Wee Willie and his mate. They heard them coming, the guys weren't trying to be stealthy, but by that time it was too late, the Sutherland boys had steamed in, fists and feet flying like a kung fu movie on fast forward. That left Sammy and Lennie ahead and I turned my attention to them. The man on the bench had looked up and was watching the action behind us with interest, his newspaper laid on his lap. He hadn't run for the hills, which bode well. Maybe he would give some assistance when the rough and tumble began.

Sammy and Lennie did pause when they saw their two mates being sorted out by the brothers, but not for long. They were here for the girl, and I clearly wasn't much of a threat. My only hope was to do the unexpected, so I grabbed Jenny firmly by the arm and swung her towards Sammy, who was unsheathing a bloody great machete from beneath his coat. She yelled a word that a young lady of her tender years really shouldn't know, but there was nothing she could do to stop herself from slamming squarely into the big man. I heard him grunt as a hard portion of her anatomy made contact with a softer section of his, the blade went flying and I launched myself at Lennie. Jerome might have learned his lesson and kept his distance, but Lennie couldn't even spell Krav Maga. He was wearing a thick jacket so body hits would not penetrate. My first punch caught him on the side of the neck and his initial look of surprise gave way to one of pain. But he didn't go down. He swung out with his right hand, but it was a wild move and I blocked it easily, then slammed the heel of my hand into his nose. Some people can strike so hard that way that the blow drives pieces of bone into the brain. I didn't hit him that hard, but I was in pretty good shape for my age and the jab was powerful enough to force blood from both nostrils. Lennie staggered back, his hands to his face and cursing like we were on cable TV.

Sammy had also been surprised by my attack, but he had already gathered his wits about him. He realised I'd given him a golden opportunity to grab Jenny, but she was no pushover. She knew she had to do something, so she fired off another barrage of expletives that would've shocked an HBO TV executive and lashed out with her foot, catching him on the shin. I heard the thud as shoe hit bone and thought, *good on you, girl.* Sammy flinched then bellowed in rage and lunged at her again.

As I whirled round from Lennie, I became aware of the man on the bench moving, standing up, the newspaper slipping from his lap, something in his left hand which was rising towards Jenny and Sammy and then there was a small noise, a spit, a cough, no more than that and I felt something wet splash my face. At first I thought some spray from the fountain had been caught by the breeze but then I saw Jenny's face, her eyes wide again, and I thought *she looks as if she's got more freckles than before* but then I realised they weren't freckles and I saw Sammy spinning towards the water, part of his head gone in a horrible mess of blood and bone, and I looked back at the guy and saw the thing in his hand was a silenced automatic and he was bringing it round to bear on me because, I realised, I was moving towards him. I didn't want to but I was doing it all the same and I wished to God I would just stop...

Then Lennie bulldozed into me from behind and I pitched forward, but as he stood there proud of himself, I heard that spitting noise again and his body jerked as his chest erupted in blood and he fell away like an extra in a Sam Peckinpah movie, all slow motion and spurting gore, his arms windmilling as he tumbled backwards.

'Jenny, get down!' I yelled, because she was still rooted to the spot, staring at Sammy's body half in the water, blood floating around his head like red oil, but the man was turning the pistol back towards her and there was nothing I could do because I was sprawled on the ground and there was little chance of reaching him in time, even if a bullet didn't reach me first...

It wasn't a spit or a cough I heard this time but an honest-to-goodness gunshot and I saw something puff at the man's left sleeve and a little spurt of blood. He didn't make a sound, in fact if he hadn't turned towards Duncan I would have sworn he hadn't even felt it. Duncan was standing a few feet away, presenting as small a target as possible, aiming a gun with a steady hand at the man. Behind him, Hamish was holding Wee Willie in a neck lock, the other man prone on the ground.

'Don't,' Duncan said.

The gunman's eyes darted from Duncan to Jenny and then to me as he weighed up his chances of managing another shot at Jenny before Duncan took him down. He looked back at Duncan and smiled. His wound must have been agonizing, but this guy actually smiled. He was a good-looking guy, but somehow the smile just seemed odd and out of place. He nodded once, a brief acknowledgement to a fellow professional is the way I saw it, and slowly lowered his weapon. He backed away, his gaze still flitting back and forth between us, alert for any kind of attack. Then, when he felt sufficiently safe, he thrust the pistol under his windbreaker and began to walk swiftly away, blood trailing down his fingers and leaving tracks on the cement.

'Let's go, Dom,' said Duncan, conveying a sense of urgency in just three words as he scanned the area, checking for any unwanted faces watching us. There was no-one, which was the first piece of good news that morning. I pulled myself upright, grabbed Jenny by the arm and dragged her away from the bodies. Her movements were leaden, as if she would suddenly seize up altogether. Hamish let Wee Willie go after exchanging a few words – no doubt threatening further bodily harm if he did not comply – and together they hefted the unconscious thug to his feet. Between them they half-carried, half-dragged him away. They had no intention of leaving any witnesses behind to talk to the police, who would already be on their way. A single gunshot might have people looking up and wondering what the hell it was, but eventually someone might decide to alert the law. Soon the park would be flooded with uniforms and we would all have to be as far away from the scene as we could. A strong word or two to the small guy and his pal would keep their mouths shut, although they would without a doubt report back to Fast Freddie. Which was fine by me, because I wanted a word with him myself.

No-one looked at Sammy and Lennie. Looks would not help them now. The aftershocks of seeing Sammy's head exploding and Lennie's chest splattering blood would stay with me for a long time. I didn't like them much, but they didn't deserve that. Even so, my *Alien* analogy crossed my mind again. There had been a chest burster after all.

'We need to find somewhere safe for Jenny,' I said to Duncan as we hurried away.

'Only one place that's really safe I can think of,' he said and I instantly knew where he meant.

Jenny was about to meet Father Francis Verne.

Chapter Eleven

The thug knocked senseless regained consciousness before we left the park and that meant we were able to walk reasonably normally back to where they had parked their white van. That was something, at least. Police sirens were already whooping their way towards the park and we didn't want to advertise our involvement in what had gone down by carrying a prostrate figure along the street. The driver's eyes widened in shock as he climbed out to meet us.

'Where's Sammy and Lennie?' He asked, but Wee Willie simply shook his head and slid open the van's side door. I saw another man lying in the back, a makeshift bandage wrapped round one blood-stained knee. Another one was groaning as skin peeled away from his reddened face and hands. I didn't know yet what had happened in the flat, but I knew they would regret ever taking on the Sutherland boys. Most people do.

Wee Willie climbed in and glared at us as his mate hauled himself unsteadily beside him. 'Fast Freddie won't like this,' he said.

'Fuck Fast Freddie,' said Hamish, relishing the alliterative qualities of the phrase. Duncan wrenched the door closed and faced the driver, who was still standing open-mouthed, his eyes darting back and forward like he was at a particularly exciting tennis match. I could understand his shock and awe. He had one guy bleeding in the back of his van, a second doing an impression of a boiled chicken and another who had clearly been through the wars, and now Sammy and Lennie were nowhere to be seen. This was not the way it was supposed to be.

Duncan stepped into his field of vision, forced the man to look at him. 'Take them back, don't speed, don't go through any red lights, don't do anything to draw attention to yourself. And don't say a word to anyone about today, clear?'

The man swallowed and nodded but Duncan wasn't satisfied, so he stepped closer and said in a low voice. 'I mean it. I find out you've spoken about this, we'll have a conversation, understand?'

The man swallowed and nodded again, his eyes conveying the message that the last thing he wanted was to have any kind of conversation with Duncan, now or in the future. He swung himself into the driver's seat, started the engine and pulled away. The wail of approaching sirens was louder now and we were close enough to the park gates to hear tyres crunching to a halt. I looked back to see two marked police vehicles parked diagonally towards the kerb and uniforms running through the gates. The cavalry had arrived, but they were too late, always too late.

'So who was that guy with the gun?' Hamish asked.

I shook my head and turned to Jenny, as did Duncan and Hamish. We all thought she knew, for some reason. I felt there was a lot this girl knew, but she wasn't telling. Her eyes roved between us and her face contorted irritably as she said, 'I don't know, do I?' The words were defiant but the voice was hoarse, subdued. Seeing a man die can get you like that. I still felt a bit delicate myself and I'd seen it before.

'It looked like he was out to get you, lass,' said Duncan, his voice gentle.

'I've never seen him before,' she insisted, some steel beginning to creep back in her tone. She was a tough cookie, this one.

Duncan nodded, knowing this was not the time or place to pursue the subject. He had a flat to clean up and a cast-iron alibi to forge for us all, and standing in the street jawing while the street was filling up with enough law to merit the opening of a doughnut shop was not getting those tasks done. He threw me a set of car keys and said, 'Take my car, Dom. I've a feeling yours is being watched.'

I nodded in agreement. I'd already come to the conclusion that I'd led that gunman straight to Jenny. He'd probably been staking out my flat and tailed me over here. I'd been so concerned over what was happening to the Sutherland brothers that I'd not noticed him.

'And Dom,' said Duncan, 'don't get a scratch on it, understand? You damage that car and I'll be very unhappy.'

I smiled. 'Duncan, you know me – Mister Careful Driver at all times.'

Hamish smiled, but Dom did not look convinced. 'Just don't be pulling any Steve McQueen stuff, okay? I want my car back in one piece.'

I knew he meant the Steve McQueen of *Bullitt* and not the artist turned film director. 'I promise to treat it as I would my own.'

'That's what he's afraid of,' said Hamish, still grinning.

We had just been through hell in the park and seen two men die, yet here we were swapping banter in the middle of Alexandra Parade. It's the way we dealt with it. Later, in quieter moments, I'm sure Duncan and Hamish would play back the scene at the pond, perhaps regret their involvement. Perhaps they would reach for a bottle of something hard and Scottish that carried the promise of freedom and clear water and mist-covered heather. Perhaps it would be enough to wash the memories away. Perhaps they would do all that. I knew I would.

I led Jenny past them and headed towards Duncan's black Mercedes. I could feel his eyes still on me, self-doubting eyes that questioned his wisdom, but I ignored them and pressed the button on the key fob to unlock the doors. I stopped when I heard Duncan say softly, 'And Dom – go the long way and keep an eye on your rear view.'

I glanced up and down the street as Jenny walked round the front of the car to the passenger door. He was right – there may have been eyes on us and we did not want them following me to the refuge. I nodded, telling him I understood, and climbed into the car.

The soft leathery precision of German engineering welcomed me like an illicit lover. I fired up the engine and heard it say in a soft Teutonic accent, *let's do this, mein herr*. I sat for a moment, my hands caressing the wheel, letting the power and opulence seep into my bones. This was the kind of motor I should be driving, not that clapped-out old Ford. This was the real Dominic Queste.

I realised that Jenny was watching me with curious eyes. I shrugged, slightly embarrassed and said, 'I love this car.'

'Do you want a moment or two alone?'

'No, it's purely platonic. Duncan would kill me, otherwise.'

I eased out into the traffic, unsure of the machine, but the controls were so smooth and perfect that a baby could drive it. I glanced in the wing mirror as we coasted away and saw Duncan keeping a watchful eye on the road. If any vehicles pulled out behind us, he would let me know. I turned left onto Cumbernauld Road, my eyes flicking from windscreen to rear view mirror, but saw nothing untoward. My mobile remained reassuringly silent so I knew Duncan had not seen anyone trailing. We were sailing towards the on-ramp to the M8, Barlinnie Prison looming up ahead of us on the right, and I kept a close eye on my speed, because in this ride it would be so very easy to break the limit without knowing.

Jenny said, 'I can't believe you threw me at that guy.'

'I had to catch him off guard.'

'Yeah, but you *threw* me.'

'I think it was more of a swing than a throw.'

'You practically picked me up and *hurled* me at him!'

'It was the only thing I could think of at the time.'

'My feet actually left the ground...'

'Don't exaggerate.'

'Next time, throw yourself.'

'It worked, didn't it? You're not hurt, are you? You didn't come out too badly, all things considered.'

She fell silent and I knew she was thinking about the bloke with the gun, reliving the deaths of Sammy and Lennie in her mind. I felt her shudder at the memory. I could not blame her because my blood was running on the tepid side as the image of Sammy's head erupting flashed in my mind – and the realisation of how close I had come to being left for dead beside the pond.

'Who was he, do you think?' she asked. 'That guy back there?

The one with the gun.'

'You're sure you've never seen him before?'

She shook her head.

'Certain?' I pressed.

'I think I'd remember him,' she said. 'Was he working for Jerome too?'

'I don't know. Jerome wants you pretty bad, but something tells me that guy's got nothing to do with him.'

She slumped into silence again, taking this in. I didn't tell her why I believed that. Jerome did want her, but he wanted her alive, if only so he could deliver some pain himself. The man in the park was not there to catch her and take her to Jerome. He had taken deliberate aim at her and the only reason she wasn't in a body bag right then was because Sammy got in the way. Our friend with the gun then took Lennie out because he was a threat and would have put one in me had Duncan not stepped in. They were collateral damage, his intended target was the young girl beside me. No, I was convinced he was another part of the puzzle that was Jenny Deavers. However, I wanted to know more about her former *inamorato*. Yes, I used the word *inamorato*. Go look it up.

'Tell me again about Jerome's drugs,' I said.

'For the last time, I don't have his bloody drugs,' she said, her voice irritable.

'Why does he think you do?'

'I don't know.' She sighed. 'It's Jerome, he thinks everyone's against him.'

'Tell me about him.'

'What about him?'

'Who is he, what is he, what's his star sign, is he a good kisser?'

I felt her give me that look again, the one I'd seen the first night we met, but I ignored it. I'm good at that. She sighed again and said, 'Jerome's...well, he's Jerome, I suppose. You've met him, you know what he's like.'

'How did you hook up with him?'

'I was dossing down in London, in a flat in Peckham.'

'Looking for the Trotters?'

There was that look again. 'Eh?' she said.

'Nothing,' I said. She was obviously not a fan of classic Brit comedy. 'So you met him when you were dossing. How?'

'At a party. Girlfriend introduced me to him. He's a good-looking guy, charming when he needs to be. He had a nice car, way nicer than this...' *Don't repeat that to Duncan*, I thought. '..and he had a nice flat. Putney.'

'Did you only stay in places in London that began with the letter P?'

'You want to hear this or not? Try shutting it for more than a few seconds.'

I decided to shut it.

'So,' she said, exhaling heavily, 'I moved in and it was okay at first. He was good to me, you know? Treated me nice. Bought me stuff, took me out. And I was happy for the first time in a long while. A very long while.'

The words stopped and I snatched a sideways glance in her direction. Her face was angled toward the floor of Duncan's pristine car, as if searching for a speck of dirt. Her eyes had clouded and I wondered if life had been happy at any time for this young girl. I didn't say anything, though. Well, not for a second or two.

'So what went wrong?' I asked.

'Nothing. Not really.' She thought about it. 'Well, me, I suppose. I get restless, can't stay too long in one place, you know? I wanted to move on but Jerome didn't want me to leave. He's very possessive. What's his is his, and I was his. So one day I just packed my bag and left, simple as that.'

'And the drugs he says are missing, what's the deal there?'

'For the last time, I don't know! He's probably just saying that to get people to help him. He just doesn't like the idea of me walking out on him. Male pride, something like that.'

'But he *is* a dealer?'

'Oh, yeah – big time. He's got contacts all over the place, people like your Fast Freddie character. Here, Edinburgh, Manchester, Newcastle, abroad, all over. He's sold more drugs than Boots.'

'And that didn't bother you?'

She shrugged. 'Nah, doesn't matter to me how he made his living.'

'You use?'

'No – mug's game, that.'

That it is, love, I thought, *that it bloody well is.*

She looked at the buildings sliding past and then said, 'I don't want to go wherever it is you're taking me.'

I didn't reply. As far as I was concerned it wasn't up for debate, but it was a free country, so she could moan as much as she liked. Wouldn't change things, though. She was still going.

'I want to go back to Saltcoats,' she went on. 'Back to my friend's flat.'

I shook my head. 'Not happening.'

'Why not? You can't force me to stay with you, you know. I'm not your slave or something. You can't just kidnap me and keep me with you against my will.'

'Jenny, you go back there, you're dead, you understand? Your boyfriend will have someone watching that flat. You go back, you're walking right into his arms.'

'You can't be sure.'

'Yes, I can.'

She thought about it for a moment. 'I still want to go back.'

'No,' I said.

'I don't see why you're doing this. You're not responsible for me.'

I didn't answer because I didn't think she would understand. It was on the tip of my tongue to tell her about Jessica's death, but I chickened out. I didn't know how to broach it. And to tell her why I felt responsible – I'd taken her aunt's money to do a job – would automatically lead me to having to break the bad news. So I simply said nothing, which is not an easy thing for me to do, and concentrated on my driving.

I had considered taking the motorway, but decided against it. I'd turned right after the flyover which crosses the M8 and headed towards Ruchazie, the road alongside Riddrie Cemetery affording us a better view of the dark Victorian bulk of Barlinnie jail on the far side of the main route between Glasgow and Edinburgh. We drove through the scheme and I turned right again, heading to Queenslie. The roads here were quieter and I would spot a tail more easily, but there was nothing to raise suspicion. When we hit the Edinburgh Road again, I turned left. Neither the girl nor I said another word until I pulled the car into the small car park in front of the Mary Ellis Memorial Refuge and we sat in silence for a few more moments. That was something of a record for me. Finally, Jenny peered at the sign above the door and asked, 'Who's Mary Ellis?'

'She was a young girl about your age who died.'

'Drugs?'

I nodded.

Jenny bobbed her head, her face grim. 'See? Mug's game. This where you're going to stash me now?'

'You'll be safe here.'

'That's what you said before.'

It was a good point well made, and I couldn't argue with her. The Sutherland brothers' flat should have been secure but I had underestimated Jerome's pull with the likes of Fast Freddie. However, there was an unwritten law in Glasgow's underbelly that no-one messed with Father Verne under any circumstances. It was a law that was enforced somewhat stringently by Duncan and Hamish, but their reputation had proved less than effective earlier that day. Father Verne, though, was a force to be reckoned with in his own right, while his work with addicts was admired and applauded by some heavyweight faces, albeit the ones who did not depend solely on the drug trade for their livelihood. Police Scotland had also made it clear that the refuge was a no-go area for the crooks. Jenny would be safe here, this time I was certain.

'What is it? Some sort of rehab clinic?' She asked.

'No, not really. It's a refuge, a place where young kids – addicts, prostitutes, homeless – can come when they feel the need, get a hot meal, a bed for the night. A respite centre, sort of. If they want they can get help off the drugs and off the streets, but only if they want. It's run by Father Verne.'

'That's who the brothers work for, isn't it?'

'Well, work *with* I think is more accurate.' I didn't see Father Verne as the employer type, doing regular staff appraisals and completing PAYE returns. I also didn't see Duncan and Hamish in the role of employees. They helped Father Verne keep the place viable, shaking funds out of people in the city who seldom if ever put their hands in their pockets for charity. They had once hinted, when we were drunk and tongues had loosened sufficiently for the truth to come out, that there was some other function they performed for the good Father, but then good sense had overtaken the liquor-fuelled need for candour and they had clammed up. I never raised it again. Some things I'm better off not knowing.

'So this Father Verne,' she said, 'he preach at these kids, or what? Tell them to get back on the straight and narrow? I mean, he's a God botherer, isn't he? That's what they do.'

I gave her a wry smile. 'Let's go in,' is all I said.

Chapter Twelve

If Francis Verne had turned up at Central Casting in Hollywood, he would have been cast immediately as a priest.

For one thing, he looked like Spencer Tracy. Had Katie Hepburn ever ventured out to the East End of Glasgow, she would have tripped over her Academy Awards to get to him. He was slightly below average height, squat in a way that suggested a powerful frame, and he had a shock of snow-white hair. His face was lined, weathered and somehow permanently tanned, which made me suspect he had a sunbed hidden away somewhere. There were scars above both eyes, reminders of his boxing days. There was a story that he and Nicholas Cornwell once went toe-to-toe in the ring. There was no-one there to see, it was something just between the two of them, but I was told there was no clear winner. I often imagined them slugging it out in an empty gym somewhere, blood and saliva spinning in the air as each crushing blow hit home, neither of them giving an inch, neither of them yielding to the other, like a pair of raging bulls.

The refuge was based in what had once been a small hotel off the Edinburgh Road between Barlanark and Baillieston. It was a two-storey building with a small car park at the side and ten bedrooms between the upper floor and an extension built to the rear. A young girl who was probably in her mid-teens watched us climb the three steps to the main door. She was standing outside, smoking a cigarette, and she told us Father Verne was in the TV room, which was on the second storey. She threw the smouldering remains of her smoke into the bushes beside the door and said she would lead us up. I let her walk ahead, even though I knew the way. I felt it was important she feel useful. The girl was stick-thin and had a complexion so sallow it was almost yellow – the famed

Glasgow tan. If I had pulled the sleeves of her sweatshirt back I had no doubt I would have revealed the tell-tale track marks where she had injected the heroin. They would have been red and irritated, like infected flea bites, because she was scratching the inside of her arms constantly. I doubted she even knew she was doing it.

She reminded me of Mary Ellis, after whom Father Verne had named this place. I'd never met her personally, but I'd seen photographs and she had the same look as this kid, as if she was being eaten away from the inside. Mary had been fourteen and had died in his arms in the aisle of his church, where she had crawled after injecting herself with a tenner bag which had proved to be far too pure for the average addict. Some young crooks had got hold of a consignment of smack and decided to market it themselves, but they lacked the necessary know-how to cut it properly. Heroin has to be watered down before it can be injected, cut with sugar, starch or even powdered milk. These neds had no idea what they were doing so the tenner bags they were punting were about 75 per cent pure H. The stuff burned through Mary's system like acid and she barely got herself into the church before she collapsed. It was a Sunday morning and Father Verne was in the middle of Mass. All he saw was this young girl staggering in the door and then folding up in the aisle. She died convulsing in his arms as he called out for someone to help, anyone, even God. But Mary Ellis was beyond help.

He had helped addicts before, but now he resolved to do something tangible. First, though, the young idiots who had been pushing the dodgy smack in the streets had to be caught. Father Verne tracked them down one by one and handed them over to the law. One or two had mysterious bruises about their person, but none wanted to admit they had been given a hiding by a Roman Catholic Priest more than twice their age.

After that, Father Verne campaigned against dealers and drugs in general. He appeared on radio and television and he gave newspaper interviews, including one to me when I was gainfully employed. He was less than circumspect in his opinions regarding the lack of attention being paid to the drug trade by the authorities and he received complaints from politicians and policemen that he had been unduly critical of their efforts. He carried right on with what he was doing. Those same politicians and policemen took their concerns to the Roman Catholic hierarchy and this brought heat from his own side. Father Verne ignored this also. He received threats from certain members of the underworld, who were unhappy with the momentum gathering among community leaders and the public at large against their trade. Father Verne paid no attention. There was a pattern forming here and it generally involved Father Verne telling anyone who wanted him to stop what he was doing or tempering his comments in any way to go and take flying fuck at a rolling doughnut. I heard him use that very expression once, when a local councillor took exception to Father Verne decrying him as a useless political carpet-bagger who put party politics before the wellbeing of his constituents. To hear a man of God giving sexual advice involving pastries was one of the highlights of my life.

Father Verne wasn't alone in the TV room. He was seated on a small settee staring up at a lanky young man who looked as if he needed hosed down and scrubbed with a broom. His skin was pasty, his clothes were just short of threadbare and he gave off the kind of musty odour that reminded me of wet towels left lying too long. His hair stuck up like a brush and he had a thin layer of fuzzy bristles on his jaw and chin, none on his upper lip, giving him the look of Shaggy in *Scooby Do*, only he wasn't as lovable. When he spoke, the words were formed on one side of his mouth, as if the other cheek was paralysed. I don't know if he affected this because he thought it was tough or if he had some kind of affliction, but it didn't help make him any more attractive. He was, to be blunt, ugly as sin.

'Look, mate, I'm no carin' if you're a Holy Joe, catch my drift?' His voice was ugly too – nasal with a distinct whine to it. 'You stay away from my lassie.'

Father Verne's face betrayed nothing. For all anyone knew, he might've been listening to the news bulletin on the TV.

The young man straightened his shoulders, jutted his chin out.

Believe me, it wasn't much of a jut. 'You hearin' me, old man? I said you keep the fuck away from my lassie.'

Father Verne stared straight into his face for a few seconds, then said in a reasonable voice, 'I hear you, Cody.' I almost laughed. Cody. Give me a break. 'Now you hear me – if Shayleen wants my help, then she will get it, and there will be absolutely nothing you can do about it. You will kill that girl if you carry on the way you're going and I won't have that.'

'You just wait...'

'No,' and the priest stood up so suddenly that Cody took an involuntary step back. He was a good foot taller than the Father, but somehow it seemed as if he was looking up at him. 'You wait. If you continue to pump her full of that shit you stick in your own arms and then pimp her out to anyone with a fiver, you *will* kill her. You want to kill yourself, go ahead, I for one won't lose any sleep, but that girl needs and wants help. And I will give it to her – I don't need your permission.'

'Oh, aye?' Cody had regained some of his composure. 'We'll see about that, old man. You watch, one morning you might wake up and find this dump of yours going up in smoke, and you with it.'

Father Verne leaned closer to the young man, his voice as frozen as his face. 'Are you threatening me?'

Cody smirked. 'I'm just sayin'.'

I saw the Father's fists clench and his shoulders tense. Cody didn't seem to care that he was close to having his face rearranged, for his sneer was still in place, but his hand crept into the pocket of his hoodie. Neds like him always have a weapon somewhere, it's a law of nature. They're so unpleasant, there's always someone ready to have a go at them. I readied myself to wade in should the need arise, though Father Verne wouldn't need my help. The day he couldn't handle an odious little shit like Cody was the day he'd have to hang up his rosaries. I saw the Father's eyes flick from Cody's face to the doorway, where I stood. He saw Jenny and he saw the girl we'd met outside. There was nothing he would've liked better than to have gone all Old Testament on the boy, but he knew this was not the time. He relaxed, let his fingers loosen. Cody's smirk deepened because he thought he'd won, but I knew different. Father Verne would never show that side of his nature to the girls. Cody saw us too, and his eyes fixed on the girl.

'Come on, Shayleen, we're outta here,' he said, striding across the room towards us. I turned and saw she had shrunk back against the wall of the corridor.

'Naw, Cody.' she said, her voice pleading, her eyes darting a plea for help in my direction.

'Aye,' he said, and reached out to grab her, but I wrapped a fist round his wrist. My fingers and thumb met, he was so skinny. He whirled towards me, tried to pull free, but I held firm. His eyes blazed with sudden anger and I tensed myself for an attack. He was no muscleman but that didn't mean he wasn't dangerous. 'Get the paws aff, bastard.'

His other hand had snaked into his pocket again and when it emerged it was holding a slice of wood with two razor blades embedded in one side. It was a makeshift weapon, but could cut a chunk out of me with ease. I didn't give him the chance to wield it. I didn't like him on principle, he'd threatened my friend and he was ugly, all good reasons for dishing out some pain. I was still holding his wrist with my right hand, so I jabbed with my left. His head snapped back, the weapon dropped, and I followed up by twisting his arm round, forcing him to slam against the wall. I jerked his forearm up his back and leaned against him. 'Cody,' I breathed. 'I've had one hell of a morning and I've not had any coffee yet. I get cranky when I don't get my coffee, so piss off like a good little boy and don't bother me any more.'

I gave his arm another twist for good measure then placed my free hand on the back of his head and forced his face against the wall as I pushed myself free. He swore a few times, but the words were cracked with tears and I knew he was struggling to remain as manly as possible. He spun round and I thought he was up for another go, but all he did was glare at me, then at Shayleen, before running off down the corridor. I heard him sob as he veered into the stairway. Shayleen watched him go then took a step towards

95

the stairway. There seemed little purpose behind the move, but she made it, and I knew she was contemplating following him.

'You can go after him, Shayleen,' said Father Verne, 'but you know what will happen. He'll beat you up and then he'll punt you to one of his pals for the price of a tenner bag.'

She looked back at him and I saw confusion on her face. She was torn between the need to protect herself and whatever bond there was between her and Cody. Tears formed in her eyes, big fat ones, moisture her body couldn't afford. She resumed her stare down the corridor while absently scratching her arm. 'I don't know what to do,' she said, softly.

'You're free to do what you want,' said Father Verne, still standing in front of the TV. This was his way. God gave everyone free will, he once told me. If this girl wanted to stay, then she could stay. If she wanted to go, then she could go. If he moved in her direction now, he might on some level be seen as trying to persuade her to remain. I knew how he worked from my own experience. True healing begins with the patient, he said. To achieve change you have to want to change.

Shayleen faced him, then dropped her eyes and nodded. She took another step towards the stairwell. 'So I can go after him?'

Father Verne nodded. 'If that's what you want. This isn't a prison, I'm not a jailer. You stay, you go, it's up to you.'

He waited while she thought this over, her jaw working as she weighed her choices, her hand now rubbing furiously at her arm. I wondered if she knew she was doing it. Jenny stared at her intently, waiting for her decision. I realised I was holding my breath. Then, finally, Shayleen nodded, turned and walked slowly in the opposite direction. We watched until she opened a door and vanished into one of the nearby bedrooms. If I listened carefully, I was convinced I could hear her crying.

Jenny and I stepped into the TV room, just as Ritt Bobak's face appeared on the screen to publicise his Christian Rally at the Scottish Exhibition and Conference Centre late in the week. He was talking about the notion of gay marriage being an abomination in the eyes of God and Man and how it would bring about the fall of western civilisation. Or at least, that's the way I took it. To be honest, he could've been saying that water was wet and fire hot and I would still have disagreed with him. I'm prejudiced that way.

I realised Father Verne was staring at me, his eyes dancing with amusement 'What?' I said.

He adopted a passable John Wayne impression as he intoned, *'I've not had my coffee yet, pilgrim, and I get cranky when I don't get my coffee.'*

I felt a sheepish grin break out. 'I didn't say pilgrim.'

'I heard the word pilgrim and it'll stay when I tell the story to all and sundry.'

I shook my head. 'And you a priest too.'

He turned his smile to Jenny. 'And this will be Miss Deavers.'

'I take it Duncan phoned you?' I asked.

His face crinkled further. 'There's not much gets past you.'

I was not surprised. Apart from phoning ahead, Duncan would also have been keeping Father Verne up to speed. Father Verne liked to be kept up to speed. I nodded towards the screen. 'You buying into this bloke?'

Father Verne turned back to the screen and said, 'Ritt Bobak? Hell no. And what is it with these Americans that they can't run for President unless they have a name straight out of *Star Wars*? Barack Obama, Mitt Romney, Rick Santorum, Newt Gingrich, now Ritt Bobak.'

I was impressed. 'You watch *Star Wars*?'

He lowered his head, looked at me under his bushy eyebrows. 'I do watch more than Bing Crosby films, you know.'

'You think he'll run for office?'

'He's certainly being groomed for it. Frankly, can't think of anything that worries me more.'

'Why?'

'Because he's a fanatic, and fanatics are dangerous, no matter what holy book they wave around.'

'So you'll not be going to see him when he's here?'

'Only if I'm dragged kicking and screaming. That man being in a position of power, let alone anywhere near the nuclear button, scares the bejesus out of me. He's a dangerous man, a very dangerous man. And if he's not, there will be men behind him who are.' Father Verne looked back at Jenny. 'But then, from what Duncan has been telling me, you've had your share of dangerous men today.'

She nodded, her eyes flicking to the TV screen, as everyone does whenever one is on. Even if you turn the sound down, your eyes are still drawn back to the flickering box in the corner, as if the static electricity exuding from the surface is reaching out and dragging you in, like the little girl in *Poltergeist*. Father Verne apologised, picked up the remote from a low coffee table at his side and clicked the off button just as Bobak was explaining that he did not believe his family should be in the public eye. 'If I run for office, *I'm* running for office – not them,' he said and flashed the interviewer the great white way that was his smile.

'I wish there was an off switch to really shut him up,' said Father Verne. 'Now, how about a bacon roll and a nice cup of tea?'

I said, 'I could murder a bacon roll and a cuppa.'

'Good,' he said, clasping me on the shoulder and putting a protective arm around Jenny, 'because you're making it.'

I knew there would be a catch. If it wasn't for his priestly vestments, sometimes I thought dealing with Father Verne was like bartering with the Devil.

Jenny asked, 'Would you really have allowed that girl to go if she'd wanted?'

'Of course,' he said. 'What I said is true, this is not a prison. She's free to do as she wishes.'

'Even if that means her going back to that guy?'

Father Verne smiled. 'Obviously I'd rather she stayed, for her own wellbeing, but I can't force her. She has to make up her own mind.'

Jenny treated me to an accusatory glance. I'd refused to let her go, after all, but then I wasn't Father Verne. Then she asked, 'How old is she?'

'Fifteen, maybe sixteen. She's not terribly sure herself. She was shooting heroin at eleven, working the streets at twelve.'

'Where are her parents?'

'Father's dead, her mother is somewhere, out there,' he waved a hand towards the wall. 'They were both addicts and drunks. They liked heroin and alcohol more than they liked her, but she had her uses. Her father turned her out himself, to make money to feed his own habit. He's burning in his own corner of hell now, I'd imagine.'

'And then she fell in with that Cody? And he did the same to her?'

'She was always with Cody. He's her brother.'

We'd reached the stairway and Jenny stopped, her eyes wide. 'He's her brother?' Father Verne nodded. Jenny chewed her lip, a sign I now knew that she was thinking of something. Sights like Cody and Shayleen could not have been new to her, not the way she had been living, but it clearly still upset her. I wondered if something in what Father Verne had said resonated in her own past.

'Happy families, eh, Father?' I said.

'World is full of them, Dominic,' he said. 'Now, how about those bacon rolls? I could eat a scabby-heided wean.'

* * *

The refuge's kitchen was well-equipped, if on the small side, and while I busied myself frying bacon, buttering rolls and boiling the kettle, Father Verne sat at a small table and spoke to Jenny.

'So, my dear,' he said, 'tell me a bit about yourself.'

Jenny's eyes shot towards me for a second then she said, 'What do you want to know?'

'Well, your age would be a good start.'

'Twenty,' she said, 'twenty-one in November.'

'A good age,' Father Verne said, but I knew he would have said that no matter how old she was. 'I remember when I was twenty going on twenty-one, life was all ahead of me. As it is for you. And your parents?'

Jenny fell silent and something stabbed at my guts. I still hadn't told her about Aunt Jessica.

'My mother's dead,' she said. 'Never met my dad.'

That was news to me and when I turned my head, mouth open, I met Father Verne's calm blue eyes telling me to keep quiet, that he had the floor. I did as I was told and took my attention back to the sizzling pig flesh in the frying pan. So Jenny's mum was an unmarried mother – Aunt Jessica kept that to herself. She had been vague about the father and I just presumed that they had divorced.

Father Verne's voice was gentle. 'Did your mother never talk about him?'

Jenny squirmed a little in the plastic chair and I thought she wasn't going to answer, or at best give him one of her patented smart-arsed replies. But she didn't. She told Father Verne what I sensed was the truth. That was the thing about him – he could make you open up.

'She said it was a one-night stand, they were both out of their heads on drink or drugs or – knowing my mum – both. He was up from London, staying with friends, and they were all at a party. They ended up alone in a bedroom and...well, you know.'

Father Verne nodded his understanding. I thought about London as I pushed the food around the pan – was that why Jenny had gone down there? To find her father?

She went on, 'Nine months later, there I was. He never came to see me, never wrote. I don't think she even told him she was pregnant.'

'Did she tell you his name?'

She nodded. 'James Quinn. He was a doctor. She said he was nice.'

So she had a name and she had a profession. The smart little bastard that sometimes whispered in my ear told me that she had without a doubt gone to London to find her dad. I wondered if she was successful. I carried them each a plate with two rolls on it and laid them on the table in front of them. Father Verne thanked me and reached for the brown sauce. Jenny nodded and reached for the red. *Vive la différence*, as the French would say. I wished them *bon appétit* and went back for my own plateful and three mugs of tea.

'And what of your mother?' Father Verne asked as he spurted the HP on his bacon. Jenny had squeezed some Heinz onto hers and she took a bite, chewed and swallowed before she answered.

'She died in a fire, when I was a girl.'

'I'm sorry,' said Father Verne.

Jenny shrugged and looked down at the roll in her hand. 'I didn't know her all that well. I don't think anyone knew her all that well, not even Aunt Jessica.'

At the mention of Jessica I felt that stabbing sensation in my stomach again. I was not looking forward to telling Jenny her aunt was dead. Father Verne did not help me much when he asked, 'Aunt Jessica?'

'My mum's sister. She took me in when my mum died. She's okay, I suppose.'

'But you still ran away.'

Jenny nodded and took another delicate bite of her roll.

'Why?' asked the priest, and Jenny shrugged. 'How old were you?'

'Sixteen,' she said.

'You've been alone since then? How did you live?'

Jenny laid the roll back on the plate and shoved both hands under her thighs, her shoulders hunched forward. She was uncomfortable with this line of questioning and I could tell she wished it would stop. During my own wilderness years I'd done things that didn't bear repeating and I wondered if she'd had similar experiences. Maybe her recent life mirrored Shayleen's and she didn't want to look into it. Her plan, I think, was to become unresponsive, to clam up and hope that Father Verne would abandon his probing.

She didn't know Father Verne, though. He didn't give up easily. 'How did you live, Jenny?'

Her eyes swung in my direction and I could see she wanted me to intercede somehow, to interrupt and halt the questions. But I was not about to do that. I had been threatened with a knife and firearms, my friends had been placed in danger, I'd seen two men gunned down and it was all because of this young girl sitting at this cheap Formica table who did not want to talk about what she had been doing for over three years. No, I was not minded to get in Father Verne's way. So I avoided her gaze and munched my food.

'Jenny,' Father Verne said, leaning forward, 'I think you have to talk about this. If Dominic or I are to help you, we need to know everything about you...'

'I didn't ask for your help, either of you,' she spat, anger burning in her eyes. 'I was doing okay by myself.'

'You were about to be knifed by your drug-dealing ex-boyfriend when I found you,' I reminded her, trying hard to keep a sharp edge out of my voice. I don't think I succeeded. 'I think your idea of "doing okay" needs to be reassessed.'

She glared at me but I didn't let it worry me. She had glared at me a lot in the past couple of days – one more did not make a lot of difference. To be honest, I was pretty pissed off with her attitude. Maybe that was why I decided to tell her.

'Jenny,' I said, hoping my voice was gentle and soothing. 'Your Aunt Jessica...'

'What about her?' she asked, her voice still hard and unyielding.

I hesitated, not sure how to put it. I'm not a doctor or a cop, I'm not used to delivering bad news. 'Jenny...' I struggled to find the words but in the end I didn't need to say anything. I suppose my face must have told the whole story. I saw tears flood into her eyes, quenching the flames of her anger.

'What happened?' she asked, her voice hoarse and strained.

'Someone killed her,' I said and saw shock flash across her face.

'Jerome?' she asked.

'No,' I said. 'It was a man called Tiger Reilly...'

Father Verne stirred at the mention of the name. 'Tiger?' I might've known an old pugilist like him would know Reilly.

I nodded. 'He was hired by someone else, though. If it means anything, I'm not sure he meant to kill her.'

'Tiger's not a hit man,' said Father Verne. 'He's muscle, pure and simple. Not a killer.'

'Well, doesn't matter what he was, he's dead, too.'

Father Verne's eyebrows shot up as he processed this. Then he frowned at the seriousness of it all.

Jenny asked, 'Did Jerome hire him?'

'He says not.'

'Do you believe him?'

'I don't know what to believe, that's why it's important that you tell us about yourself.'

She looked at me then Father Verne, then down at her plate and the remains of her food. She was finding all this hard to take and despite my growing annoyance with her, I suppose I couldn't blame her. She'd had a hell of a time, and now she'd found out that her only relative was gone. Although I'd have preferred a more profound film, a line from *Thoroughly Modern Millie* popped into my mind: *so sad to be all alone in the world.*

The phone in the office next door rang and Father Verne said to me, 'Answer that, will you, Dom?' I nodded and with a final look at Jenny, stood up. When I left the room Father Verne was leaning across the table and talking to her in a soft voice. If anyone could get her to talk, it was him.

I entered the office and picked up the receiver. After I'd said hello, Duncan's voice greeted me. 'Dom? Everything okay?'

'Everything's fine, Duncan.'

'Jenny settling in?'

'She's with Father Verne now,' I said. 'He's trying to get her life story.'

'Good luck to him – Hamish and I tried to find out more about her last night but she clammed up. We didn't want to push too hard in case she did a runner. Can you leave him to it?'

'Sure, I think I'm in the way anyway.'

'Good, Hamish and I are done here – we're going to pay Fast Freddie a call, thought you'd want to come.'

'You thought right.'

'Right – meet us at his place in half an hour. And Dom...'

'What?'

'Don't use your mobile. I'm calling from a neighbour's house.'

Duncan's neighbours – what a gang.

'You think someone might be listening?'

'Maybe. It's not just you tabloid journos who know how to hack mobiles, you know.'

And then he was gone and I felt vaguely insulted. I'd never tapped a phone in my life. The only electronic means I'd ever used to obtain someone's personal information was phoning Directory Inquiries. Still, I resolved to take his warning to heart and avoid using my mobile.

I returned to the kitchen and told Father Verne and Jenny that I was going out for an hour or two. Father Verne nodded but Jenny didn't even acknowledge my presence. I jerked my head, asking Father Verne into the hallway and he nodded. When he came out I said in a low voice, 'Keep an eye on her, Father. Don't let her out of your sight. She's a runner.'

He glanced back into the kitchen and shook his head. 'I think she's had enough of running for now. She's a smart girl – she knows she's safer with us than out there on her own.'

I grimaced to show I was uncertain. 'I wish I had your faith, Father.'

He grinned and patted me on the shoulder. 'It's in the job description.'

And then he turned and went back to sit in front of Jenny. I watched them for a moment, she sitting staring at the cold food and he watching, waiting patiently, certain in the knowledge that sooner or later she would tell him what he wanted to know.

As I settled myself into the car I saw Shayleen standing in the street, another fag wedged in the corner of her mouth, right hand working at the scabs on her left arm. She must've slipped by us when we were eating. I watched her for a full minute as she pondered where she was going to go. She looked up and down the street until finally she decided and began to walk towards the city. *You've lost one, Father,* I thought, but then she stopped and stood still, her back to me, her head down as if she had forgotten something. Eventually, she turned and walked slowly back towards the refuge, the cigarette butt joining the first one in the bushes before she pushed through the doors.

As I pulled away, I wondered if there was something in this faith thing after all.

Chapter Thirteen

Freddie Fraser had been a tearaway all his life, which came as no surprise to anyone as his father was a thief, his brother was a thief and his mother was known to be somewhat sticky-fingered as she wandered round C&A in Argyle Street. She was said to have the speediest lifting technique in the city, with jumpers, shirts, trousers being transferred from the shelves to under her coat in the blink of an eye. She once walked in a slim Glasgow 'hairy' and left looking as if she was eight months pregnant. No-one stopped her. Legend has it that the store manager even held the door open.

So when wee Freddie also turned to thieving, no-one was unduly shocked that he proved to have a talent for it. After all, it was in his genes. However, he also had two other skills that could not be explained by his DNA. First of all, he had a propensity for violence that was not shared with his father or his brother, although his mammy had been known to throw a punch or two when she was out of her head on Red Biddy, a mixture of cheap wine and meths popular among Glasgow's hairy class. Freddie might have been small and thin enough to model clothespoles, but he was a nasty little shit when riled.

His second talent could have done him some favours if he had worked at it.

Freddie Fraser could run.

I've never seen him do it myself, because by the time I made his acquaintance he was in his sixties and was running things rather than running in them, but by all accounts he was like the Six Million Dollar Man with his arse on fire. He could run like the devils of hell were after him, as my granny used to say, and given his other activities that may well have been the case. As a child I used to read a comic character called Alf Tupper, I think in *The Victor*.

Alf was a working class, whippet-thin runner known as the Tough of the Track who won all his races despite having been up all night making briquettes to save a friend's business, missing his bus to the stadium, being knocked over mid-race by a poncy upper-class twit and losing one of his raggedy running shoes. When I heard about Freddie Fraser winning medals at school for running I tended to see him as that hard-nosed little guy from the back streets sticking two fingers up to the ruling classes. As I learned more about Freddie, though, it became clear that he was more likely to stick those two fingers into their eyes and then rob them blind.

His running ability, which proved useful in his day job when fleeing the law, brought him the nickname Fast Freddie and Fast Freddie he has remained ever since, even though nowadays he was unlikely to break into a gallop, or anything else for that matter. Fast Freddie Fraser was a prime example of a bad boy made even worse, thanks to his foresight in jumping on the heroin band-wagon in the early 1980s which allowed him to put his breaking and entering days behind him. Now he had those two fingers of his in more pies than a crooked baker. Drugs, extortion, identity theft, counterfeit goods – if it was bent and it was profitable, you'd find Fast Freddie's fingerprints all over it. Not literally, of course, because he was careful nothing could ever be traced back to him.

He based himself in the office of a discount carpet warehouse near Bridgeton Cross, one of the many legitimate enterprises he owned. They made him a tidy profit, but nothing like the millions he had raked in over the years importing substances destined for the veins or noses of the city's users. He sat at a large desk that dwarfed his skinny little body and I wondered if he was over compensating for something. I'd heard a rumour that there was another reason they called him Fast Freddie – his staying power with the ladies was nowhere near Olympic class. Of course, I would never dream of asking him if it were true, querying the love life of a Glasgow crook can be hazardous to one's health. Behind him a large picture window looked down on the warehouse floor, where his army of salesmen punted cut-price floor coverings. He stared across the vast, empty expanse of his desktop at Duncan,

Hamish and myself, his dark little eyes narrowed and glittering, his face carrying more lines than a script for *The West Wing*.

'You were out of order, Freddie,' said Hamish, who tended to do most of the talking in situations like this, Duncan preferring to sit quietly and look menacing, something he did quite well. He scared me, and I was his pal.

'How do you work that out?' said Freddie, his voice harsh and guttural, as if he'd had more than a sip of his mammy's Red Biddy back in the day.

'Sending your boys to our house. Well out of order, Freddie.'

Freddie shrugged, as if he didn't care. Which he probably didn't. You didn't get to his position in Glasgow's underbelly by giving a toss about what was, and what was not, out of order. 'Worked out all right for you, didn't it? One of my guys is laid up with a shattered knee, one's got a face like Freddie fuckin' Krueger, another one's punch drunk and what else?' He stared off into the middle distance as if trying to recall. 'Oh, aye – two are dead!'

'Not our doing,' said Hamish.

'Aye, I know – otherwise we'd no be sittin' here havin' this wee chat.'

Duncan shifted slightly in his chair at the veiled threat and Freddie's slitted eyes shifted in his direction. 'And don't you be tryin' anythin' on, Duncan Sutherland,' warned Freddie. 'I'm no they lads, get me? I've got enough boys in this building to grind you like coffee, know what I'm sayin'?'

Duncan did not reply. He held Freddie's stare, his face expressionless. Freddie seemed to be waiting for Duncan to say something, but if that was the case he was disappointed. Finally, the small gangster looked back at Hamish. He asked, 'So what are you wantin?'

'Leave the lass alone,' said Hamish.

Freddie sighed and sat back in his big chair. He looked like a ventriloquist's dummy in repose. I resisted the impulse to peep under the desk to see if his little feet touched the floor. 'No can do,' he said. 'Made a promise to a mate.'

'Break it.'

Freddie shook his head. 'A promise is a promise and my word is my bond. Jerome wants that lassie really bad, know what I mean? And Jerome and me, we're in business together. Wouldn't be fiscally responsible of me not to help him out.'

'She's just a girl, Freddie,' I said and those hard eyes slid to me. Freddie had nothing but contempt for users, even if he made his money out of them. He had even more contempt for former users like me, probably because he no longer made any money out of us. He stared at me for a second and his mouth tightened into a slit.

'Shut the fuck up, Queste, the big boys are talking,' he said. I tried holding his gaze as Duncan had done but, God help me, I didn't have enough Clint Eastwood in me. I struggled against the overwhelming need to drop my eyes and was relieved when Hamish spoke up and bailed me out.

'Break it to Jerome that he's lost this one,' he said. 'You're not getting the lass, Freddie, we mean it.'

Irritation made his face crease even further. 'What the fuck is she to you? Eh? She's just a wee tart that ripped my mate off. You shaggin' her or what?'

Hamish shook his head sadly. For Freddie, there always had to be an angle, a sound financial reason for doing things, or in this case sexual. He might say he was doing a favour for a pal but Freddie did not have pals. There were people from whom he made money, people with whom he made money and people who did not make him any money. Those in the last category held no interest for him. Hamish and Duncan were actually helping out a mate – in this case me – and that was that. Whatever their past, whatever they may still get up to, the Sutherland brothers were loyal to their mates. That was something Fast Freddie would never understand and that was why Hamish did not respond.

Hamish stood up, Duncan followed. I felt the need to make it unanimous.

'Don't send any more of your boys,' said Hamish. 'We've put the girl in a safe place now. Leave her alone. Take my advice – disappoint your pal Jerome. There's nothing but pain if this goes any further. And don't even think about putting any of your pals among Police Scotland's finest onto us. We're covered for today's drama and it won't work out well for you. '

Freddie smiled, but he didn't find anything particularly funny. Hamish was suggesting that he might be tempted to grass to the law and he didn't like that. He was an informer when it suited, but he didn't like to be reminded of the fact. However he decided to let it pass and simply said, 'Who killed my boys?'

'We don't know,' I said. 'Maybe you should ask your pal Jerome.'

'What's that supposed to mean?'

'Well, maybe Jerome decided not to put all his eggs in your basket. Maybe he didn't have enough faith in you to bring him what he wants, maybe he's got a back-up plan.'

Freddie's eyes narrowed even further until they were practically closed. I knew that meant he was really pissed off, possibly at the thought of Jerome playing both ends against the middle but more likely at me for putting the thought in his head. I didn't believe it myself, but I was still smarting from him making me feel as small as his willy was reputed to be.

'Think about it, Freddie,' I said, unable to help myself, as we turned towards the door. Then I pulled a *Columbo*. I turned back and said, 'Oh – one more thing. Seen much of Tiger Reilly lately?'

Freddie's brow furrowed. 'Reilly? No spoken to him in months, why?'

'Well, sorry to tell you, but the only way you'll speak to him in the future is by visiting a spiritualist.'

The lines above Freddie's nose deepened. 'What the fuck you on about, Queste?'

'He's dead, Freddie. Someone strung him up from the yardarm late last night over by the Riverside Museum.'

'They hung him? Why'd they do that?'

'Dunno – maybe they'd intended to keelhaul him, but only reached the letter H in the maritime dictionary. H for hanging, for hoist, for heave-ho, me hearties.'

'Who would want to do that?' Freddie was sincerely perplexed. A kicking, a stabbing, a shooting he understood, but leaving a man dangling from a spar was not the Glasgow way.

'I think the same guy who shot your boys today. Tiger was working for whoever he's working for.'

'How the fuck do you know that?'

The truth was I didn't know it for certain, it was just a hunch. Another word that starts with H. But I wasn't about to tell him that, so I ignored his question. 'Tiger wasn't working for you any more, was he?'

'No, dropped him months ago. He was getting too fond of the sauce, made him unreliable. You can't depend on an alky or a junkie. Even an ex-junkie.' I guessed that last bit was for my benefit but I ignored it.

'And you have no clue who he was working for now.'

'Anyone who would give him beer money, I heard. You really want to know, why not ask his ex?'

'He was married?' I was genuinely surprised. I thought Tiger Reilly was just a bit player whose function was to menace and break bones. I never thought he might have a back story of his own.

'Aye, to an auld slag who used to hang around the boxing matches. Lives down near the Barras.'

'Don't suppose you have an address?'

He smiled. 'Aye, but I'm no giving you it. You fancy yourself as a detective, go detect.' His smile broadened, proud of himself, and I knew this particular interview was over.

As we made ourselves down the dull stairwell to the rear exit, Duncan said, 'You didn't tell us about Tiger Reilly.' He kept his voice low, for sounds echoed up and down the bare brick walls and none of us put it past Freddie to be lurking somewhere above.

'Been a bit busy today, Duncan, what with high-speed dashes across town, being chased through the park and guns going off everywhere.'

Duncan nodded, 'Fair enough. So who killed him?'

'Beats me. I had words with his fist at Jenny's Aunt Jessica's...'

'What was he doing there?'

And then I realised I hadn't told them about Aunt Jessica either, so I gave them a quick *précis* of the events up the West End and my subsequent excursion with DCI Cornwell to the Tall Ship. By the time I had completed my tale, we were outside and heading towards the car park. We paused beside Hamish's Vauxhall Astra, which had more dents on the bodywork than the surface of the moon. It must have pained Duncan to be seen in his brother's car. When I reached the bit about identifying Tiger's body, they both shook their heads.

'That's not right, that,' said Hamish. 'That's not the work of local lads. Too extravagant.'

I said, 'That's kinda what Nick Cornwell said. He inferred it was meant as a warning to me.'

Duncan said, 'And you think it's the same guys who were behind the shooter in the park?'

'Well, let's put it this way – let's hope so. If any more bad guys get involved here, I'm going to need a cast list.' They both nodded as they thought about this. I went on, 'That guy at the park – did he look ex-military to you?'

They looked at each other and frowned. Duncan said, 'Could've been. He handled the weapon like a pro, didn't seem flustered at all. He could've been Regiment...' The Regiment, the SAS, trained killers. 'What made you think of that?'

'Something Jerome said this morning – about these ex-military types looking for Jenny.'

'And you believe him? He's not exactly what you'd call a solid source.'

'True, but that guy today did look he would be at home in camouflage gear, didn't he?'

Hamish said, 'So why would ex-Regiment blokes be looking to kill a teenage girl?'

I shrugged. This was becoming very complicated, extremely messy and decidedly nasty, but I was not about to walk away. I don't like people pointing guns at me. I don't like police officers telling me to keep my nose out of things. I don't like being threatened in my own home, be it ever so humble. I'm funny that way. I looked at the brothers and knew they were in for the duration, for all the above reasons. They're funny that way too. I suddenly felt all warm and fuzzy at their loyalty. Thankfully Hamish spoke before I felt the need to hug them and tell them I loved them. Pals or not, I think they would have battered me like a haddock there and then.

Hamish said, 'Does Jenny know about her aunt?'

I nodded. 'Told her before I left the refuge.'

'How'd she take it?'

'Stunned, I suppose. But it's hard to tell with her, she's a deep one.'

Duncan said, 'So what do we do now?'

'I'm going to find Mrs Reilly, see what she knows. Can you two get over to the refuge? I don't trust that wee sod Fraser not to make a play for Jenny there.' They both nodded. 'First I need to find a phone book.'

Hamish laughed as if he found the whole idea quaint. 'Phone book? Where you living, like? The seventies?'

Duncan handed me a sleek-looking mobile. 'Here,' he said, 'this is for you. The number's taped on the underside, we've already got it programmed into ours.'

I took the slim wedge of black plastic as Hamish said, 'It's better than your old one. It's internet ready, so you can use it to look up directory inquiries.'

I pressed a button and the phone's screen lit up like George Square at Christmas. 'And how exactly do I do that?'

Hamish sighed and took it from my hand. 'Give it here, man. Honestly, Dom, you're like one of those Amish blokes or something.'

He then pressed a flurry of buttons and within seconds I was able to look for all the Reillys listed in the East End. Of course, the one I needed could be ex-directory, but it was a start. As I walked towards the Mercedes, Duncan pulled open the passenger door of Hamish's heap and then said, 'Be careful, Dom.'

I smiled. Maybe a hug was on the cards after all. 'I'm always careful, Duncan, you know that,' I said. 'But thanks for the concern.'

He pulled a face. 'Yeah, get over yourself. I meant with my car.'

He can be all heart, can Duncan.

Chapter Fourteen

Sometimes finding people is so easy you feel embarrassed to admit it. Sometimes it takes shoe leather and a brass neck. Ginty Reilly was a case in point. Freddie had said she lived near to the Barrowlands, the legendary ballroom, concert venue and weekend market, so when I got back to the car I went through the online listing and let my fingers do the initial walking. I jotted down the addresses and then headed over there to start knocking on doors. Freddie had said she was Tiger's ex, so I had to assume that she still retained her married name. If she hadn't, I'd have to rethink my entire strategy.

I parked in a side street opposite the glass-fronted '60s-style Barrowland building, which looked desolate on a weekday. I remember well the occasional visit to the market on a Sunday afternoon with my dad and sister. Mum would sit at home, lost in her own thoughts as usual, not caring whether we ever came back. I remember those days out as happy days, probably because she wasn't there. My mother had a way of bringing dark clouds with her wherever she went. Dad would go off to find whatever bargain he was looking for and we kids would wander among the myriad of stalls in the collection of buildings and streets surrounding the actual Barrowland. It was a world of adventure for a young boy, the sights, the sounds, the smells, all carrying with them a promise of something magical. Of course, a lot of what was being sold was a load of old tat, but it didn't seem that way for an impressionable boy. Street traders hawked their wares at the top of hoarse voices, enticing housewives to part with their cash and buy a real china dinner service, *32 pieces, straight off the boat from Hong Kong, look at the lovely willow pattern on this, hen, and it's going for not ten quid, NOT five, NOT four, but TWO quid, two quid the lot, can't say fairer than that, and I'll even throw in a box to carry it, how about that?* And then money would be waved in the air and the trader and his helpers passed among the throng, exchanging boxes of dishes for coin of the realm.

Those streets were empty as I walked through, heading for the first address on my list. The first Reilly was a 21-year-old student with a stud in her nose, long black hair and a sleepy look. She didn't even say anything when I asked her if she knew a Walter Reilly, just slammed the door in my face. The next one was an angry man who I'd roused from his bed. He was a night porter at a city centre hotel and he took none-too-kindly to my waking him up and promptly advised me to go away and have sexual relations with myself. The third wasn't even called Reilly, she was a jovial-looking woman of indeterminate years who told me that she'd bought the flat off Ginty the year before.

I asked, 'Don't suppose you'd have her new address, would you?'

The woman was jovial, but she wasn't stupid. 'Aye, son, but not sure I should tell you. Why you looking for Ginty?'

'It's a legal matter,' I said, the lie falling easily from my tongue. I'd used it before. 'She's not in any trouble, but I really do need to find her.'

Her eyes narrowed. 'A legal matter? You a lawyer, then?'

'No,' I said, smiling, 'if I was I'd be better dressed.'

'You one of those whatchamacallits, then? A parrot legal?'

My smile was genuine. 'Something like that. We just need to contact Mrs Reilly. It's about her ex-husband.' It was close enough to the truth to be believable and she bought it.

'Oh, well. Suppose there's no harm in telling you where she is. You seem like a nice lad.' I could've kissed her for that alone. She rattled off an address which was only a few minutes away by car. I thanked her and turned away, knowing she would probably phone Ginty and warn her. Didn't matter, I didn't think Ginty would leg it.

She lived in a ground-floor flat in a red sandstone tenement running between London Road and the Gallowgate. I parked Duncan's car outside the closemouth. I scanned the walls and lampposts for traffic restrictions, but saw none. Wouldn't do to end up getting a ticket, not with Duncan's car. I stepped into the gloom of the close, stopped at the first door on the right and rattled the letterbox. It sounded very loud in the quiet of the building.

The door opened and a woman's face appeared in the gap left by the security chain. I had expected what Freddie had called an old slag, but this was a willowy blonde, her face thin and drawn, She had obviously been crying.

'Mrs Reilly?' I asked, and she nodded. 'I'm very sorry to trouble you like this, but I wonder if I could have a word?'

'You the bloke who spoke to wee Ella?' Strong Glasgow accent, voice a bit thin thanks to the weeping, but deep and husky. This was really not what I had been expecting – *good on you, Tiger, son.*

'Yes,' I said, the word bouncing up the stairway like an argument. I lowered my voice. 'I'm here about Tiger.'

'He's dead,' she said, and I saw tears well up in her eyes again. They were blue, I noticed. *Jesus,* I thought, *get a hold of yourself.*

'I know. That's what I want to talk to you about.'

'You're not police.'

'No, I'm not,' I said solemnly. When all else looks hopeless, tell the truth. Words to live by, along with Hakuna Matata.

She said, 'The police have already been here.'

'I know,' I didn't know that, but it sounded better. 'But there are a few things I'd like to ask you.'

'Ella said you were working for a lawyer.'

For some reason I didn't want to hoodwink to this woman. 'I'm sorry, I lied.'

She nodded, recognising my honesty, gave me the visual once over. 'You from the papers?'

'No. I knew your husband.'

That made her think twice. 'You knew Walter?'

'Well, I knew him as Tiger.'

She looked me up and down again with suspicious eyes. Part of me wished they were lascivious eyes, but the rest of me told that part to behave himself and remember he was out.

She asked, 'Were you in the fight game?'

'No,' I said, giving her my best grin, the one I usually reserved for old ladies, tax inspectors and sheriffs. 'I met him when he was working for Fast Freddie Fraser...'

Her eyes hardened and she said, 'That bastard!'

'You'll get no argument from me there, Mrs Reilly. I've no love for Freddie either. I'd call him a bastard too, but that would be hard on the rest of the bastards.'

I could tell she was warming to me. Her eyes had lost that concrete look. 'What's your name?'

'Dominic Queste,' I said and a quick smile plucked at the corners of her mouth.

She asked, 'Really? How'd you get a name like that?'

'Changed it by deed poll,' I said.

'You changed your name to Dominic Queste? What was your name before?'

'Erasmus Shittybreeks.'

Despite everything, she laughed. She had a nice laugh and I was glad I'd been able to lighten up the mood. I heard the chain rattle off and she said, 'Come in, Erasmus.'

I stepped inside and waited while she locked and chained the door again. She led me down a narrow hallway to the front room, which was bright and airy and filled with the kind of pine furniture you used to buy at Habitat. The place was so clean it gleamed. I wished I'd brought my sunglasses.

She motioned for me to sit in a peach-coloured armchair with wooden arms and she settled herself on a matching three-seater settee. She absently picked up a throw cushion and hugged it as she looked at me. Now that I could see her clearly, she was even better looking than I'd first thought. The hair was honey-blonde and hung down to her shoulders, her face slightly lined but that only served to add character. I think I was falling in love – which is not an unusual occurrence. Generally a half-decent looking woman merely needs to smile at me and I'm lost. I'm easy.

'Sorry,' she said, 'do you want tea or anything?'

God help me, but I was about to ask what the 'anything' covered. I held myself in check. Flirting with a woman who had only that day become a widow was low, even for me. 'No, I'm fine,' I said. 'Thanks, though.'

She inclined her head in acknowledgement and then said, 'So you said you wanted to talk about Walter.'

I couldn't get used to thinking of the bruiser I knew as Tiger being called Walter, but I pressed on regardless. 'First of all, I'm very sorry for your loss.'

She shrugged and pulled the cushion tighter to her body. I've never been so jealous of soft furnishings in my life. 'Thanks, but to be honest it was only a matter of time before someone did him in, the poor bastard. There were times I thought it would be in the ring, but when he went to work for Freddie Fraser I thought... well...you know what Freddie's into.'

I nodded. 'Who has he been working for lately?'

She shook her head. 'I don't know. We split about, oh, four, five years ago. But we still stayed friends. All he told me last time I saw him was that an old army pal phoned him up with some work, that's all.'

An old army pal – there's the military connection again. 'Who was this pal?'

'Robbie Freeman. They were in the Royal Highland Fusiliers together.'

'Not the SAS? Or Special Forces?'

She laughed again. It really was a nice laugh. 'Walter hated the army and he was a rotten soldier – he'd never've got a look-in with those guys. Why do you ask that?'

'Just wondering. So this guy Robbie...'

'Freeman.'

'Yeah, Freeman. Did he keep in regular contact with Tig... Walter?'

'Not what you would call regular, every now and again maybe. Sometimes he had work for him, you know?'

'What kind of work?'

She shifted uneasily in her seat. 'Knowing Robbie – and knowing Walter, for that matter – it was nothing legal. You knew Walter, you knew what he was like. That's what finally did for the marriage in the end, the black part in him. He was just becoming too violent, you know?'

Indeed I did. I could still feel the weight of his fist not only from the encounter at Aunt Jessica's, but also from when it had crashed into my nose all those years before. It still bent slightly the wrong way thanks to that. 'So did Walter give you any idea what the job was?'

'Strong-arm stuff is all he said. Well, what else would it be? Walter could be a sweetheart but he wasn't the brain of Britain, if you know what I mean. But when that black part of him took over – and the drink? He wasn't the man I married.'

I'd never thought of Tiger Reilly being a sweetheart, but then with guys like him you never do think of their private lives. Everybody needs someone to love and love them in return, I suppose, and this slim blonde in front of me once saw something in the old pug that others never would.

As if she had read my thoughts, she said, 'I know what he was like to other people, all muscle and fist, but Walter wasn't like that with me, not at first. He was really a very sweet guy, very loving, very gentle.' I saw the tears dam up in her eyes again as she spoke. 'They say that he killed a woman, the police said it. It was bound to happen, sooner or later. He changed in the past few years, working for Fraser, doing the things he told him. I couldn't take it and I threw him out. He took it very well, like the old Walter knew it was the only way.'

She shook her head and fell silent, perhaps thinking about her Walter and happier times. I was about to say something, anything, when she started speaking again, very softly. 'Sometimes we'd just sit here on this couch, cuddling, watching the telly. I'd put my head on his shoulder, he'd stroke my hair, dead soft-like. It was like being caressed by an angel's wing, you know?'

I nodded, even though the caresses Tiger had given me were not like any part of an angel's anatomy, unless angels had big rough hands with knuckles made of iron.

'And when we were out he always held my hand. Some men don't like that kind of public display, but not my Walter. Always took my hand. Always gentle with me. Always loving.... Used to be, anyway.' She blinked and a couple of the tears burst through to trickle down her cheek. She gave me a shy smile and wiped them away with her hand. 'I'm sorry,' she said, 'you must think I'm a right old softie.'

'No,' I said. 'I don't think that at all.' I really found it difficult to marry the two images together. To me, Tiger Reilly was a bruiser who broke bones for a living. But here was this woman in a nice clean flat who said he had once been gentle and loving. Two sides of the same guy. But then, I suppose we all have secret parts of ourselves that we only allow certain people to see. There had been someone like that for me once, long ago, but I screwed that up the same way I screwed up everything else in my life. I hadn't thought of Louise for a long time, but sitting here with this attractive woman and talking about Walter and the life they once had together, she came back into my mind. Louise Paton, dark-haired, dark-eyed but so eternally cheerful if I could have mainlined her I would never have needed to go a-snorting. But my personality can take a turn to the dark side for no reason at all – my mother's legacy and hence my love affair with Charlie - and I knew that I was not right for her, so I distanced myself. She never understood it and she tried to get through to me, but by that time I was too far gone and I did not want to take her down with me. Last I heard she had married and was living in Inverness. I hoped she was happy. I hoped she had found herself a Walter Reilly to watch telly with and to stroke her hair. And I hoped he never turned into Tiger Reilly.

'This Robbie Freeman,' I said, putting memories of Louise from my mind, something at which I had become very adept. 'Any idea where I'd find him?'

She stood up. 'I've got a phone number in my book, that any good?'

'That'll do fine,' I said, and watched her move over to a side-board, pull open a drawer, rifle around inside. She must have been in her late forties or early fifties, but she really did look after herself. I had spotted an exercise bike folded up in the corner and I'd lay good money that it was used regularly.

I gave myself a mental slap to behave. The woman's ex-husband was not even cold yet and I was eyeing her up. *What the hell is wrong with you?* But I knew what it was. I hadn't had any female company for six months and that had been a frenzied coupling in the back of the car with the wife of a cop who had asked me to find out who he was shagging on the side. I think she just wanted to pay him back somehow. I knew I shouldn't have done it, but an erection has a mind of its own and none of it is conscience. The payback was for her peace of mind only, she assured me. She wasn't going to tell him, which was a relief because I had enough trouble with the law without them ganging up on me for making a cuckold of one of their guys. Even though he was humping anything with a pulse. And yes, I used the word cuckold.

Ginty turned back with an address book in her hand and rattled off a city centre number, which I scribbled down on the back of an envelope I'd fished out of my jacket pocket.

'Why are you so interested in this, Erasmus?' She asked.

I knew she would ask that sooner or later, and I still was not sure what I was going to say. I hesitated for a second then said, 'I was working for the woman they say Walter killed.'

She blinked at that. Once, twice. Then, her voice hoarse, 'Who was she?'

I sighed. 'A nice lady, lived up the West End. She hired me to find her niece.'

'And did you find her?'

'Yes, and she's in trouble. There are men who want to hurt her. I'm trying to find out who they are and stop them.'

She swallowed and sank onto the wooden arm of her Habitat couch. 'And...and do you think Walter killed this woman client of yours?'

I stared at her for a moment, considering a lie. But something inside me clearly did not want to be untruthful with her. 'I don't think he meant to,' I said, and my words prompted the tears to tumble from her eyes again. 'I'm sorry,' I said.

She shook her head, turned away and swabbed her face with a tissue she plucked from the sleeve of her cardigan. I wondered if

I should say anything further as I stood up. 'Mrs Reilly,' I said, but she did not turn to face me. 'Thank you for this. And I really am sorry for your loss.' It sounded lame. Christ, it was lame. 'Listen, would you mind giving me your phone number? Just in case something else occurs to me? Or so I can keep you informed?' If she doubted my motives, she didn't show it. She rhymed off her number, which I scribbled down on the envelope too. Then I took out my new mobile, read the number taped to the back and scratched it out, tore that section off then laid it on the small occasional table beside the armchair. 'That's my number, in case you ever need to just talk, or anything. Don't hesitate to give me a call, please.' My mouth was still open as if I could say more, but my brain wasn't co-operating. I couldn't decide whether I was being a nice guy or hitting on her. I turned and headed for the door.

As I walked down the corridor to the front door, I heard her sobbing again. I paused with my hand on the handle of the front door and thought about going back. But I didn't. I'd done enough as it was.

Chapter Fifteen

I thumbed in the number Ginty had given me and was connected to an answering machine for Elite Security Services. I cut the connection then fumbled my way through the internet procedure, looked up Yellow Pages online and found the company had a city centre office, in Gordon Street. I wheeled the car round and headed for the Gallowgate, passing the Barrowland again on my left then on the right the Saracen Head pub – the Sarry Heid, as we call it, reputedly the oldest pub in the city – and from there to Glasgow Cross. I turned left onto the Sandgate, eventually passing the old High Court buildings on my right and the archway at Glasgow Green on my left, then turned right before I hit the river and carried on to Clyde Street. I hate driving through the city centre, even in a car as opulent as Duncan's. It's so stop and go, with traffic lights at every junction. I wished I'd brought some CDs with me, but I had to settle for Radio 2. It was the oldies hour on the Steve Wright Show and when I clicked it on The Legend of Xanadu by Dave Dee, Dozy, Beaky, Mitch and Titch was just beginning. At least that was something, a favourite from my childhood.

The song, as music often does, awoke memories. My father sitting quietly while my mother screamed at him because he was half an hour late from work, his features blank, his muscles tightened to prevent any expression, for to react was like throwing petrol on a flame. And my sister and I in the other room, turning up the radio to try to drown our mother's voice out, her screeching, harpy voice as it told him how worried she was, how he should've phoned to say he was going to be late, that she'd phoned the hospitals because he was never late. It sounded like concern, but we all knew different. It was all about her. It was always about her.

I forced the memories back into that locked room in my brain reserved for all the bad things in my life. This was not the time for me to be confronting old ghosts. I'm very good at fighting those memories down. It was never the time.

I parked the car in the St Enoch Centre multi-storey and walked up Union Street to Gordon Street, which runs alongside Central Station. Glasgow's city centre is not that big a place and can be covered on foot by any reasonably fit person, as long as you're not attempting any of the steep hills that lead up to Sauchiehall Street from Argyle Street beyond the railway bridge known as the Hielanman's Umbrella.

I found the doorway leading to the offices of Elite Security wedged between a building society and a cut-price bookstore. The hallway was gloomy and cold, not that it was overly warm in the street. An old-fashioned lift stood beside a wooden board listing the companies with office space in the building. Elite was on the fifth floor, which figured. The lift was broken, which also figured. A grimy doorway to the right led to the stairs and I had no option. I could have scaled the exterior walls like Spiderman, but I'd left my web-slinging gear at home.

My breath grew increasingly laboured as I reached each new floor, and I don't know whether I was imagining it or not but the temperature did seem to be dropping. It was a brisk spring day outside, but that did not explain the tumbling mercury inside. The exertion of climbing the stairs generated heat but I was most definitely aware of a nip in the air of the stairwell.

I now know what it was. It was cool and perhaps even damp in that stairway, but it was not any colder than the hallway downstairs. On some level I was picking up something in the ether, a vibration, a warning that something was just not right.

I reached the fifth floor and paused to catch my breath before I pulled open the door. I could feel my heart pounding in my ears and I was sweating a little, but not too much. Not bad for a fifty-something who never worked out. My mind flashed to Ginty's exercise bike and that sent my train of thought chugging to the rowing machine in a cupboard in my flat. It was, in the phrase of second-hand car salesmen the world over, hardly used.

Every now and again I took it out and looked at it, but putting it together just seemed like too much effort and it was placed back in its prison again. I feel it's the thought that counts. Even so, as I stood on the landing panting like a steam train idling at a station, I resolved to do something about myself.

The corridor beyond the door was as dark and gloomy as the one at street level, although it had a series of doors leading off into individual offices. I checked the nameplates on the wall beside the door as I moved along, looking for Elite Security. I passed an inquiry agent, (*get him with an office and everything,* I thought), two insurance brokers and a furrier. There was also a bespoke tailor, an import/export agency and a family law specialist. Elite's headquarters was behind the door at the far end, beside two obviously empty offices.

The door lay slightly open and I rapped my knuckles on the wood. I'm British, it's something we do. If I see a queue I always feel the need to join it. I always expect it to rain. And I never barge in somewhere, even if the door is open. I had a flashback to standing outside Aunt Jessica's house and felt the hairs on the back of neck beginning to form a queue of their own. My spider sense was really tingling now. Something was wrong.

I gave the door another knuckling, but there was no sound from within. I glanced along the empty corridor, as if there was a sign telling me what to do next, though I knew I should have just turned and walked away again. Yeah, like that would happen. I sighed and slowly pushed the door open.

I found myself in a small square area with another three doors leading off. I had expected to be met with a simple office, but clearly this place was bigger than I thought. The one directly ahead was lying open so I shoved it with the back of my hand to reveal what was obviously the nerve-centre of the security operation. The weak sunlight did its best to burn its way through two dust-speckled windows looking out over Gordon Street and I could see the dark, ornate facade of Central Station across the way. There were posters on the wall of buff men in combat gear policing jungle terrain and deserts. Obviously, this security firm did not provide retired cops to guard building sites. Two desks sat side-by-side, cutting the room in half. A computer and a telephone with an array of buttons sat on one, and I guessed this acted as a reception area. Behind the desks, three green filing cabinets filled the wall beside another open door and I could see a light shining weakly through the gap.

'Mister Freeman?' I said, and waited. Nothing. I flashed back to Aunt Jessica's house once more. It was like *déjà vu* all over again. I stepped between the desks and saw the computer was on, a half-written letter on the screen. A cup sat beside the keyboard, the tea inside untouched. I laid the back of my fingers against the cup and found it was still warm. Not boiling, but still drinkable. I paused at the rear door. My Britishness came out again and I rapped at the frame. After all, maybe he was in there getting his secretary to take something down. Ooh, Matron.

'Mister Freeman, you in there?' I called, but no answer was the loud response. That's what the silence was like now, a scream. Or maybe it was my spider sense shrieking like a frightened schoolgirl. I pushed the door open and looked inside.

Robbie Freeman was in there. He was sitting in a large false leather swivel chair behind a desk, his eyes open, his mouth slack, the bullet hole in his forehead little more than an angry flea bite. The blood and brains splattered across the chair were more telling. Blood also oozed from two wounds in his chest. A tubby little woman in her forties I took to be his secretary was sprawled across his lap. I couldn't see from my angle but I knew she would have similar wounds. One to the head, two to the chest. Kill shots. Professional.

I fumbled in my pocket for my phone. My hands trembled and I knew it wasn't because of my exertions climbing the stairs. Finding dead people was becoming so frequent I should wear a hood and carry a scythe. I was about to hit 999 when I heard a soft footfall behind me and I turned, the phone halfway to my ear.

The man from the park stood beyond the double desks, his pistol raised and levelled at me. He had obviously been lurking behind one of the other doors. If he recognised me he didn't show it. In fact, he didn't show anything. His face was immobile as he aimed the silenced pistol at me and I knew he would have no hesitation in taking me down.

'The girl,' he said, his accent American, so that blew the SAS theory, although he could've been an ex-Navy SEAL or Delta Force, or any number of US special forces I know only from movies.

'Safe,' I said. 'Somewhere you can't get her.'

I saw amusement in his eyes and I feared there might be nowhere she would be safe from this man. I had overcome my initial shock by then and I noted that his left arm hung slightly at his side, the sleeve of his windbreaker holed by Duncan's bullet and ringed by blood. I wondered how badly hit he was.

'Who are you?' I asked. I didn't really expect him to reply, I just wanted to keep talking. Maybe he wouldn't notice what I was trying to do with the phone in my hand. I wasn't used to these keys and I hoped to God I was hitting the right ones.

The smile in his eyes seemed to widen, as if I had asked a stupid question, and then froze. Right then I knew he was not going to indulge in idle chit-chat and I was about to join Freeman and his secretary. I punched the last button and prayed I'd done it correctly. Thankfully I had.

The phone on the desk beside the computer rang. It was a shrill, strident sound and it cut through the silence between us like a siren. He flinched slightly, his eyes flicking towards the phone. That's what I had hoped would happen when I hit the redial button. When his eyes left me all too fleetingly, I seized the chance to leap into the office, slam the door and duck down, my weight pressed hard against the wood. I had no idea what I was doing, but it seemed like a good idea. I heard the suffocated *phut* of the pistol and a bullet splintered the door just about where my head had been a second before. A key hung from the lock and I twisted it just as I felt his body being thrown against the door. I rolled away as fast as I could and another three shots pummelled into the wood. I scrambled behind the desk, coming face-to-face with the dead woman, blood streaming down her upside-down

126

forehead from the single wound between eyes that stared at me as if to say, *Get the bastard*. I hauled open drawers as the kicks at the door grew in intensity. Thankfully, it was made of solid wood with a sturdy lock and they both held but I knew that wouldn't last forever. I wrenched at the drawers, telling myself that an ex-soldier in Robbie Freeman's line of business was bound to have something I could use. I needed a weapon, anything, a letter opener in a pinch, but ideally a gun. But the only thing I could find was a staple gun, which was about as much use as an umbrella in a radiation storm.

And then the door frame began to splinter.

I threw myself across the room just as it began to give. A hand poked through the gap, a hand with a gun, so I rammed my body against the door, wedging the hand against the frame. I heard him grunt and that gave me some satisfaction. He tried to pull free but I kept the door tight against his flesh. He pushed against me from the other side and I surmised his bad arm prevented him from giving it his all. I strained back, forcing the edge of the jamb into his wrist. If I was to get out of there under my own steam, I had to make him drop the gun and then keep him out. I had a gut feeling that my limited expertise in Krav Maga would be next to useless against him, even with one arm injured. But no matter how hard I pushed, he still held onto the pistol. *What the hell is he*, I thought. *The Terminator?*

And then he began to twist his wrist to bring the muzzle around to face me. It must have been excruciatingly painful, for I could see the flesh scraping away under the wooden edge and leaving a bloody trail, but he did it. I couldn't duck and I couldn't step out of the way. I did the only thing possible. I still held the staple gun so I jammed it onto his hand and pressed down. I heard another satisfying grunt as the twin prongs of metal bit into his flesh, so I did it again. And again. I jammed them into the soft tissue between his thumb and forefinger where it was stretched tight round the handle of the pistol. Finally, with maybe half a dozen of the little buggers nipping at him and drawing blood, he let the weapon fall and jerked his hand through the gap.

The door, with my weight still against it, slammed shut. I kept very still, my breathing laboured, the stapler held out like a pistol as I listened for movement, fully expecting him to throw himself at the wood again. But there was no sound from beyond the door. I visualised him standing on the other side, knowing I had his gun now and wondering if I would use it. I didn't want to touch it, though. It had just been used to kill two people and there was no way I was going anywhere near it. Fingerprints, DNA, gunshot residue – hell, any one of them would see me in the frame right and proper. He didn't know that, though. For all he knew I had the thing in my fist and was ready to put a bullet in him if he tried anything further. At least, I hoped that's the way his mind was working.

I don't know how long I stood there with my shoulder against that door, waiting for him to attack again, before I began to suspect he was gone. Of course, he could have been waiting for me to come out. Or he could have been lying prostrate, having succumbed to staple poisoning. But my spider-sense told me he had fled.

I eased the door open and peered into the main office. Empty. I swung the door fully open, every nerve on the alert for another assault. But he was long gone.

I exhaled long and loud and sank into the nearest chair. My new-found skills of self-defence using office supplies were exhausted and the adrenalin was no longer pumping, I felt I was going to drop. My hands still trembled as I dialled 999 on my mobile. My voice sounded shaky and strangled as I asked for the police.

After I had given them all the details they asked for, I wanted to remain in the chair because I was too exhausted to move. However, I needed to have a quick look around first. I'd already had a look in Freeman's desk drawers and there was nothing of interest. The filing cabinets were my best bet. There were three of them and I scanned the labels on the front of each drawer until I found the one that read M-R. I jerked it open and was glad to see each folder was neatly labelled. I flicked them one by one, looking for a file marked 'Reilly', but there was nothing there. That puzzled me. Everything else in the office was neat and tidy, a place for everything and everything in its place. Why no file for Tiger? I cast my eyes around the front office in case there was another bundle of folders awaiting attention, but there was nothing. If there had been such a file, I'd bet my complete collection of James Bond soundtracks that the Terminator had already taken it before I got here. I jiggled the mouse to awaken the computer and glanced at the text file on the screen, but it was simply a letter to Freeman's landlord about an approaching lease renewal. He wouldn't need that now, I thought.

I moved quickly back into Freeman's office, fully aware that I was running out of time. There was an old-fashioned writing bureau behind his desk so I slid it open and poked around inside. If there was something there I'd never find it, not in the time I had available. I closed the lid again and turned to the desk. I did not want to disturb the bodies at all – I was in enough trouble – so I peered over them at the large sheet of blotting paper on the desk top. Who uses blotting paper now? Then I realised that for Freeman it was a glorified notepad. I raced through the scribbles with no clue as to what I was looking for, simply hoping that something would reach out and strike me as significant. Finally, one thing did catch my attention, a note just beside Freeman's dead hand.

Tiger – Excelcis.

What the hell was Excelcis? And what did it have to do with Tiger? And who had sent the Terminator to kill Freeman and the woman?

The only thing I could say with any degree of certainty was that I was buggered if I knew.

Chapter Sixteen

The two uniforms were in the process of taking me to Glasgow City Centre police office in Stewart Street when they received a call diverting us instead to Glasgow West End, where Detective Chief Inspector Nicholas Cornwell wished to interview me. I swore they had a look of pity on their faces as they told me.

I ended up back in the same interview room I'd been in the night before. Christ, was it really only the night before? Talk about packing a lot into your day. Nick played the usual waiting game, but it didn't worry me at all. In fact, the solitude and the silence gave me the chance to take stock of the story so far in an attempt to put everything in its place.

I had been hired by Aunt Jessica to find her wayward niece, Jenny, who it seemed had been bumming around between Glasgow and London for a few years. Jenny's mum had been about as warm as a week in Siberia and had killed herself either by accident or design in a house fire. Her father was a doctor living somewhere in London but it was as yet unclear if Jenny had made contact. While living in London, Jenny had become bedroom buddies with Jerome Kingsley, drug dealer and all round nasty bit of goods. Kingsley was in cahoots with Fast Freddie Fraser, who had supplied the muscle and the contacts to help trace Jenny, who may or may not have half-inched a bag full of cocaine before she left. Jenny denied it, insisted Kingsley's a possessive sort and that's why he was after her. Hmm. Maybe, but Jenny was far from forthcoming with anything, let alone the truth, so maybe she had stashed the gear somewhere and planned to make a fast buck punting it.

So she was on the run from Kingsley, and by extension Fast Freddie, but someone else was after her – my pal the Terminator, an American Special Forces type who could take a bullet in the arm like it's a midge bite and who killed without compunction. Jerome had mentioned other ex-military types who had been asking about Jenny down the Smoke. Aunt Jessica was killed by Tiger Reilly, who was working for an old mate called Robbie Freeman, another ex-army guy who ran a security firm which specialised in mercenaries. Again, more former military personnel. Tiger was killed, perhaps as a warning for me to keep my nose out of whatever the hell was going on, but more likely because I'd seen him, he could be identified, and if he was picked up he'd no doubt roll over on whoever hired him. Robbie Freeman and his secretary were also both murdered, and the file relating to Tiger removed. It all sounded to me like someone was tying up loose ends.

The question, of course, was who was that someone? Kingsley? Maybe, but what did he have against Aunt Jessica? He'd seemed genuinely surprised when I told him about her death. Tiger had worked for Fast Freddie, so was the diminutive Glasgow gangster playing some kind of double game? No, instinct told me he was a bit player this time round and, anyway, murdering women was not his style.

So why was the Terminator after Jenny? What the hell wasn't she telling me? And Excelsis? What in the name of the wee man was that? And what did it have to do with the price of fish, if anything?

I was snatched out of my expositional fugue when the door was thrown open with the kind of drama you'd expect in an old Bette Davis movie, and Cornwell and Theresa Cohan swept in. They looked serious. Hell, Nick always looked serious, but she looked grim. I wondered if I should be worried.

'So, Queste,' said Nick as he sat down opposite me, just like old times. 'Looks like we should start calling you Typhoid Mary. People are dropping around you like flies.'

'If you're looking for another statement, Nick, I already gave one at the office.' Which was true – I'd given two detectives more or less the full skinny back at Gordon Street before the uniforms whisked me away. Obviously, I didn't tell them everything.

'You're in big trouble, sonny boy,' Cornwell said, making me smile. *Sonny boy*. I wasn't that far behind him in years. He frowned. 'This isn't funny, you know. Four people are dead.'

I didn't say anything. I wasn't being tight-lipped or tough. The truth is I was suddenly too scared to say anything. Nick was his usual gruff self but I sensed something else – he was enjoying this. And if that was true, then I must be in trouble. The seriousness of my situation had finally dawned on me and I was decidedly uncomfortable.

'What?' Cornwell was smiling now that he saw my expression change. 'No snappy comeback? No funny remarks?'

I shrugged, forcing myself to adopt my normal devil-may-care attitude, even though my arse was making buttons. 'Don't want to waste my material. Thought I'd save it for my one-man show.'

'Good idea. You can do it for the other inmates at Barlinnie.'

That shocked me further, but I was determined not to show it. I looked from Cornwell to DC Cohan, who was leaning against the wall behind him, watching me intently. She still had that grim look on her face. I really was on dodgy ground here and I had to tread carefully.

'Why am I here, Nick? Gordon Street is city centre, you're West End. Why you involved?'

'The first two murders were on my patch, that makes me very involved. And I've made it my business to be alerted whenever the name Dominic Queste pops up – so whether it's a traffic ticket or yet another murder, I'll hear about it. Four corpses, Queste, and you're the common denominator. And there was a double shooting in the East End this morning that I'd bet my pension you know something about. We're going to check the ballistics from that incident with the bullets from Gordon Street. I'll up the ante with my wife's pension and say there'll be a match. And if we place you at the locus...' He smiled, as if that prospect would make his day.

'Can I remind you, DCI Cornwell, that I've not been charged with anything?' I said, wondering where the hell my officious tone of voice had come from. 'I'm here as a witness.'

'Aye – for now.'

I gave him a small laugh. 'You don't really think I killed Robbie Freeman and his secretary, do you?'

He sidestepped my question and asked one of his own. 'Why were you there?'

'Following up on enquiries for my client.'

'Your client's dead.'

'I told you, I feel obligated.'

He grunted, telling me what he thought of my obligation. 'So what took you to Elite Security?'

'Tiger Reilly was old mates with the dead man. Sometimes he threw him some work. I think Tiger was working for him when he killed Mrs Oldfield.'

Cornwell gave me another grunt, which I think was designed to signify that I was not telling him anything he did not know. Then he sidestepped again. 'Where's the girl?'

I put on my most innocent face. 'What girl?'

Exasperation got the better of him. 'Jesus, Queste, don't play the innocent, it doesn't suit you. Jenny Deavers, Jessica Oldfield's niece.'

I considered lying again, telling him that I had no clue, but I sensed it was time to come clean. Not about everything, though.

'She's safe,' I said.

'Where?'

'I don't think I need to tell you that.'

'I think you do.'

'Then we'll have to agree to differ.'

He sighed and glanced over his shoulder at DC Cohan. Then he turned back to me and hunched forward in his chair, his hands clasped before him on the table top, just as he'd done the night before. Maybe he was praying for the strength not to indulge in some head ripping.

'Look, Queste,' he said, his voice low, 'all hell is breaking loose out there. Jessica Oldfield, Tiger Reilly, Robbie Freeman, Mary Sullivan, all dead...'

'Mary Sullivan?' I asked.

'Robbie Freeman's partner,' he explained. So she wasn't his secretary. I'm a sexist pig, obviously. 'Then there's the two blokes out in Alexandra Park, shot in broad daylight. Now, my gut tells me that's got something to do with all this too. My gut tells me that you know more than you're saying. My gut also tells me that the girl is central to it all. So what do you say?'

'I'd say better get to a doctor – that gut of yours has far too much to say for itself.'

He sighed, but I saw the line of his jaw harden. I couldn't blame him. If I'd been sitting where he was, having to deal with a smart-arsed guy like me, Cohan back there would already be phoning for an ambulance. To his credit, Cornwell kept his temper.

'You need to let me bring the girl in, Dominic,' he said. 'You need to let me protect her, to find out what the hell is going on in my city.'

It sounded reasonable and if I had been sensible, I would have told him where she was. But no-one ever said I was sensible and anyway, I was a bit stunned at him using my Christian name. Threw me right off my stride.

'I'll tell you what I'll do, Nick,' I said, leaning in closer myself, and clasping my hands in an identical fashion. 'Once you let me go, I'll speak to her, ask her if she wants to come in, and if she does I'll bring her right to you. Deal?'

He looked at me through those cold, grey eyes of his and said, 'What makes you think I'm going to let you go? We've got you standing over two recently dead bodies and I'll bet your prints and DNA are all over that place. We've got the gun too. Not looking good for you, is it?'

I shook my head in disagreement, feeling the ground becoming firmer beneath my feet again. 'I didn't touch that gun, so there'll be no prints or DNA of mine on it...'

'So you wiped it clean.'

I shook my head again. 'You'll find the shooter's prints on it, although I've a feeling you won't get a hit.' I wasn't convinced they'd find a ballistics match with the weapon used in the park, either. The Terminator was a professional and unlikely to use the same weapon twice. I didn't mention that, though. I went on, 'Also, your scenes-of-crime people swabbed my hands for GSR. You already know I'm clean. And if I shot them, why the hell did I phone you lot and then sit about waiting for you to arrive?'

'Maybe you thought you were being clever.'

'No, that would just be dumb. You know me, Cornwell, I know my way around this kind of thing. I know I'd be the prime suspect.'

'Prime suspect? That is indeed what you are, Queste,' he said, softly, and he was smiling again. He was enjoying this.

'Okay,' I said, not really expecting him to put it quite so bluntly. 'Then charge me or let me go. Either way, I'm not saying another word unless my lawyer is present.'

Cornwell glared at me for a full minute, probably weighing up the chances of him losing his pension if he smeared the interview room with my blood. Then he seemed to relax and stood up, nodded at Cohan, and walked out. To his credit, he did not slam the door. Theresa gave an audible sigh and sat down in his recently vacated chair.

'You need to see sense, Dominic,' she said, her soft Irish accent strangely soothing. 'DCI Cornwell wants what's best, you know.'

'If this is the good cop to his bad cop, it won't work. I've seen *NYPD Blue*.'

She smiled and gave her head a little shake. 'No, this is just good advice. We need to find Jenny Deavers and we know you have her. We think she's in trouble.'

I turned sideways in my chair and looked at the door behind me. I leaned against the wall and twisted my head to face Theresa. 'You know something, don't you?'

'We know a lot of things.'

'About Jenny, I mean.'

'Of course we do. We're not the clods you think we are.'

'I never said you were clods. What do you know?'

'Why should I tell you?'

'Because I think that's what this little game is all about. Nick knows I didn't kill anyone, he knows it's not my thing. So he's putting on the pressure, trying to get me to spill. But he also

135

knows I'm not likely to tell him, so he brings in the gentle touch. That's you, by the way.'

She gave me that look. 'Yeah, I cracked that code.'

'I think you're supposed to tell me a thing or two in the hope that I'll tell you where Jenny is. Then I'll be sprung from here – I'll lay odds that if Eamonn's not out there already, he's not far away. You can't hold him back for long, you know. He'll tear the place down brick-by-brick. Nick knows he's on thin ice holding me in here without legal advice and Eamonn's the man with the blowtorch.'

She smiled. 'You're pretty bright, you know that?'

I shrugged modestly. 'There are teachers who would disagree with you, but I'm not stupid. I've been down the town, you know? I'll admit he had me going at the start of our little session but I wasn't thinking straight, I've had a hard week. So let's cut the bullshit and tell me what Nick wants me to know and I'll be on my way.'

'And the girl?'

'I meant what I said – I'll give her the option. She's a big girl, Theresa – she can make up her own mind.'

She thought about this and then nodded. 'Okay. We dug around in her background, found out about her mother – you know she's dead, right?' I nodded. 'Well, she had some pretty interesting friends. Big Tam McCutcheon? You heard of him?'

I nodded. 'He was a big man back then. If there was something crooked going on, he was part of it. And if it wasn't crooked he was giving it a right good twist.'

'He was before my time, but that's what everyone says. Anyway, Bernice Deavers was very much involved with him and others like him. She was a bit of a girl, by all accounts. Liked men. Liked the dangerous ones. And they liked her. But she got in too deep, learned things she shouldn't, maybe saw some stuff, and our lot got to hear about it. She was pulled in and she named a couple of names.'

That made my eyebrows do a double Roger Moore. 'She ratted on Big Tam? That wouldn't have done much for her longevity.'

She shook her head. 'No, not him, two of his rivals. Now, it may be that it was an arrangement she had with him, maybe not. Whatever it was, about a month later, she wound up dead.'

I sat back in the chair, taking this in. 'You think she was murdered, don't you?'

She shrugged. 'The boys back then thought her death was a bit convenient for certain parties, sure. But there seemed nothing suspicious about the fire. Seemed like an accident, pure and simple. The old story – smoking in bed, probably pissed out her head, maybe drugs. Place was gutted, body burned to a crisp. The question is how much did the daughter know of all this?'

'She was just a kid.' I thought about this, though. It seemed slim but all it took was one nutter to take it into his head that it was time to punish the family. 'What about the two faces she fingered?'

'One's dead, choked on his own vomit after an overdose, the other's in the pokey down south for firearms offences. He'd moved to Manchester when he decided our lot was paying far too much attention to him.'

'I take it you've spoken to him?'

'Of course, we don't sit around, you know.'

'And?'

'He's been well warned, don't worry. He's pleading innocence but…' She shrugged, pulled a face, telling me that a crook's word isn't worth the breath it took to say it. 'Okay, so we start to thinking about the father, who turns out to have been a medical student up here from London. James Quinn. We run a trace. Turns out he spent some time in the army.'

She caught something registering with me. 'What?' she asked.

'Nothing,' I said, cursing my lack of a poker face.

'No, not nothing – something. What?'

I sighed. 'There's an ex-army thread running through all this, somehow. Tiger was ex-army, Robbie Freeman was ex-army, his firm recruited mercs.' I stopped it there. No need at this stage to talk about the shooter, lest it implicate me somehow in the Alexandra Park events. 'The father wasn't SAS or anything?'

'No, Royal Army Medical Corps. He left three years ago, went into private practice to dish out suppositories to the upper crust in St John's Wood. Doing well for himself.'

I waited, but she remained silent. I suddenly felt like an Agatha Christie fan who finds the last page is missing. 'Is that it? No more?' I asked.

'Your turn. Who do you know is after this girl?'

So this was going to be like *Swap Shop*. I hated *Swap Shop* but I decided to play anyway. 'There's this bloke called Jerome Kingsley, ex-boyfriend. He's a candyman from the Smoke.'

'He's a what?' The words were coated in a mocking, Irish laugh. What was it about the phrase that people found funny?

'A drug dealer from London,' I said. 'He's in Glasgow and he says she took some of his gear. He wants it back.'

Theresa frowned and I could see her impression of Jenny Deavers changing from lost girl and potential victim to drug-dealing scumbag. 'And did she take his drugs?'

'She says not. She says he's a possessive arsehole and he just didn't like the idea of her walking out on him.'

Theresa nodded, her face telling me that she could well believe that all men are possessive arseholes...no, scratch that – *all* men are just arseholes. Thank God I'm just a boy.

'Right,' I said, 'the father, Dr Quinn, Medicine Man. You speak to him?'

'Budgets don't allow us to jet off to London these days, but we asked our colleagues in the Met to look him up. I suppose we'll be asking them about this Kingsley guy too now.'

'And?'

'And what?'

I could feel the frustration crinkling my face, even though I knew she was winding me up. 'Jenny's dad. Did the London police come back to you? Did they speak to him? Has he had any contact with her recently?'

'No, they didn't speak to him. That's the thing.'

'What's the thing?'

'He wasn't in his home or his surgery. He hasn't been seen for two weeks. Dr James Quinn has apparently vanished off the face of the earth.'

Chapter Seventeen

While I languished in the comforts of Glasgow West End police station, Duncan and Hamish decided to retrieve my car from where I had left it that morning. The medium for the return of my somewhat rusty chariot was one Twitchy McGlinchey, an absolute legend in lower criminal circles. When he was still a teenager he had the reputation for being able to steal any make or model. He loved to drive at speed and often nicked vehicles just for the hell of it. Sometimes he stole to order – once or twice for police officers who wanted their cars taken and trashed for insurance purposes. Car security being what it is these days, he was now used more as a driver. He was called Twitchy because his body jerked of its own volition, as if someone was applying a cattle prod to his nether regions, but put him behind a steering wheel and he became as fast and furious as Vin Diesel. It was a curious transformation.

They sat up the hill in Hamish's beat-up Vauxhall and checked out the perimeter. They could see my car where I'd left it further down the street.

'It's a wonder it's still here,' opined Hamish. 'A strange car in this street.'

'No self-respecting thief would want it,' said Twitchy, which was true but cruel. If I'd been there I would have taken issue, as the old bus had plenty of life in her yet.

Duncan craned his neck to scrutinise the immediate area. 'Don't see anything out of place, do you?'

'We'll know soon enough,' said Hamish. 'You know what the deal is, Twitchy?'

Twitchy sighed, his face showing exasperation through a myriad of little ripples as he recited, 'Aye, nick the motor, drive the motor, make sure no-one's following the motor.'

'Apart from us.'

Twitchy's head inclined slightly, a spasm jerking his jaw to the side. 'Apart from you.'

'And if you do notice anyone?'

Twitchy looked at Hamish as if he had just tumbled off the water biscuit that had carried him up the Clyde. 'Lose the bastard and head for Father Verne's place.'

Hamish nodded in satisfaction and turned back to his brother. 'Sounds simple.'

Duncan cleared his throat. 'Let's hope so.'

Twitchy climbed out and walked down the hill towards my car. I often thought he walked like Walter Brennan in *To Have and to Have Not*, a sort of hop, skip and jump motion that was caused by whatever affliction he suffered from. Some said it was a form of Parkinson's Disease, but that didn't explain why it vanished completely once he nestled in a driver's seat.

He reached my car and opened the door with little difficulty. I'd given Duncan my keys before I parted company with them that day. That was why Twitchy was so unconcerned about taking the car – if the law had felt his collar, he knew he had permission to drive it away. He didn't care if anyone watching began to follow him, for Twitchy could lose a tail before it even knew it was lost.

The brothers watched my car nose out into the traffic towards Edinburgh Road and waited to see if anyone followed. They didn't wait long. The blue four-wheel drive had been parked about six car lengths way on the opposite side of the street and they both spotted it at the same time as it edged out.

'Here we go,' said Hamish, firing up his engine.

* * *

Two hours after Twitchy, Duncan and Hamish set off on their quest, I nestled deep into the soft leather of Eamonn's Audi and let the strains of Vivaldi's 'Four Seasons' soothe my jangled nerves. I have always been partial to The Four Seasons, even when they ditched Vivaldi and took up with Frankie Valli. I mentioned this to Eamonn as we pulled into Dumbarton Road and he gave me a look that showed he was well in touch with his feminine side. Mind you, the line was weak, even for me, but he needed to cut me some slack – I was a little man who'd had a very busy day.

Eamonn had lost no time in springing me once Theresa had told me everything her boss wanted, namely the info on James Quinn. Nick's message was coming through loud and clear – he was worried, as people connected to Jenny seemed to be developing a serious case of death or vanishing, and he wanted her in protective custody. I asked Theresa if he was worried about me, and it made her laugh. If I can bring a little sunshine into someone's day, I'm happy.

We were heading into the city centre so I could retrieve Duncan's car from the St Enoch Centre before it closed. Dumbarton Road was, as usual, busy, so it was stop/start all the way, which gave me time to fill Eamonn in on just about everything. Again, I didn't tell him about Alexandra Park. He was a lawyer and he did not want to hear about such things.

He's a good-looking guy, is Eamonn. Tall, tanned and with dark hair showing grey at the temples. He wasn't smiling as he listened intently to my tale, but I knew if he did I'd be treated to a glimpse of teeth so white pedestrians would think the sun had come out. He took care of himself with such precision that there was a rumour he was gay, a rumour I believe begun by police officers who, like Nicky, held a deep dislike for him. I happened to know he was not homosexual. His wife once confided in me, thanks to an excess of gin and tonic, that Eamonn's sexual urges were so huge she was thinking of sub-contracting the marital duties. I knew that Eamonn had already taken care of that particular task, as he was regularly showing off his briefs to a nubile young lawyer who turned many an ageing head at the Sheriff Court.

His face was grim as he watched the road and listened to me talk. We were passing Kelvingrove Art Galleries on the left, its red sandstone bathed in the dying of the light, when he said, 'You're in over your head, Dom.'

'Tell me about it.' It was true. I'd been in dodgy situations before, I'd encountered violence and death, but nothing like this. The body count here was on the scale of a Big Arnie movie.

'You have to get the girl to go to the police,' said Eamonn. 'They'll protect her.'

I sighed. 'I know. I can't force her, though, if she doesn't want to go.'

He nodded in agreement. 'True, but you must make her see sense. Duncan and Hamish are good at what they do, but if what you're telling me is even halfway accurate, this might be even too big for them. This fellow in the Gordon Street office, the ex-military type?'

'The Terminator,' I said.

There was a flicker of a smile when he heard that. 'That what you're calling him?'

'I considered Humphrey but rejected it.'

'Listen, and understand,' said Eamonn. 'That Terminator is out there. It can't be bargained with. It can't be reasoned with. It doesn't feel pity, or remorse, or fear. And it absolutely will not stop, ever, until you are dead.'

That made me laugh, which felt good. I felt as if I hadn't laughed in such a long time. I had never pegged Eamonn as a big movie fan, but sometimes he surprised me.

'Yeah, but I'm not Sarah Connor in this scenario,' I said. 'It's the girl.'

'That's why you need to bring her in. You can't protect her. You're not Kyle Reece, Dom.'

I had to agree. I was no soldier. I'd been on the run for two days, I hadn't eaten in hours, and I'd been shot at more often than a road sign on a hillbilly highway. I was done in, washed out, bone weary. Time to do the sensible thing, for once. I slipped my phone from my pocket and switched it on. Eamonn glanced down at my hands and said, 'The police take that from you while you were in there?'

'Yeah, why?'

'Don't use it,' he bobbed his head in the direction of his iPhone nestling in a holder of its very own on the dashboard. 'Use mine. You never know what they've done while they had it. At the very least they'll have a list of all the numbers you've dialled or have called you.'

Eamonn's paranoia was legend. He did not trust the police as far as he could throw the Chief Constable. Sometimes he took it too far – I really couldn't see some sergeant in Partick slipping a bug into my phone – but I was too tired to argue. Anyway, just because he was paranoid did not mean they weren't out to get me.

I slipped the iPhone from its holder and studied the dial to work out how to work it, then put in Duncan's number. It bounced immediately to voicemail because, although I didn't know it at the time, they were retrieving my car and seeing who tailed it. I didn't leave a message. It occurred to me that if Eamonn was right we'd all need to get new phones again. I was certain this would pose no problem, as Duncan and Hamish had a seemingly inexhaustible supply of mobiles.

I poked out the number of the refuge. It rang about ten times before Father Verne answered.

'Hi Father, it's me,' I said, aware of the weariness in my voice.

'Dominic – where have you been? I've been phoning you for hours,' I didn't like the note of desperation in the good Father's voice. I liked his next words even less. 'Jenny's gone,' he said.

I sat up straight and was aware of Eamonn giving me a sideways look of concern. 'What happened?'

'I was dealing with a young boy who had just arrived and when I looked into her room, she was gone. We'd heard you had been arrested and I think she panicked. I'm very sorry, Dominic, I feel responsible...'

Sometimes faith can be misplaced. But I didn't say that. He sounded cut up enough as it was. 'Not your fault, Father. As you say, your place isn't a prison. Where were Duncan and Hamish?'

'Out retrieving your car. I thought she had settled in but obviously not.'

'She's slippery, Father. She also doesn't know what's good for her.'

The priest's voice was strained. 'I should have stayed close by her. She could be anywhere by now.'

I had an idea where she could be heading and I glanced at the clock on the dashboard. 'How long has she been gone?'

'About two hours, maybe a touch more.'

I nodded, knowing there was only one place she would head. I was going to get some more sea air.

Chapter Eighteen

True to form, Twitchy ditched whoever was tailing him before they knew it. Duncan and Hamish first became aware that my car had vanished from the head of their covert little convoy when the four-wheel drive slowed down almost to a standstill as its occupants wondered just what the hell had happened. One minute the Ford was idling at a set of traffic lights, the next it had turned right and entered some kind of parallel universe. The advantage Twitchy had, of course, was that he knew these streets as only a seasoned car thief could. He knew a twist of the wheel would take him onto a road with a number of quick turns both left and right – and whatever road he took led to lanes and alleys into which a nimble-fingered driver could steer a vehicle like mine and seemingly disappear from view. Hamish drove past the four-wheel drive and pulled in, keeping it in his wing mirror. The flash motor crawled along as its passengers tried to work out where their quarry had gone.

'I'll bet they're sitting in there scratching their heads,' said Hamish with a grin. 'Face it, lads – he's gone.'

'How many in there, you think?' Duncan wondered.

'Two that I can see. Of course, there could be a couple of midgets in the back seat.'

'How likely is that?'

'I dunno – I knew a wee fellow a few years back who was the most vicious bastard I've ever come up against. Used to stab guys in the groin with a sharpened umbrella. The Tiny Terror of Tyneside, the papers called him. He's dead now, though.'

'Unlikely he's in the back of that car, then.'

Hamish conceded that point with a shrug and watched as the vehicle passed them and began to pick up speed. 'So what now?'

'Stick with them, see where they take us.'

'They might've spotted us as we passed.'

Duncan nodded. 'We'll take the chance. They might've been too busy looking for Twitchy to bother about us."

Hamish craned his neck to study the sky. 'We're losing the light.'

Duncan looked up. 'We'll see where they take us for as long as we can. Keep a good few lengths between us, though.'

Hamish gave his brother a withering glance and turned the wheel to the right. 'Okay, and you can keep an eye out for an old granny while we drive.'

Duncan frowned. 'What?'

'Maybe you want to go teach her how to suck eggs.'

* * *

It was fully dark by the time I reached Saltcoats. I'd hoped she would see the sense of staying in the refuge, but Jenny had wanted to get back to whatever flat she was living in since I'd met her, so I was guessing she would make straight for the seaside. I parked outside the tenement building I'd seen Jerome leaving that first night. The problem was I didn't know which flat she'd been staying in. I could have gone on the knock, but I'll be honest, I really did not feel like it. However, I couldn't think of anything else to do, short of stand out in the street like Marlon Brando in *A Streetcar Named Desire* screaming her name.

First, though, I needed to arm myself. I'd not wanted Jenny to come back here because if Jerome had been anything like the professional I felt he was, he would've had someone watching the place for her return. That someone would have been instructed to let him know as soon as she appeared. I'd looked into Jerome's eyes and I knew he wanted to deal with her himself, especially after the debacle at the Sutherland brothers' flat. I needed an equaliser. I sprung the boot to see what goodies Duncan had stashed there. I don't know what I expected to find, but I was disappointed, for the immaculate storage area was empty. I flicked open a side panel and found the emergency jack, wrapped in a plastic cover. I pulled the tyre iron free, an L-shaped chunk of heavy metal which would just have to do. The boot closed with all the efficiency and class that German engineering demanded and I headed for the doorway to the building.

Before I entered I checked the exterior windows for lights. The two ground-floor flats were both dark, there was one light on the first floor left, another second floor right and then both flats on the top floor. Jenny could be sitting in the dark but I doubted it, so that meant I had a fifty-fifty split. That was one of my lifelines gone. If only I could have phoned a friend. If Jerome was already in there, and chances are he was, I knew we were going to have some kind of showdown. I'll be honest, the idea clenched my colon. I thought about giving the Sutherlands a call, but it would take too long for them to get here. It was all down to me. The problem was, which flat?

I tucked the tyre iron behind my back as an old man leading a small dog, a Westie, stepped past me and into the close. The dog halted in its tracks and glared at me with a malevolence that belied its size. A bark grew from a growl and the man jerked at the dog's lead.

'Jessie,' he scolded, 'behave yourself! I'm sorry, mate, she's a crabbit wee bitch.'

'That's okay,' I said, forcing a smile but never taking my eyes off the dog. Never trust a wee dog, I'd learned. They have a tendency to be ankle-snappers.

'Learned it frae ma wife,' the man said, as he half-dragged the dog down the passageway. His voice was thick with liquid and his breath came in fits and starts between the words. 'She was a crabbit wee bitch an' all. God rest her soul.'

He fished in his trouser pocket for his keys and headed towards the door at ground-floor left.

'I wonder if you could help me,' I said, still keeping my distance from Jessie, who was standing in the middle of the passage with her legs wide apart, like a solitary Spartan guarding Thermopylae, giving me a belligerent look that said, 'You shall not pass.' If Gerard Butler had had Jessie as one of his *300*, the movie would've been half as long. I unfolded Jenny's photograph from my pocket with my free hand and held it out. 'Seen this girl at all?'

The old man peered at the picture then regarded me with suspicion. 'You a friend of hers?'

'Wouldn't say that,' I said. 'Her name's Jenny Deavers. She's a runaway. I've been hired to take her home.'

'What you like, then? Some sort of private eye? A gumshoe? A shamus?' He gave a laugh that rattled round his throat.

'Something like that,' I said. 'I know she's staying up this close, maybe with a pal, but don't know which flat. It's important, mate. Her family's worried sick and they want her home.'

He narrowed one eye and took a step back, perhaps to see me better. 'How do I know you're no some sort of pervert, or something?'

I looked as innocent as I could. 'Pal, believe me, I haven't got the energy for that sort of thing. All I want to do is get this lassie home to her maw and then get myself to my bed. It's been a long day, know what I mean?'

He thought about this for a moment, while Jessie eyed up my shin for a tooth sharpener, and then nodded. 'Nae skin off my nose,' he said. 'Second floor on the left.'

'Second floor on the left,' I repeated and stepped gingerly round Jessie to get to the stairs, keeping the tyre iron hidden behind me. 'Thanks, mate.'

'Aye. That's second-floor left as you go up the stairs, mind, no as if you're facing the building. It's on your left as you go up the stairs.'

'Right,' I said, already climbing the stairs and recalling it was one of the flats I'd seen with lights on. 'Thanks.'

'Aye,' he said and then went into his own home, dragging Jessie behind him. She tried to stand her ground but failed. I wondered if the old man would lend me the dog to take upstairs with me, because I'd bet she'd be handy in a rumpus.

I took the stairs two at a time and paused outside the door to catch my breath. I dropped to my knees, eased open the letterbox, peered through. I could see a long hallway with a couple of doors

148

leading off and another at the far end with light bleeding underneath. I could hear the faint rumble of a man's voice, could've been Jerome, so stealthy and sneaky was the way to go. There were two locks, a Yale and a mortise. The mortise had a key lodged in the other side so I hoped only the Yale was locked. Praying no-one would chance across me – my position would be hard to explain – I carefully laid the tyre iron down on the rough doormat and groped inside the pocket of my jacket for my lock-picking kit. One of the many advantages of knowing the Sutherland brothers was they had access to equipment and skills that ordinary folk did not. The lock-picking kit had once belonged to a veteran housebreaker who gave it all up when arthritis mangled his fingers into gnarly twigs. The old man even showed me the tricks of his trade. Picking a lock isn't easy – it's all to do with tension, touch and torque – but I managed to ease the five bars that kept the door in place back into their springs within a few minutes.

I carefully closed the front door behind me, ensuring it made no sound, and crept down the dark passage. The door was ajar and I came to a halt in order to peer through the gap. I could see Jenny sitting on a wooden chair, her face taut with fear. She was looking straight at the door but she did not see me. Her attention was on something else just to the right of my eyeline, which I guessed was Jerome.

'See, darling, I don't like being ripped off,' he was saying. 'I can't abide a thief, me. Hate 'em. With a passion. Especially when they steal from *me*! From *me*!'

Judging by his voice, he was building himself up to a frenzy, and that was not a good thing. Something would have to be done soon, but the problem was I didn't know how close he was to the door, whether he was right behind it or far enough away for me to burst in and catch him by surprise. I also didn't know if he was on his own or had turned up team-handed. If I was lucky, the element of surprise could work if he was on his tod, but if he had some of Fast Freddie's guys with him I would be in serious trouble. I wondered if I had time to nip down and borrow Jessie for a few minutes.

Jerome stepped into view slightly, just his left shoulder, but at least I knew where he was. 'You had no call to do what you did, darling. No call. You took my gear and you took my money and that is something I cannot forgive.'

That was interesting – so Jerome was telling the truth when he said that she'd taken his stuff. Or, at the very least, had gone missing when she did. That meant Jenny was lying when she said he simply didn't like her leaving him. I wondered what else she had lied about. And there was money missing too. Jenny had some questions to answer.

'Jerome...' she began.

'Shut your mouth!' he yelled. 'You just shut your mouth, bitch!'

Tears erupted from Jenny's eyes, but she struggled to retain her composure. Someone else was sobbing though, another girl I couldn't see. Jerome was breathing heavily and I could tell from his taut shoulder muscles he was struggling to regain control of himself. 'Now,' he said, 'you can talk, but only if you're going to tell me where my gear is. And my fifty grand.'

Jenny's lips tightened and she wiped the tears from her cheeks.

'I'd talk if I were you, girl. Otherwise your little friend here? She's going to lose an ear. Then if you still don't talk, she's going to lose another ear. Then her nose. Then her eyes, her lips. And it'll be your fault, Jenny, darling. Because you're a lying, thieving, scheming *bitch!*'

I guessed he was holding Jenny's friend but she was obscured by his broad back. I pictured him pressing that big bloody knife to her face and maybe he was bluffing, maybe he wasn't but if I was going to do something, I'd have to do it now.

I didn't have enough information about the layout of the room to formulate a plan so my best bet – my only bet – was to pile in and let the adrenalin carry me through. It was rife with danger – I still didn't even know if Jerome had company. But as the wise man said, needs must. The wise man also said fools rush in, but I didn't want to think of that now.

I took a step back and kicked the door fully open. Jerome whirled but I clunked him on the chin with the tyre iron before he knew what was happening. He wheeled away, letting the twenty-something girl go, but still retained the knife, which was not good at all. I moved in after him and swung again, catching him squarely on the shoulder. He yelped and twitched away, jerked round to face me, but I wasn't letting him off the hook. I had already stepped in closer and the iron landed with a thud on his temple, sending his eyes rolling back in his head and the knife slipping from his hand. He swayed back, blood dripping from a cut on his chin, but he kept his feet and I could see that there was fight in him yet so I cracked him again, this time on the nose, and I swear I heard something snap. He slumped to his knees, his hands to his face as blood streamed through his fingers and dribbled down his chin, while more oozed from his temple. He groaned when he looked up and saw me moving in once more. He held out one hand to try to ward me off, but he didn't have the strength and my final blow caught him square on the jaw. I think I may have dislocated something in there, but he didn't feel it because he moaned softly and slumped to one side.

My breath was hot and heavy as I stood over him, the tyre iron half raised in case he moved, but he was out cold.

'Jesus,' I heard Jenny say. 'Have you killed him?'

I looked at her as she comforted her still-sobbing friend and felt fear stab at me because it was just possible I had. That was the danger when you let your instincts dictate your actions in these situations. Fight or flight can become fucked very easily. I dropped to one knee and felt the side of his neck for a pulse, relief flooding through me as I found it strong and steady. I shook my head and Jenny set her pal aside to launch herself from her chair to deliver a series of kicks to Jerome's chest.

'Bastard! Bastard! Bastard!' she spat, before giving him another kick for good measure. I let her vent. She was barefoot so she wouldn't do him further damage.

'Happy now?' I asked as she stood over him, glaring at his prone form. She didn't answer and I turned to her friend, who was sitting on the floor beside the chair, watching us through John Lennon spectacles with round, terrified eyes. She was on the chubby side, her brown hair hanging loose. 'What's your name, miss?'

She swallowed, unable to speak. I could see she was having trouble taking all this in.

'Miss?' I said gently. 'What's your name?'

'Lesley,' she said, whispered almost.

'Okay, Lesley, I need you to find me something to tie this guy up with. String'll do, or if you've got it, some tape. Can you find me some?'

She nodded and hauled herself to her feet. She turned to a door which led to a small kitchen, then stopped and looked back at me. 'We need to call the police.'

Not on your life, I thought, but that wasn't what she wanted to hear. I gave her a reassuring grin and said, 'All in good time, Lesley. First we need to secure him, okay?'

She nodded and carried on towards the kitchen. 'And stick the kettle on,' I said. 'I could murder a cuppa.'

Chapter Nineteen

As I wrapped Jerome's hands and legs in enough string to tie up Christmas Trees for the whole of Saltcoats – followed up with copious amounts of sticky tape – I listened as Lesley tearfully outlined to Jenny what had happened. It seemed Jerome had paid the girl a visit after our encounter in the street the night before. He had her address because Jenny had somehow managed to leave her phone when she packed up and left his flat. In that phone was Lesley's number, and it was very easy for a man with Jerome's contacts to get the address that went with that number. He came back to the flat after we got away and introduced himself to Lesley. He was a good-looking fellow and could be charming when he wasn't threatening to rearrange her into a Picasso painting. He convinced her to let him know when Jenny showed up again. So much for my belief that he'd had someone watching.

'He told me he was your boyfriend from London, Jenny,' Lesley said as I ripped off another mile or so of tape to wrap around Jerome's slack mouth. 'He said he really wanted you back...'

'Don't worry about it, Lesley,' said Jenny. 'He's a bastard, that's what he is.'

'He said he missed you. He seemed so nice.'

'He's not nice, he's a bastard.'

'He asked me to phone him when you came back. He said he loved you and he couldn't function without you.' I don't think Lesley was trying to convince Jenny of anything. I think she was justifying events to herself. She needed to know that even though she had done the wrong thing, it was for all the right reasons.

'Bastard,' Jenny said again, just in case we hadn't got the message.

Lesley was crying now. 'I'm so sorry, Jenny – I really believed him! I just wanted you to be happy and he's so good-looking, and he seemed so nice, well-dressed, you know?'

Jenny went to her friend then and hugged her. I noticed that the pudgy girl looked at Jenny with a tenderness that was really quite touching. Lesley, I realised, was hopelessly in love with Jenny, and I think Jenny knew it and she used those feelings whenever she felt the need.

'You shouldn't have come back, Jenny,' I said. 'You could have got both you and Lesley killed.'

Jenny shot me a look that told me I was a bastard too, but to be honest I really didn't care what she thought. Jenny was no innocent victim here, after all. She had put her friend in harm's way without a second thought. And I hadn't forgotten about the drugs and the money. My eyes flicked to two hefty sports bags in the corner.

'What was so important that you had to come back?' I asked.

'I told you before, my stuff.'

'And what stuff would that be?'

She shrugged as she stroked the weeping Lesley's hair. 'Just stuff.'

'Uh-huh,' I said and stepped over to the bags. 'This it here?'

'Leave that alone!'

I ignored her and stooped to unzip the first bag. She flew across the room but I straightened and gave her a look that was ferocious enough to stop her in her tracks. Lesley looked scared and I felt bad for her, but I was pissed off with Jenny, for lying to me about the drugs, for putting her friend in danger, for being a pain in the arse. People were dying around her and all she wanted to do was get back to collect a bag of cocaine and fifty thousand in cash. Oh, yes, I was well pissed off with her. I swear if she had taken another step towards me I would have decked her. She caught the heat in my expression and kept her distance.

She watched through surly eyes as I flipped open the bag then picked it up and emptied the contents on the floor. T-shirts, blouses, underwear, socks and two pairs of jeans tumbled out. No drugs, no cash. I threw the bag aside and turned to the second one. I glanced at her and saw she was watching me now with ill-concealed hate. I opened the second bag, knowing in my heart this was filled Jerome's product and his green. I gave her a triumphant smile and upended it. The smile froze as a succession of photographs, letters and documents flooded out.

I wasn't pissed off any more. I was embarrassed.

'Satisfied?' she asked, managing to inject enough venom into that one word to fell a grizzly.

I didn't know what to say. I stooped to pick up some of the photographs. They were all of a good-looking woman with jet black hair, a few of them with a little girl who looked like Jenny. The woman wasn't smiling in any of those pictures and there was no physical contact. I recalled the photographs I'd seen in Jessica's house of the same woman.

'Your mother?' I asked.

'Yes,' she snapped, snatching the prints from my hand before kneeling to gather everything together.

I felt like something you'd scrape off your shoe as I asked, 'Are the letters hers too?'

'Yes. They're letters she received from my father. This is all I have left of her.'

She scooped the envelopes together carefully, tenderly, and I tried to help her stuff everything back into the bags but she slapped my hands away. 'Leave it,' she snapped. 'You've done enough.'

'I'm sorry,' I said. It was weak, but it was the best I could do.

She crammed a handful of letters into the bag. 'What did you expect to find anyway?'

'Jerome's drugs.'

She sighed and said, 'I told you, I don't have his bloody drugs.'

'But you did take them?'

She didn't answer as she pulled the last of the photographs and sheets of paper to her and thrust them back in the bag. She zipped it up then stood to give me a defiant look. 'Yes,' she said. 'I took his drugs.'

'So where are they?'

A small smile then. 'At the bottom of the Thames. I threw them off Westminster Bridge.'

'And the money?'

'I didn't even know there was money in the bag. I grabbed the first one I could find to piss him off.'

'Why?'

'Because he was suffocating me. And he cheated on me. He's a bastard.'

'So I hear,' I said, still slightly ashamed, although it did occur to me that if she had told me she'd dumped the stuff in the river before, it would have saved all this drama. I didn't say that, though. This was no time to be right.

* * *

We couldn't leave Jerome, so we piled him into the back of the Mercedes. First we covered the back seat with a sheet borrowed from Lesley – there would have been hell to pay if any blood had wound up on Duncan's soft leather. Jerome was coming round by then, so he was able to walk, albeit unsteadily, down the stairs. Eamonn's paranoia had taken root in my mind and I still hadn't even switched on my mobile, let alone use it, so I used Lesley's phone to call Duncan. I told him I was using a landline because my mobile may have been compromised and he didn't ask any questions. I said I had a package that needed some medical attention so he told me to head for the hospital and he would phone ahead. When Duncan said hospital, he didn't mean we should take advantage of the delights of the NHS. It was street speak for Doctor John Brewer, a tame GP who accepted cash for treating low-level injuries under the table.

I threw Jenny's precious bags into the boot and watched as the two girls embraced at the closemouth. I promised Lesley she wouldn't be implicated in anything and it was a promise I intended to keep. She seemed like a nice girl, and I decided I'd protect her even if Jenny wouldn't.

Jenny was still steamed as we headed back to Glasgow. My shame at turfing her unmentionables out on the rug aside, I was feeling pretty much the same. She had lied to me, after all. She had sucked Lesley into her problems. And she had run away. Jenny Deavers was not my flavour of the month.

We drove in silence for much of the journey, which suited me fine. I kept a weather eye on Jerome in the back, but he was bound up like a masochist's wet dream and unable to move. His eyes, though, were alert again. I had checked his injuries while he was out cold and I didn't think I'd broken anything, but it sure as hell wasn't for the want of trying. He would be aching like buggery, that much was certain.

Jenny's voice startled me. 'That stuff is all I have of her.'

I knew what she was talking about, of course, but she told me all the same. 'My mum. That's all that was left from the fire that killed her. Photographs, letters, my birth certificate, a few other things. She kept them in an old tin, a biscuit tin. That's how they survived.'

'Do you remember much about her?'

She nodded. 'I remember she really didn't have a lot of time for me. She wasn't abusive or anything, she took care of me, I was always fed and clothed and given things, but that didn't change things. I was an inconvenience to her. I got in the way of her life. I don't think she ever really loved me, I was just there and I think she wished I wasn't. She was fond of men, very fond of men, and having a little girl around was difficult for her, even for one night stands. And she had a lot of them. Aunt Jessica was the same, maybe not with men, but neither of them were capable of any real warmth, let alone love.'

'Your aunt regretted it, I think.'

Jenny thought about this. 'Maybe. Too late, though.'

She fell silent again and I knew she was lost in her memories of an unhappy childhood. My feelings towards her began to thaw once more. No wonder she was a self-centred bitch sometimes – she probably had to be from an early age. A little girl living with a mother who neither wanted her nor, by the sound of it, took much trouble to conceal her feelings. Naturally, it made me think of my own childhood and of a mother who was so wrapped up in her own disappointment with life that she barely noticed the little boy who needed her attention. I was a mistake, as Mommy Dearest often told me. She had never wanted me, had done everything she could to get rid of me, short of heading up a back alley for an appointment with a beefy woman and a knitting needle. My sister June was older than me, so seemed not to need as much attention or even notice as our mother slid deeper and deeper into herself. At least, that's what I thought at the time. Years later I discovered I was wrong – June noticed, she felt it, she hated her for it as much as I did. I had one advantage Jenny did not have – my father was around and he tried to keep things as normal as he could. Even so, I convinced myself that I really was a mistake, but not in the way my mother meant. I was certain there had been some sort of mix-up at birth, that I was actually part of another family, a better family. The fact that I was born at home made no difference, an error had been made. And as my mother's madness grew, I more and more wished I was someone else, somewhere else, anywhere but in that home with its frozen silences punctuated by frequent bursts of hysteria. I think that was why I became such a movie fan. They offered me an escape, a sanctuary. I could sit in the darkened cinema and be taken away from my life and placed somewhere else, even if only for a couple of hours.

My gaze flicked to the rear view and I saw a pair of eyes glittering at me. I'd forgotten about him for a few minutes. 'You okay back there, Jerome?'

The tape around his mouth prevented any speech, but he could still grunt, which he did. I don't know how he made a solitary rumble sound like a threat, but he did. It's all in the eyes, I suppose.

'She's not got your gear, Jerome,' I said. 'I think you should know that.'

His eyes told me he didn't believe me.

'It's true,' I went on, happy to be talking about this rather than thinking about the past. What is it they say? The past is a foreign country and they do things differently there? That's true, I suppose, but the past is also home and sometimes you can't help but go back. You might not want to, you might not enjoy it when you're there, but you're drawn there against your will. I checked the road ahead and then flicked back to Jerome. 'She took your stuff all right but she doesn't have it. Do you, Jenny?'

Jenny was looking out of the passenger window to the darkness beyond and did not respond. I answered for her. 'She chucked it in the river before she left London.' Another glance at Jerome as his eyes slid towards the back of Jenny's head. 'So there's lots of little fishes having a part-ay down the Smoke on your product. Wouldn't be surprised if they didn't get so high they turned into flying fish.'

I could tell by the heat in Jerome's eyes that this was not what he wanted to hear. I smiled at him in the mirror. 'It's over, Jerome. Your stuff's gone, so's your cash. You can't get it back and hurting Jenny won't change things. There's no profit in this for you any more. Chalk it up as a loss and move on. Get me?'

He looked back at me and I could tell he was far from convinced. Concentrating on the road, I played my final card. 'Let me put it this way. I'm going to take you to see a doctor, get you patched up. Then my friends are going to put you on the first train back to London. You will not get off that train and come back to Glasgow, am I clear? Because if you do, my friends will put a bullet in your head without even thinking twice. They're none too fond of drug dealers at the best of times, but if you irk them in any way, they could take you into a severe dislike, you catch my drift? And, Jerome?' I made sure he was paying attention. 'Listen to me when I say this. You might think that your connection with Fast Freddie will save you, but it won't. Fast Freddie won't be able to save you. God almighty will not be able to save you. You come back here, you're a dead man. I promise you.'

He stared at me for what seemed like an eternity before he finally nodded. I believed he meant it.

I was wrong.

Chapter Twenty

Doc Brewer lived in a large detached sandstone villa on the South Side of the city. At today's prices it would probably set you back almost a million smackers, easy, but the GP had lived there since he was a boy. His father had been a doctor and his grandfather had been a doctor, so it was a family home rather than one bought from his own NHS labours, although I understand GPs can make a healthy living out of the unhealthy. Of course, the good medico had a lucrative sideline in under-the-counter care, thanks to the likes of Duncan, Hamish and other denizens of the city's dark side. For a consideration, Doc Brewer treated cuts, bruises, even knife wounds. Depending on the severity of the wound he had to treat, his fee ranged from the substantial to the considerable. He drew the line at bullet wounds, though, which still had to be dealt with at a hospital, no matter what legal heat might emanate from turning up at A&E.

The Sutherland brothers were waiting for us in the driveway and the first thing Duncan did was cast an appraising eye over his car. He looked surprised when he found no bumps, scratches or bullet holes.

'Really didn't expect you to hand it back in one piece, Dom,' he said, and I think I detected something akin to awe in his tone.

'Got to say, Dunc,' I said truthfully, 'neither did I.'

Hamish hauled Jerome none-too-gently from the back seat. 'Out you come, sunshine. If you're a good boy and take your medicine, you might get a lollipop.'

Jerome really didn't look as if a lollipop would cut it, but he allowed himself to be led into the house by Hamish. Duncan glanced at Jenny in the Mercedes and motioned me to step out of earshot.

'You really worked him over,' he said. There was no judgement in his tone, merely a statement of fact. Nevertheless, I felt a twinge of shame, as I always did in the aftermath of my brutal inner self showing its face. But Jerome had stepped over a line when he threatened Lesley in that way. I couldn't say for certain if he had any intention of following it through, but something told me that with this guy, a threat made was more like a cast-iron promise.

Duncan saw I had no wish to discuss it further. 'We got your car back, although God only knows why. I'd put it out of its misery if I were you.'

'Lot of life left in the old thing yet,' I said.

Duncan's eyes rolled to tell me that he doubted that very much indeed, and asked me why I'd not been using my phone. I gave him a quick rundown of the events in Gordon Street, my trip to the cop shop and Eamonn's dire warning about the bugging and hacking abilities of Police Scotland's crack team of lawmen and women. Duncan nodded gravely at this and said, 'I'll get you a new one tomorrow. I'll get us all new ones tomorrow. This guy today, the Terminator, he was the same guy from the park, right?'

'Either that or he has an identical twin.'

Duncan's eyes were thoughtful as he joined up some dots. 'We followed the people who were following Twitchy, until he gave them the old sliperoo. Tracked them to one of those big hotels down on the riverside, you know, near the Exhibition Centre?'

'Was the Terminator one of them?'

'Nah, a guy and a woman, but they gave off a Special Forces vibe, just like the Terminator. They're a bit over confident, though, didn't pay attention to their surroundings. Probably think we're hicks up here.'

I hoped the Terminator wasn't working alone, because if there was yet another party involved I was going spit the dummy so far out of the pram it would require satellite imagery to find it. I couldn't take any further questions or complications. I ran a hand over my eyes and down my face.

'You look done in,' Duncan said, ever the master of under-statement.

'Yeah,' I said. 'I feel as if I've done the Iron Man challenge, the Glasgow Marathon and swum the Channel all in one afternoon. I need some sleep and I need a shower. I also need something to eat. My belly thinks my throat's been cut.'

Duncan nodded and glanced back at the car. 'What about the girl?'

'I don't know if she's hungry.'

Duncan grimaced. 'You know what I mean. What are you going to do with her?'

'Back to Father Verne, I suppose. Tie her up in a room, if that's what it takes to make her stay put.' I had asked her on the way up if she wanted to be delivered into police custody. The offer was flatly turned down. This news would not please Nick, but into everyone's life a little rain must fall.

Duncan trusted me one last time with his precious car to drive across the city to the refuge while he and Hamish dropped the newly patched-up Jerome at Central Station to catch the late train to London.

Jenny looked as drained as I felt by the time we reached the refuge. She evidently did not feel the need to apologise to Father Verne for doing a runner earlier in the day, so she lost the points she'd gained when she spoke about her mother. The priest and I stood in the corridor after she had closed the door to her room without a word.

'Can we lock her in?' I asked.

Father Verne shook his head. 'You know there're no locks on these doors. It's my first sign of trust in the kids who come here.'

'Is that the faith thing again?'

He nodded and touched my arm to lead me away from the door. 'That poor girl's exhausted,' he said. 'I don't think she's going to run off again. Not tonight, at least. You don't look too hot yourself. Drink?'

'A whisky would be nice,' I said. 'And if there's a roll and sausage around, I'll have that too.'

Father Verne smiled. 'I'll even make it for you.'

That was music to my ears.

* * *

I devoured the final morsel of the two rolls Father Verne had rustled up for me and sat back before I took a sip of single malt. Square sausage and Laphroaig malt might not be on the menu in the top restaurants, but the way I felt that night, it was Michelin-standard fayre. I asked him if he'd made any headway in finding out what Jenny had been doing during her years in London. He shook his head.

'She's a deep one,' he said, 'but self-sufficient, I would say. She's capable of looking after herself with a single-minded determination that's quite worrying in one so young. I feel certain she's had some experiences, though, met people she would've been better off not meeting, like Mister Kingsley.'

I chewed on my food and thought about this. Maybe there was something else she'd got herself involved with down south that I didn't know.

'Does the word Excelsis mean anything to you, Father?' I asked.

'It's Latin, Dominic, of course it means something to me.'

'What does it mean?'

'Roughly it means highest, as in *Gloria in Excelcis Deo* – Glory to God in the Highest. Why do you ask?'

'It was scribbled beside Tiger Reilly's name on a blotter in the Gordon Street office today.'

'The Gordon Street bloodbath?'

I gave him a frown, not used to him talking in such dramatic terms. He smiled. 'It hit the evening paper,' he explained. 'Excelsis, eh? Well, poor old Tiger certainly will not be greeting his Maker, God rest him. I think he's heading in a totally different direction. What do you think it means in relation to our current situation?'

I sipped my drink again. 'The Terminator looks ex-military, and Elite Security specialised in recruiting mercenaries and former soldiers for security work, so it could be a code word.'

Father Verne nodded. 'A code word for what?'

'God knows.'

'I'll ask him, shall I?'

'It certainly couldn't hurt.' I sat back in my chair and closed my eyes, felt myself beginning to drift.

Father Verne's voice floated through to me. 'You could always ask himself, you know?'

I smiled, shook my head. 'God and I are no longer on speaking terms. Father, I have sinned...'

There was a pause then before his voice came through again, quieter now. 'We all have, Dom, and yet He still cares. That's the beauty of it.'

I forced my eyes open again and smiled at him. He was always trying to get me back into the church. 'You keep trying, Father. Maybe one day you'll win. Just keep trying.' My eyes slid closed again. 'God loves a trier.'

And as I floated off into sleep, I swear I heard Father Verne say, 'He loves us all, Dom, even the sinner...'

* * *

Father Verne had a full house, so I had to make do with dossing on a couch in his office. I have no memory of being helped onto it and covered up with a blanket, but someone got me out of that chair and walked me to it. It wasn't grandma's feather bed, but it wasn't the worst place I'd ever crashed. During my lost time in the thrall of various narcotics, I slept rough in underpasses, sheds and, for a period, in the centre of some thick bushes in Queen's Park. *Skippers* were what we called them on the streets. That was when I was at my lowest, before Father Verne found me in the gutter, near death. Correction – I was dead, more or less, and he brought me back to life. I couldn't bring myself to follow a religion, but I did know that resurrections were possible.

All the same, I was as stiff as Richard Todd's upper lip when I woke up. I could smell bacon frying and hear voices drifting down the hallway from the kitchen. I hauled myself upright and stretched, my muscles protesting so much they practically carried placards. I thought about dropping to the floor and giving myself twenty, but decided against it. Getting up from the couch had been a hard enough struggle and I didn't want to tempt providence by lying on the floor. I contented myself with another stretch, making my tendons creak and crack like a breakfast cereal. Exercise is overrated anyway.

Duncan and Hamish were at the table wolfing down a full Scottish breakfast when I stepped into the kitchen. I just knew Hamish was going to call me Sleeping Beauty.

'Morning, Rip Van Winkle,' he said through a mouthful of potato scone.

I grumbled something that was unintelligible even to me and moved to the coffee pot to pour myself a pick-me-up.

'He's a delight first thing, isn't he?' said Duncan.

'Obviously a morning person,' said Hamish.

'Such a cheery chappie.'

'A ray of sunshine.'

'Blow it out your arse,' I said as I sat down at the table, my voice still hoarse from sleep. What my words lacked in wit, they made up in sincerity. 'Jerome get off okay?'

'Ah, another cheery chappie,' said Hamish. 'Aye, he got off just fine, muttering all sorts of threats, of course. Never heard such language. I waved him bye-bye as he pulled out.'

I nodded, satisfied, and sipped my coffee. It tasted good and I felt my natural *bon homie* creeping back. 'Any of that bacon left?'

'Plenty, bonny lad,' said Duncan. 'We brought in some supplies this morning. You want the full boona? Bacon, eggs, potato scone, beans, tomato, mushroom?'

'All of the above, except the tomato.'

'Toast? Juice?'

'Yes, please.'

'Good for you, lad. I like to see a healthy appetite in the morning. But you'd better get started making it, because we haven't got a lot of time.'

The brothers grinned at me as I pulled myself to my feet, cursing under my breath. So much for pals, I thought. Duncan was still chuckling to himself as he laid a new mobile phone on the counter beside me. 'Here,' he said, 'try not to let anyone hack into this one.'

'I'm not sure anyone hacked into either of my other ones.'

'Neither am I, but let's not take the risk. As Lawrence of Arabia used to say, *trust in God but tether your camel.* ' Duncan laid a card beside the phone. 'That's the new number. You'd better give that to anyone who had the old one.'

The only person I'd given my number was Tiger's widow, Ginty. Irrespective of my motivation, I had meant what I said when I offered my help whenever she needed it. I couldn't do that if she didn't have my new number. I asked Duncan to keep an eye on the food frying on the cooker and went back to Father Verne's office, where I fished the slip of paper out of my pocket on which I'd written her number and dialled it. She answered on the fifth ring and I said, 'Hi, this is Dom... It's Erasmus.'

'Jesus! I've been trying to get you since last night.'

Normally that would have made me smile, but the urgency in her voice told me there was something wrong.

'There's been a guy here, asking about Walter, asking about you.'

'Police?'

'No, but he wasn't a ned either. Tall bloke, good-looking, American accent, something wrong with his arm. He held it by his side, kind of stiff-like. Like it was broke or something.'

The Terminator, had to be. Tiger's next-of-kin would be in the file he'd taken. 'Are you okay?' I asked. 'Did he hurt you? Threaten you?'

'No, I'm fine. But, listen...there was something about him, Erasmus. He's dangerous, you know?' No kidding, I thought, but she wanted to emphasise her thought. 'I've been around neds and crooks and gangsters all my life, but this guy? He gave me the jim-jams, you know what I'm saying? If he's looking for you, it's not good for your health.'

The concern in her voice made me feel warm inside. Then she chilled me again.

'The reason I'm saying that,' she went on, 'is because he left me a number in case you got in touch again. Says he wants to speak to you.'

I tried to keep my voice steady when I said, 'You'd better give me it, then.'

She read out a mobile number, then said, 'You sure you should be in touch with a bloke like that?'

'Mrs Reilly...'

'Ginty. I think now that I'm your social secretary we can be on first-name terms.'

'Ginty, believe me when I say that I really don't want to talk to him, but I think it's best that I do.'

'Okay,' she said, and fell silent.

'Okay,' I said, and fell silent.

We were silent together for a few seconds. I tried to come up with something witty to say but to be honest all I could think about was the Terminator. Finally, I said, 'As long as you're okay, Ginty. And listen – I've got a new mobile number...' I read it out. 'But if you haven't got a pen you can dial 1471 and get it then.'

'Okay,' she said.

'You can phone it any time, if you ever need anything.'

'I phoned the other one and you never answered.'

'Yeah, well, there was a problem with that one. But listen, I'd better call this guy, see what he wants.'

'Okay. And Erasmus?'

'Yeah?'

'Come by any time you're passing.'

'I will.'

I was smiling as I hung up. I was still smiling as I dialled the Terminator's number. He answered almost immediately. 'Mister Queste,' he said. That surprised me and my smile died.

'How did you know it was me?'

'The only person who has this number is Mister Reilly's widow. I knew she would give it to you.' He was American, but there was no regional accent, no southern drawl, no western twang, no northern snap. His tone was colourless, business-like, measured. I could've been talking to a machine.

I asked. 'How did you know I'd left contact details with her?'

I heard a small laugh. 'I know a lot about you, Mister Queste, especially your weakness for good-looking females.'

'That's unfair. I know next to nothing about you.'

'And that's the way it'll stay, believe me.'

'Still, puts me at a disadvantage.'

'Oh, you're extremely disadvantaged. In fact, the phrase "out of your depth" springs to mind.'

'Really? So how's the arm?'

The small laugh again. 'It was a scrape, nothing more. It'll heal. Do you still have my gun?'

'Police have it. They'll have found your fingerprints by now, I'd imagine. Maybe some DNA.'

That brought another laugh. He could be a cheery bugger, for a machine. It was followed by a confident, 'I wish them luck.' Which meant his fingerprints and DNA weren't on file, certainly not in this country. Which meant he'd never been arrested. Which meant the police weren't going to be much help in that regard. Which meant this guy scared the living shit out of me.

'Anyway, Mister Queste,' he said, 'enough idle chit-chat. I want the girl.'

'Why?'

'Because she's my target, Mister Queste, I thought you would've worked that out by now.'

'Who hired you?'

The small laugh became a full-throated guffaw. 'Ah, Mister Queste, you don't expect me to answer that, do you?'

'I dunno – I thought maybe you'd be so surprised by the question you'd answer without thinking.'

'I don't do anything without thinking. The girl. I want her.'

'She's too young for you.'

'Give her to me. It would save your friends a lot of pain.'

'My friends?'

'I told you, I know a lot about you. I know where you live, I know where you drink, I know where your friends, those brothers, stay. I know about that priest and his home for fallen children.'

'She's not at any of those places.'

'Yes, she is. And I'll make you a promise – hand her over and no-one else needs to be hurt, even though I owe that pal of yours a bullet hole.'

He was bluffing. Clearly he knew a lot about to me – too much for my comfort – but he couldn't know for certain where she was. That was what I told myself and I was almost convincing too. Almost.

'I give you my word as a gentleman,' he said.

'Gentlemen don't kill innocent children.'

'Gentlemen kill anything that moves, otherwise what's hunting season for?'

Okay, he had a point there, but Jenny was no grouse. 'You're not getting her.'

He sighed, something almost sad in the sound. Made a change from the laugh, I suppose. 'Oh, I'll get her, Mister Queste.'

And then he hung up. No goodbye, no final threat, no evil laugh, just a dead line. I jumped to the window to scan the car park and road beyond. I saw no mysterious cars or vans lurking, well, mysteriously. But as I studied the world outside the refuge, I couldn't shake off the feeling that eyes were studying me.

I told Duncan and Hamish about the conversation as I wolfed down my breakfast. It takes a lot to put me off my feed and, as I'd said the night before, I felt as if I'd not had a decent meal in a week. The brothers registered the Terminator's warning with irritation. Like me, they don't like to be threatened and seldom react well.

'This is pissing me off good and proper now,' said Duncan.

'Yeah,' said Hamish.

'We've been on the back foot from the beginning here,' Duncan went on, 'and that pisses me off too.'

'Yeah,' agreed his brother.

'It's time to take control.'

'Yeah,' said Hamish again, smiling.

I asked, 'What do you suggest?'

'Take the fight to them this time,' answered Duncan, glancing at Hamish, who nodded his agreement. At least he didn't say "yeah" again.

Chapter Twenty-One

Father Verne categorically refused to have Hamish accompany him to the hospital to visit a sick parishioner. He had agreed to take Jenny with him, but there was no way he was going to turn up with a bodyguard. So we hatched a plan to lure any watchers away from them. Shayleen was about Jenny's height and build and she agreed to act as a decoy. She wanted to head into the city anyway and we could be her transportation. I wondered if she was heading back to Cody, but didn't say anything as it wasn't my place. I could tell the thought passed through Father Verne's mind too, but he also remained silent. The faith business must be hard going sometimes. Jenny was unwilling to co-operate – of course she was, it wouldn't be in her nature to simply give in to something that was being done for her benefit – but she finally agreed to swap clothes with the girl. A baseball cap was the final touch to conceal the difference in hair colour.

I had to admit it was a good fit, and hopefully from a distance it would fool even the Terminator. We left first, making as much of a show of getting into Duncan's car as we could without actually turning it into a pantomime. Father Verne and Jenny would wait until we had left, then call a taxi to take them to Gartnavel General.

We took an extended tour of the city, meandering down roads, taking long diversions, all to make anyone following that we were trying to shake them off. I sat in the back seat with Shayleen, who stared through the car window, but I felt didn't see much of what slipped by. I don't know what world she was in, but it wasn't this one. She rubbed at her left arm incessantly and I feared she would scrape off the skin if she kept it up.

I wondered if some conversation would distract her and asked, 'So what's your plan, Shayleen?' Her face swivelled to meet mine and I could see she wondered what I meant. 'In the town? Where you going?'

She shrugged. 'A wee wander, that's all. Bit cooped up in that place. Needed a change, you know?'

She was still scratching at her forearm and I thought I'd try to direct approach. 'You're not going to make a buy, are you?'

She looked down at her arm, stopped rubbing, and smiled. She looked a lot younger when she smiled. 'No, no way. I'm done with all that, been off it for weeks. Don't miss it. Anyway, no got any cash.'

I searched her eyes for signs of a lie, but saw nothing. That didn't mean anything, though, for users can be consummate liars. They often have to be in order to survive. It's as if the narcotics that have taken over every fibre of their being has made them into the greatest salesperson ever. If they told you night was day, you might catch yourself reaching for your sunshades.

'Want my advice?' She waited, knowing I was going to give it whether she wanted it or not. 'Stay away from it. And stay away from your brother. He's bad news.'

She looked away at the mention of Cody. 'He's okay,' she muttered.

I shook my head. 'I know his type. He's trouble. You've got the chance here to get out of it, if you stick with Father Verne. You go back to Cody, you meet up with him today...' She looked back at me and I knew I'd hit the nail on the head. 'Jesus, Shayleen, you *are* planning on meeting him!'

'He's my brother,' she said, but there was no strength in her voice. 'I'm just going to say goodbye.'

'He's a waster and he's not good for you.'

'He's my brother,' she repeated, and this time her words carried some steel. 'We're family. You not got family?'

'I've a sister.'

'Then wouldn't you want to say goodbye if you were walking away?'

The words *my sister isn't a drug-dealing pimp* were ready to leap off my tongue but I swallowed them. The feeling that she would be drawn back into the life by her brother wouldn't leave me but whatever I said would make no difference. What she did was no business of mine, I had my own troubles, so I simply nodded and lapsed into silence. Duncan and Hamish had seemingly not paid any heed to our brief conversation. They both stared straight ahead, Duncan behind the wheel, Hamish slouched in the passenger seat, but I knew they were both on the alert for any sign of a tail.

Duncan weaved through the streets and finally dodged between two buses to pull into the kerb to allow the girl to dart from the car. She had already taken off Jenny's denim jacket and ditched the baseball cap so she wouldn't be recognised as she walked away. She didn't say goodbye, didn't thank us, didn't say anything. She just threw the door open and shot out. As we pulled away from the pavement I watched her merge with the pedestrians and finally vanish. Perhaps she was telling the truth and just wanted to wander around the shops as a change of scene. Or perhaps she was heading right back into her old life. I don't know how Father Verne did what he did – I knew he couldn't imprison these kids, but to just let them come and go freely must be nerve-wracking for him. *You don't know this girl*, I told myself, *she is not your responsibility. You have enough on your plate.*

'You can't help someone who doesn't want to be helped,' Duncan's voice was gentle and he was twisted round in the driver's seat, looking at me.

'Then why are we doing all this?' I answered, unexpectedly feeling emotion burn at my eyes and claw at my throat. 'Jenny sure as hell doesn't want us helping her.'

Duncan jerked his head to the side. 'Maybe so, but this is personal now, for me and Hamish anyway. They came to our home. That's not on.'

I stared into the crowds again. 'So we just forget her? Because I'll bet Father Verne won't.'

'He'll give her space. He knows he has to let them go, otherwise they won't come back. If they come back then they're serious about wanting help.'

I wished I'd said more to her before she climbed out. I wished I'd pleaded with her to stay with us, let us take her back to the refuge once we'd done our business. But Duncan was right, it had to be her decision. I hoped she made the right one.

* * *

It was one of those hotels that have sprung up in Glasgow over the past ten, fifteen years and the citizenry doesn't understand why. It seemed to us that for a while a flash new boarding house was built on just about every spare piece of city centre ground, although the economic downturn had seen such enterprise tail off. This one was a 200-bedroom monster with fine views across the river to the Science Park as well as the headquarters of the BBC and STV.

It was a grey day and the water was correspondingly dull and choppy. As we stood in the car park, I felt as if I'd wandered onto the set of some science fiction film from the '60s or '70s, *Logan's Run* or *Fahrenheit 451*. The architecture here is futuristic, if not downright weird. The flying saucer that was the Hydro concert venue was the former, the Armadillo-shaped Clyde Auditorium provided the latter. It was, though, a mixture of the old and the new Glasgow, with the old city represented by the stark skeleton of the Finnieston Crane behind us and the domed brick of the Rotunda bar and restaurant which was once the northern entrance to a series of tunnels under the Clyde. Further on was the Crowne Plaza Hotel, which was more upmarket than this brand-new one, but only in the way that Buckingham Palace is more upmarket than, say, 10 Downing Street.

We were standing beside a spotlessly clean Range Rover with tinted windows. It may have been the one I'd seen outside Aunt Jessica's house the night she died, but they all look alike to me. This had been the vehicle the brothers had followed after Twitchy shrugged it off like dandruff from his shoulder. They had watched a man and a woman climb out and head into the hotel and Duncan had memorised the registration number so he would know it again, there being a plethora of such vehicles dotted across the open space. Duncan pointed out the pair had betrayed their expertise in their choice of parking space. There were CCTV cameras at various vantage points, but the marked bay they had chosen was equidistant from them all, and far from the hotel, even though there were a number of spaces near the entrance, so although anyone coming or going would be recorded, the image would not be clear. Unless the lenses were top of the line hi-def numbers, which was highly unlikely. If they worked at all.

When we arrived, the Range Rover was hemmed in by a tall blue van on one side and a large lorry on the other, from which two heavily muscled and bearded men who, despite the chill in the air, were unloading an array of sound equipment in t-shirts. We'd watched them trundle the gear across the car park towards the Rotunda, and they hadn't returned. While we waited, a white Ford Transit parked in front of the four-wheel drive and the driver also headed to the Rotunda. I wondered what was going on in there, but forced myself to focus. Another off-road vehicle rolled up beside it, why I couldn't say, because there were plenty of other spaces available. The driver, a smart-looking redhead in a business suit, walked off on lethal-looking high heels towards the Hydro, talking to herself. At least, I thought she was talking to herself, but then I saw the Bluetooth receiver stuck in her ear, which always makes me think of the Borg in *Star Trek*. The redhead was in touch with the Collective. Technology. Resistance is futile. The upshot was that the vehicle that formed the object of our attention was well wedged in and obscured from view on three sides. Which suited us right down to the ground.

'Okay,' I said, 'so what do we do now? Hang around here until they come out? Could be here all day.'

Duncan looked around to ensure no-one was watching then nodded to Hamish, who produced a large brick from under his jacket and proceeded to throw it at the windscreen. The missile bounced off the glass like it was made of rubber.

'Jesus, man,' said Duncan, 'put some muscle into it.'

A somewhat abashed Hamish retrieved the brick and tried again. This time the glass shattered and almost immediately the vehicle's alarm sounded. Duncan started to walk towards the hotel.

'Where you going?' I asked.

'To report an act of vandalism,' he replied.

Duncan was back with us a full ten minutes before they appeared. The man and woman were dressed identically in grey sweatshirts, tracksuit pants and expensive trainers made by the nimble fingers of slave labour in the Far East. I wondered if they had been roused from the gym. A hotel like that was bound to have a gym. The woman had the solid look of someone who could break my back between her legs. Maybe she was the Terminator's sister, I thought. The guy was bald and built like a brick shit-house's bigger brother and I could easily visualise him in camo gear stalking the Predator through a South American jungle. No sign of the Terminator, though, which was disappointing.

Hamish and I had hidden ourselves behind the blue van while Duncan lurked at the rear of the lorry. The man and woman inspected the damage to their vehicle with no visible sign of emotion. Maybe it was a rental. They didn't even register surprise when Duncan stepped into view, his automatic pistol held loosely in front of him. No need to point the thing, just let them know it's there. Also, the cameras may have been straining to capture the image, but there's no mistaking a gun being levelled. It's not as if Duncan could pretend it was a TV remote if his collar was felt. The man's hand, however, did twitch towards his waistband at the rear of his sweatpants but stopped when Hamish moved from out behind the van and said, 'Not a good idea, bonny lad.'

They twisted round to face us, their faces still blank. Maybe they *are* cyborgs, I thought. Their expressions remained frozen even though they could see Hamish's gun held double-handed in front of him, barrel aimed at the ground. They knew, though, that it could come up very quickly. Two pairs of eyes flicked to me, saw I had no weapon and was therefore no threat, so they focussed all their attention on the brothers.

'Sorry to bother you, but we were wondering where your pal was?' Duncan asked, ever so politely.

'What pal would that be?' It was the woman who spoke. I expected her to be American, like the Terminator, but she wasn't. She was Welsh, by the sounds of it. I wondered if you got Welsh cyborgs.

'The American bloke with the moustache and the sore arm,' I said. She turned back to me and looked me up and down, as if she was thinking of buying me. I saw the notion of denying all knowledge flicker and die in her eyes. She looked bored, as if she'd had guns pointed at her all her life, which she probably had.

'Sykes? Haven't seen him for two days.'

Sykes, so that was his name. I felt deflated. Sykes was such an ordinary name for such an extraordinary man. Sykes. I decided that from now on I'd call the woman Hattie and the other guy Derek, after Jacques and Guyler respectively.

'You expect us to believe that, lass?' Hamish said, and she shrugged, telling him to believe what he liked.

'He works alone,' she said.

'So why are you here?' I asked.

'To see the sights of your fair city,' she said. 'Wonderful architecture, has Glasgow.' She nodded at the smashed window. 'I take it you fellows did this?'

'Got your attention,' admitted Duncan.

She nodded. 'That it did. Scuppered our security deposit, though.' So it was a rental.

We stood there for a few quiet seconds, not sure what to do next. We had convinced ourselves that Sykes would have been here, but he wasn't. Hattie and Derek looked relaxed as they watched us, although his eyes darted back and forth, waiting for a chance to pull the pistol he had tucked away behind his back and start blasting. Hamish spotted it too, so he said, 'Maybe we should lose that gun, mate. Just reach round, thumb and forefinger, and pluck it out. Drop it to the ground and kick it over here.'

Derek glanced at Hattie, who nodded her consent. Obviously she was in charge, but by the sounds of it had no jurisdiction over Sykes. I had the impression that Sykes was a law unto himself. An outlaw. A maverick. It should have made me warm to him, but it didn't.

Derek did as he was told, the gun clattered to the tarmac and then made a scraping noise as he used his heel to propel it towards us.

'Kick it away under that van there, Dom,' said Hamish and as I did as I was told, I saw Hattie's eyebrow arch at my name.

'Dom?' she said. 'So you're Dominic Queste?'

I toed the pistol as far as I could under the dirty blue van beside me so if things went pear-shaped they'd need to scramble to retrieve it. When I spoke I felt a tremble in my voice. I couldn't help it, I was nervous. 'You've heard of me? I'm flattered.'

'Don't be,' she said, and I knew from the slight smile that she had taken note of my quivering voice. She looked back at Duncan. 'So that makes you the Sutherland brothers.' It wasn't a question, it was a statement. Maybe Sykes had not been bluffing when he said he knew all about me. I was glad we had convinced Father Verne into taking Jenny with him to visit a parishioner in hospital. However, with Sykes not here I did wonder if he was up to something elsewhere. I began to grow extremely nervous.

'What about you, lass?' Duncan asked. 'You got anything on you that you shouldn't in this law-abiding town?'

She made a show of looking down at her loose-fitting sweatshirt and trackie bottoms. 'You're welcome to frisk me, if you want.'

Duncan grinned, letting her know that he had no intention of getting within an arm's length of her. She looked as if she could pound him into hamburger without breaking sweat. 'What's your interest in the girl?' Duncan asked.

'I have no interest in the girl,' said Hattie.

'Then why do you want her dead?'

She smiled. Ordinarily it would have been a pleasant smile, but this was not an ordinary situation. 'Sykes wants her dead. We've got other fish to fry.'

Other fish to fry? What the hell did that mean?

Duncan let it pass though. 'I take it you're professionals?'

'Through and through.'

'Who are you working for?'

She shook her head and tutted. 'Mister Sutherland, you disappoint me. You know we're forbidden to kill and tell.' She looked around at us all and then said, 'So, it looks like we've reached an impasse. We're going to tell you nothing and you're not going to shoot us.'

'We could hurt you a bit,' said Duncan.

'You could try,' she said, and we all knew that any kind of physical contact would end very badly for the good guys. And the brothers were not going to shoot anyone unless they had to. She saw the looks on our faces and smiled again. 'Well, boys, it's been a pleasure chatting to you but I think we'll head back to our rooms now. I've got to contact the rental company about this wanton act of destruction.'

'Don't think so, darlin',' said an Irish voice from behind me and I turned round to see Wee Willie aiming a gun in our general direction. He was backed by another two goons, each with a sawn-off shotgun, and a large figure with his head swathed in bandages like an unfinished Egyptian mummy. But I could see the eyes and they were red and angry and glaring straight at me. Jerome hadn't taken a telling after all, for there he was, large as life and with an even larger revolver. I know nothing about guns, but it looked like a Magnum .44 to me, one shot from which I knew could blow my head clean off. And I really did not feel lucky at all. Obviously he had got off the London train at the first stop and contacted his old pal Freddie. And here he was, like a bad penny. They hadn't followed us from the refuge, of that I was certain. No-one would've evaded the brothers' eagle-eyes. So how did they know where we were?

So there we all were, we were armed, they were armed, Hattie and Derek in the middle. Duncan and Hamish still had not raised their weapons so we didn't have the full Tarantino but it would not take much for the bullets to start flying. My nervousness was now verging on panic.

'So, Queste,' Jerome said, his voice muffled by the layer of bandages. 'You were full of big talk last night, about me getting a bullet in the head if I came back. Well, here I am.'

'It's early yet, Jerome,' I said, struggling to keep my voice even. I was nervous before, now I was downright skittish. Guns, guns, too many guns.

'That's all it was, big talk,' Jerome said. 'Trying to be the big man in front of the girl. Well, if only she could see you now, shaking like a leaf. Where is she?'

I said, 'Not here.'

His eyes narrowed. 'I was told you'd have her here.'

'You were told wrong.' Wee Willie glanced at Jerome and if ever a glance was uneasy, it was that one. Someone had told Jerome that we'd have Jenny here. Someone else knew we'd be here. It didn't take a mastermind to work out who.

Jerome's grip tightened on the pistol as he took this in. He was seriously pissed off now and that was not a good thing for my health. He breathed out through gritted teeth. 'Okay, we'll get her, don't you worry about that. Plenty of time for that little cow. No, Dominic, you're not so big now, eh? Not when you can't creep up and cold-cock me. Not when...'

I didn't find out what he was going to say next because the side of his head erupted and he pitched over like a sack of potatoes. I had no idea where the bullet came from, didn't even hear anything, but I was aware of Hattie and Derek lunging behind the Range Rover, she snatching a pistol from under her sweatshirt and he plucking what looked like a tiny revolver from a holster round his ankle. At least, it looked tiny in his hand. Duncan dropped to the ground, using the lorry beside him as a shield, while Hamish threw me down just as a bullet whipped past me and thudded into the blue van behind us. Wee Willie and his sidekicks seemed to freeze, not knowing what the hell was going on, and one of them paid the price as a bullet ploughed into his chest, throwing him back like a rag doll. Willie and the other one moved then, dropping their weapons and hitting the concrete with the enthusiasm of a lover. This had all the hallmarks of Sykes, the Terminator. Hattie thought so too, for I saw her poke her head over the bonnet of the four-wheel drive and call out his name then duck back again when a bullet slammed into the bodywork near her face. I'd still not heard any shots, so he must have been using a silencer. My eyes slid towards Jerome's body, which was twitching as his nerves refused to die. I'd told him he would get a bullet in the head but I hadn't meant it. I felt sorry for him.

Then another bullet pinged off the tarmac beside me and I started to feel sorry for myself.

Wee Willie and the other thug cowered, their weapons abandoned as they covered their heads with their arms. Most Glasgow thugs are used to sudden acts of violence – get in, get it done, get back out again – and aren't equipped for extended gunplay. This was out of their league. A movement at the bonnet of the Range Rover drew my attention and I saw the big guy pop up to squeeze off a couple of rounds in what he believed was Sykes' direction before something red plucked at his shoulder and jerked him to one side. Then another splash of scarlet flew from the centre of his chest and he tumbled back out of sight.

'Sykes!' I heard the woman yell. 'For God's sake, what are you doing?'

Another round punched into the four-wheel drive in response. 'Shit, Sykes!' I heard her shout.

I didn't stop to think why he was shooting at his own people, all I wanted to do was keep my head down. I glanced at Hamish and he was doing the same. Neither he nor Duncan had loosed off a round, still mindful of the cameras that were possibly recording this for posterity. Fast Freddie's men remained paralysed with fear. I wouldn't have been surprised if their personal hygiene had slipped ever so slightly. I know I felt like pissing myself.

Then the shooting stopped. Nobody moved. Nobody dared.

Time slowed as we waited for another hail of bullets.

Nothing.

Hamish was the first to move, rising carefully to his feet. He remained at a half crouch as he peered round the side of the van, then scanned the perimeter. He nodded to me and I pulled myself up, my body tense and wary as I waited for a slug to punch into me. Duncan ventured into the open and he raised a hand, telling us he was okay. Hattie rose slowly, her eyes watchful. Fast Freddie's boys took the opportunity to leap to their feet and scamper away. I watched them go, expecting to see them felled by another two expert shots but they were allowed to leave unharmed. They piled into a blue Vauxhall Vectra and sped away. There was a strange silence as the rest of us stared at each other. Duncan, Hamish and Hattie remained on the alert though, their eyes watchful, their weapons ready. Speaking personally, I was just glad it was over.

I didn't see Sykes until it was too late.

Neither did Duncan.

Sykes stepped into view behind him, his gun at waist level, and fired. I yelled a belated warning but my friend jerked forward, blood spurting. Shock shut my mind down but Hattie was made of sterner stuff, for she bellowed Sykes' name and ran round the bonnet of her car, gun raised. She got off one shot and missed, but Sykes seemed unfazed. He fired once and her forward momentum came to a sudden halt as the bullet tugged at her shoulder, spinning her round. Sykes fired again and this time there was a small explosion of blood at her thigh and she went down.

Hamish was the first to move, surging towards the gunman, but a bullet careening off the concrete at his feet forced him to a sudden halt. 'Easy, big guy,' said Sykes, politely. 'I've no interest in killing you, but that doesn't mean I won't.'

'You shot me brother,' said Hamish, his voice low and rough-edged.

'Yes, I did. I owed him that,' said Sykes, holding up his left arm, the one Duncan had shot at Alexandra Park.

'I'll kill you,' said Hamish.

Sykes smiled, backing away. 'Somehow, big guy, I doubt that.'

Then he turned and sprinted between the cars. Hamish moved quickly to Duncan's side, kneeling beside him. I watched Sykes go while shouting to Hamish, 'How is he?'

'There's a lot of blood, a lot of blood,' he said, a sob breaking his voice. 'It looks bad, Dom...'

Cold rage pulsed through my body then. I'd had enough of this, all of it. I'd had enough of being shot at, threatened, beaten. This had been the final straw. I was done.

I was moving for a full minute before I realised what I was doing, weaving between the parked vehicles after Sykes, a mist covering everything except the back of the man I was pursuing. A running man attracts attention so Sykes was walking, although at a brisk pace. I didn't care if I attracted attention so I ran at full pelt. He reached the entrance to the covered walkway over the motorway and threw a look over his shoulder when he heard my footfalls pounding behind him. He picked up his speed and vanished into the overpass and I followed, climbing up over the expressway, the cars streaming below visible through the tinted Perspex tunnel. About midway he stopped and turned, the gun at his side. He held up his injured arm, telling me to come no further.

'This is very unwise,' he said. I was panting but he wasn't even out of breath.

'Why?' I wheezed.

'Why? Because I could kill you without a qualm.'

'No,' I said, still trying to catch my breath. I don't know what I meant to be honest, it just came out. I waved a hand back towards the car park. 'Why?'

His gaze flicked through the Perspex to the scene of the shootout. Sirens reached us as police flooded into the area.

'Your friend shot me, I told you. And I always pay my debts. As for the rest? I would have thought you'd be grateful to me for dealing with that big guy. He was, I think, about to shoot you.'

'You told him we'd be here.'

He nodded. 'It was time he was out of the picture. He was beginning to annoy me. I knew your friends would come back here today, men like them are so predictable. And I saw you all leave the refuge. I had another task to complete but I let Mister Kingsley know. I must say, he reacted with impressive speed.'

'And your friends? You killed that man, wounded her.'

'They're not my friends. Sometimes allies, often competitors, never friends.'

'But they were here to help you.'

'No,' he said, 'they were here to kill me.'

That stunned me. I'd thought they were part of his team.

'Why?' I was getting tired of saying that, but it was all I could think of.

He smiled. 'It seems I'm out of control. They had been assisting me in this contract, but now they're a tag team to take me down. You were the conduit to the girl, the girl the conduit to me. They followed your car, hoping it would lead them to her and they could then use her to draw me out. But they weren't good enough. Neither were your pals, by the way. While they were following the tag team, I was following them. I tracked them here to the hotel first, then back to the refuge. If the girl had been there, I'd have fulfilled my contract. But she wasn't there.' So Jenny running away to Saltcoats had turned out to be a good thing after all, for Sykes had scoped the refuge out while she was away. He continued, 'She had to be with you, so I paid Mister Reilly's widow a visit. Fine looking woman. Too good for that thug.'

'You hired him.'

'My clients hired him for local muscle. They showed a severe lack of judgement, I must say.'

'Did you kill him?'

'Yes. He had proved to be something of a liability. '

'Did he kill the woman?'

'Yes. I had to leave them alone for a time while I ran an errand and stupidly left him to get some information out of her.'

'What information?'

'Where you were. I knew she had developed cold feet over the whole enterprise. Reilly was meant to scare her a little, but I'm afraid his lack of restraint got the better of him. I blame myself, for there was no need for Mrs Oldfield to die.' He reconsidered. 'Well, certainly not in that way. Mister Reilly had outlived his usefulness and, to cap it all, he let you see him. So he had to go.'

He spoke so matter-of-factly about death that it set the hairs on the back of my neck marching like the Grand Old Duke of York's men. 'What errand was so important that you had to leave?'

'Dropping someone off somewhere. Someone who didn't need to witness Mrs Oldfield being questioned.'

'Who were you dropping off?'

He smiled but there wasn't much humour in it. 'That doesn't concern you.'

I sighed. This guy would only tell me what he wanted me to know. 'And the tag team back there, they helped you strike Reilly to the yardarm?'

'Yes, they had their uses.'

'Not now, though.'

'No, not now. They should've known better than to come after me.'

'But you didn't kill the woman.'

'No.'

'Something between you, maybe?'

He didn't answer. I didn't expect him to. I don't know why I was standing there in that plastic tunnel high above the rumble of traffic, chatting to a psychotic killer as if we were discussing the weather. I don't know why I took after him in the first place. It just seemed to be the thing to do. The air outside our Perspex world was filled with the sound of sirens and I was aware of blue lights flashing below as policed cars zoomed towards the car park. Sykes saw them too, for he began to back away. I felt I had to keep him there, give the boys in blue the chance to arrive. Someone was bound to have seen me chase him up here. At least, that's what I hoped.

'What about that man and woman in Gordon Street?' I asked.

'They had supplied Mister Reilly to us – faulty goods, I would say. They needed to be punished for that alone.'

His words chilled me to the bone. My voice was hoarse when I said, 'So you killed them both for that?'

'That and because they would not give up his file on Mister Reilly, which I thought would contain some reference to my employer. I had to take it.'

'And the woman?'

He shrugged as if she was inconsequential. 'I'd say collateral damage but that would imply she was innocent. She was as guilty of poor standards as her partner.'

I felt my anger turn as cold as my blood. 'You tried to kill me too.'

'Yes, I saw you as a threat to my contract.'

The sirens had converged now and we both looked towards the car park. Blue uniforms swarmed across the space, armed units leading the way.

Sykes continued to back away. 'Time to go. And if you want some free advice, don't follow me any further.'

I tried the quick-fire approach again. 'What does Excelsis mean?'

He raised an eyebrow at that, an amused smile tickling his lips. 'Where did you hear about that?'

I told him, deciding it didn't matter where I learned it but also to show he wasn't as clever or as thorough as he thought. I regretted being so smart when he raised the gun a fraction higher and said, 'I should kill you just for knowing that.'

I'd been matching his backward movement but this brought me to a sudden halt. It hadn't occurred to me that he could've shot me at any time but he hadn't. 'Why don't you? I mean, you would've done it before, why not now?'

'You are no longer a threat to me. And I've no contract in your name.'

I experienced a movie flash then, *Three Days of the Condor* with Max Von Sydow's cold-blooded hitman telling Robert Redford he had no arrangement regarding him. Except this was no movie. The deaths here were real. And Sykes was no actor, he was a real-life killer.

'You shot at me back there,' I jerked my thumb over my shoulder to the crime scene in the car park.

'I shot in your direction. My bullets only go where I want them.'

The events in the car park replayed in my head. It was true, he could've killed me at any time. But he hadn't. He would've happily taken me out in the Elite office, but I'd been lucky. But now something had changed and I didn't know what. I tried again. 'What is Excelsis?'

He shook his head. He wouldn't tell me.

'They want you dead, what do you owe them now?'

'Rule number one – never reveal the principal. No matter what.'

'Then what about the girl? Why do they want her dead?'

He shrugged. 'Not my business. I never ask why, just who and how much. But it doesn't matter now.'

'What do you mean?'

'Didn't I tell you?' He smiled. 'The job's over. I told my client an hour ago that the girl's dead.'

Chapter Twenty-Two

My voice was cracking by the time I had finished telling it for the umpteenth time, but the cop standing over me still wasn't satisfied. I couldn't blame him. I seemed to be at the centre of a body count usually reserved for men with masks and chainsaws and even though I was being reasonably candid about everything I could understand his frustration.

I had wandered back down the covered the walkway towards the car park and into the waiting arms of two burly coppers, both dressed in riot gear and sporting machine pistols. As soon as they saw me they began screaming at me to lie down on the ground with my hands on the back of my head, fingers laced. I did as I was told. I was too tired to do anything else, the adrenalin that had pumped me up for my pursuit of Sykes now purging my system like the blood I'd seen on Duncan's chest.

I asked them how my friend was but they didn't answer, one of them too busy immobilising my hands with a plastic zip tie, the other standing over me with his weapon trained on the back of my head.

'My friend,' I said again, as they hauled me to my feet. 'How is he?'

'We're not here to answer questions, pal,' said one. 'But you're going to answer a shit load of them.'

I should have known they wouldn't tell me how Duncan was. Maybe they didn't even know. They hauled me to my feet and threw me up against a wall bearing plastic advertising hoardings while they tightened the fastenings on my wrist and patted me down for weapons. The grinning face of Ritt Bobak shone back at me, a picture of health and right-wing madness. Perfect, I thought, feeling nauseous just getting up close and personal with a photograph of that creep. As the cop's hands roamed over me, I idly scanned the print on the poster. I wasn't conscious of doing it, the poster was there, I was there, my mind was churning with thoughts of Duncan falling forward, the blood spurting from his body, then Sykes' voice calmly talking about death and dropping the bombshell that Jenny was dead. The advertisement carried details of Bobak's Scottish tour, his appearance here at the conference centre, then Edinburgh, Aberdeen, Perth. Finally, my eye lit on a single word. Suddenly everything was blocked out as I focussed on it, the sirens, the traffic, the shouting, the hands of the two police officers, even Sykes' revelations. None of it existed anymore. All I saw was the single word in the small print at the foot of the poster.

Excelsis.

Then I was dragged away, forced round, the cops pushing me ahead of them, my hands firmly tethered behind my back, one of them prodding me enthusiastically with his machine pistol. I got the message and walked towards a waiting van.

They took me across the river to Govan Police Station. Partick would have been closer, but the station in Helen Street is one of the most secure in the city, hell, the entire country. Street lore says that it is designed to withstand a siege, although you don't get many *Assault on Precinct 13* events in Glasgow. The modern building, nestled between Bellahouston Park and the M8, is where they hold terrorist suspects when the need arises, so it has to be damn near impregnable. I was no terrorist but given the amount of violence that had surrounded me in the past few days I understood their thinking. I was grateful for the respite the ride across the river afforded and also consoled myself with the knowledge that it took me further away from Nick Cornwell. My mind was also racing with the implications of my new discovery. So Excelsis had something to do with Ritt Bobak? But what the hell did some crackpot American evangelist have to do with all this? And why did he want a teenager from Glasgow dead?

They took all my possessions from me, including my new mobile phone, and I thought Duncan would have to find me yet another new one soon. My thoughts came to a dead halt then and I swallowed back the bile that rose in my throat as the image flashed of Duncan pitching forward, blood streaming from his body. I tried to go to my happy place but to be honest, I always had trouble finding one.

So they led me to the interview room where the only light was the stark white one above the small table and planked me down in the uncomfortable plastic chair, my wrists still tethered by the plastic strap. Then they left me alone. I thought about Hamish, wondered if they'd brought him to Helen Street too. Chances were they had and he would be sitting in a similar room and desperately trying to find out about Duncan, who may have been dead by then, for all I knew. It kept coming back to that, Duncan being dead. No matter what, my mind circled that particular drain. Duncan dead. Duncan lying on a table somewhere. Dead. Aunt Jessica, Jerome, Sammy and Lennie, Tiger, Derek – the mercenary Sykes gunned down in the car park – and the nameless thug he shot. All dead. Too much death. And then there was Jenny and Father Verne.

When the silent, grim-faced suits filtered in, the first words from my mouth were about Duncan but neither of the two men answered. The uniform who arrested me had already said it – they weren't here to answer questions, they were here to ask them. Knowledge is power, after all, and police know that all too well. When I saw Nick Cornwell step into the room, I was so glad to see a familiar face that for a fleeting moment I forgot to be worried.

'Nick, you need to tell me how Duncan is,' I pleaded, but he ignored me and vanished into the shadows where I heard the scrape of a chair being moved. 'Nick?' I said again and then felt my teeth grit with anger. Surely he wasn't playing silly buggers. I tried his full title. 'DCI Cornwell?' Still nothing from him.

I felt the plastic tie being sliced and my hands were free. I rubbed my wrists as a figure stepped into view and took off his jacket, draping it over the chair across the table. He had been one of the first two to enter, a big man, powerfully built and I didn't fancy taking a beating from him. I was glad the police didn't go in for that sort of thing as much now. He dropped a folder onto the table top but didn't open it. I figured I knew everything that was in it anyway. After all, it would be all about me.

And then Eamonn came in, pulled a chair to my side and sat down. He gave me a smile that should have been reassuring but somehow wasn't. I was both glad to see him and utterly terrified. The big detective pressed a button to start the video camera which was perched on a bracket high up on the wall. This was being recorded. The detective cautioned me. This was big boy's games now.

'I'm Detective Chief Inspector William Rae,' said the detective, his voice betraying Highland roots. 'I'm based here at Govan and I'll be asking you a few questions about recent events. Also present are DCI Nicholas Cornwell from Glasgow West End as well as DI Thomas Libberton from Govan CID.'

I glanced into the darkened room but apart from the vague sensation of bodies, the occasional cough and the fact that I'd seen them come in, I wouldn't have known anyone was there.

'So, Mister Queste,' said DCI Rae. 'This is a mess. A hell of a mess.'

I couldn't disagree with him but there was only one thing on my mind. 'Duncan Sutherland, how is he?'

He gave me a long, hard look, then said, 'Worried about him, are you?'

'Of course I'm worried about him. He's a mate.'

'You often lead your mates into mortal danger, do you?'

That stung because I knew that everything was my fault. I had taken Jenny to the boys in the first place, drawing them into a situation that had proved to be beyond even their considerable expertise. And now Duncan may be lying dead on a slab somewhere. There it was again, that dark thought snaking through everything. Jenny. Father Verne. I thought about Sykes' words. I needed time to think, to process.

I swallowed hard. 'Look, I'm happy to co-operate...'

A grunt issued from the depths of the darkness and I knew Nick was expressing doubt about my co-operation in his usual manner. I ignored him. Eamonn also cleared his throat, as if he was going to advise me against saying anything. I ignored him too. 'But I'm not going to answer any questions until I know how he is.'

Rae laid both hands on the table top and loomed over me. 'Mister Queste, you're in no position to be making any demands. You're in deep trouble, you have to know that. Wherever you've been, you've left a trail of death and destruction behind you.'

'I've not killed anyone.'

'We'll see what you've done or haven't done, shall we? Now, I suggest you answer anything I ask with complete candour. If you don't, things can get very difficult, do you understand?'

Eamonn decided he'd gone too far. 'DCI Rae, Mister Queste has already stated he'll co-operate fully with your investigation. He is well aware how serious this is, so threats of that kind are totally unnecessary.'

Rae didn't even look at Eamonn. He kept his eyes on me. I made a show of closing my mouth tightly and stared back at him with as much defiance as I could muster. I sensed he was a decent man, a good cop, and he really wanted to get to the bottom of these events, but I was determined to stand my ground. I had to know about Duncan. He must have seen what I'd hoped was a steely glint in my eye for he glanced off into the darkness and said, 'DCI Cornwell?'

There was a pause then I heard Cornwell clearing his throat. 'He'll live, Queste,' his voice rumbled from the gloom. 'He's in hospital, but the bullet hit him high on the shoulder and didn't touch any major arteries or organs. He was lucky.'

I felt the tension ease from my body and I smiled. Lucky, hell – Sykes had told me his bullets go only where he wants them. Duncan had only winged him so he did the same.

'Satisfied?' Rae asked, and I nodded. 'Good, let's get started then. Suppose you start from the beginning, tell us everything.'

I nodded and took a deep breath. 'It started when Jessica Oldfield asked me to find her niece, Jenny Deavers. She'd run away when she was sixteen and her aunt wanted her back...'

And out it all came – tracing her to Saltcoats, the tussle with Jerome Kingsley, finding Aunt Jessica dead, Tiger Reilly, Fast Freddie Fraser, Sykes, the lot. I did not mention Excelsis, though. That was for me to deal with. And I still didn't link Alexandra Park to it all, for they were looking for an excuse to charge me and attempting to pervert the course of justice would make an early Christmas present. I didn't tell them Duncan and Hamish were armed in the car park and curiously the cops didn't mention it, so something had happened there. I didn't tell them everything that Sykes said on the covered walkway before he turned and loped away. I could have run after him, but frankly I was too busy processing what he had told me.

Even with my omissions, it was quite a story and if I hadn't lived through it I doubted I would have believed it. When I stopped talking DCI Rae didn't move or say a word, he simply stared down at me with those hard, clear eyes. Then he made me start again. After that, he took a break and the entire audience filed out, Nick giving me his trademark glare. A uniform brought me a coffee from a vending machine and another paper cup with water. He also dropped onto the table a packet of sandwiches that looked as appetising as cardboard. I ate them, though, and drank the coffee which was so vile farmers could have used it as sheep dip. Eamonn stayed with me, tried to get me to clam up, told me to give him time to find out exactly what was going on but I shook my head. It was time I got the bulk of it out. I needed to purge myself of as much of it as I could.

When Rae and the gang returned, he made me tell the story a third time, trying to catch me out in slight differences in the narrative, trying to find where I was lying.

'Were you armed today, Mister Queste?' He asked after I'd completed it again.

'No,' I said.

'Were either of the Sutherlands?'

'Did you find anything on them?'

'No.'

'Well, there you are, then.' So the CCTV obviously did not

show them holding anything. We'd done well there. I wondered what Hamish had done with the weapons.

'The two people you lured out of the hotel...'

'Hattie and Derek.'

'Yes. Their real names are Jane Cowan and Samuel Robinson. Do you know them?'

'I told you, no. They had been following my car and we wanted to know why. We also thought they could lead us to Sykes, who had threatened us and threatened Jenny.'

'When our officers arrived at the locus they found Mister Robinson was armed to the teeth, as was one of the other dead men...' he looked at the file on the table top, flicked a page, 'Jerome Kingsley. How did you and your friends keep them at bay without weapons of your own?'

I shrugged. 'Harsh tones?'

He gave me a tough stare that seemed to go on forever. Cops are good at that. 'You think this is funny?'

I shook my head.

'Damn right it's not funny. You lured them out of their hotel room, you vandalised their car. They were highly trained ex-military personnel. You were a threat of some kind and yet you say this man Robinson did not draw a weapon at any stage in the conversation. Don't you find that strange?'

Something niggled at my brain as he spoke. Something about the way he was talking about the scene in the car park. 'Maybe they didn't see us as a threat. Maybe they thought they could handle us without firepower. You'd need to ask them.'

'Short of using an Ouija board, no-one will talk to Mister Robinson, while Ms Cowan is declining to answer any questions.' He waited to see if I had anything else to say. When I didn't he continued, 'Ms Deavers. She seems to have vanished, as has Father Verne. Do you know where they are?'

I had to be careful here. 'No. Sykes told me he had completed his contract, that Jenny was dead. I'm worried that he also disposed of Father Verne.'

Rae nodded. 'We've checked the refuge, his church and the

hospital he was visiting. He made his visit, but nothing after that. Someone thought they saw a priest and girl climbing into the back of a black transit but they couldn't be sure. You know anyone with a black transit?'

I shook my head.

'If it is this guy Sykes, what's his deal? Who's he working for?'

'I don't know.'

He leaned in closer, his face close to mine. I could smell a mixture of stale coffee, cigarette smoke and yesterday's after shave. God knows what he could smell from me. 'I think you know more than you're saying, Queste.' Rae said then paused as he studied me closely. I held his gaze as best I could.

'There's something you're not telling me, isn't there, Mister Queste?'

'I've told you everything.'

'I doubt that. You're pretty much a maverick, according to your file. You're often not forthcoming with the police. You don't play well with others. I doubt very much that you're telling me everything.'

I didn't reply. I didn't see the need. He wouldn't believe me anyway. With good reason.

'Let's go over it again, Queste,' he said.

'We've already been over it three times.'

'And we'll keep going over it until I've got it straight in my head,' he said. 'Why were they after the girl?'

'I don't know.'

'Who is this guy Sykes?'

'I don't know.'

'You made him up, didn't you?'

'No, check the CCTV tape from the car park. He'll be on it.'

He didn't say anything. He hadn't mentioned anything about the CCTV at all. Curious. That niggle grew in intensity. He sighed and straightened up, running his hand through his hair. I saw him glance to the side, as if taking instruction from one of the unseen figures.

'Seven dead, Queste,' he said, and he let it hang there for

a second before he went on. 'Nine if you include the two in Alexandra Park, which I know is connected to all this. And the common denominator is you. You know more than you're saying, of that I'm certain. Nine dead. How does that feel? To know that your actions led to the deaths of nine people?'

I didn't answer. I knew he was trying guilt trip me into making some form of confession, but I wasn't going to fall for it. The truth was most of those people would have died anyway. I didn't cause their deaths and I could not have prevented them. Aunt Jessica knew too much. Tiger Reilly was a liability. The man and woman at Elite Security were dead as soon as they heard about Excelsis. The world was better off without Lennie and Sammy, to be honest. Jerome Kingsley might have been alive today if he'd done what I told him but he made a choice and he lost. Robinson and the other thug who got it in the car park took their chances too. You play with guns, they go off.

The thing was, I knew the body count was higher. There were other victims out there, either not found or not connected to this. Sykes had told me that, among other things, before he ran off and before I was lifted. But I wasn't ready to share that just yet either. Rae was right about me – I don't play well with others.

Eamonn sprang me as soon as he could. When it came down to it, they had nothing really to charge me with. I'd been present when acts of violence had occurred but there was no evidence that I had committed any.

It was cold outside, but I hunched into my jacket as if I was freezing at the North Pole. Eamonn gave me a worried look and said, 'You look done in, Dom.'

'It's been a busy few days,' I said. He did not reply, simply nodded and pressed the remote on his key fob to unlock the doors. We climbed in and he said, 'Where to? Home?'

I shook my head. 'Is Hamish with Duncan?'

'Yes. The police released him about an hour ago. He told them nothing and they had no reason to keep him, same as you. At best you're witnesses. For the moment, at least.'

'Take me to them, then.'

He nodded and started the engine but before he moved off he turned to me and said, 'This isn't over, is it?'

I thought about it. 'Almost there,' I said.

Chapter Twenty-Three

Duncan was sitting up in bed reading a newspaper when I turned up at the door to his room. He had been given a private room, which was lucky for the other hospital patients because he snored like an adenoidal pig. There had been a policeman on the door until they had decided that our side had not broken any laws, or at least they couldn't prove we had broken any laws. Now he was unguarded and I stared at him for a second, grateful that his wound was not as bad as I had first feared.

He looked up at me as I lurked in the doorway and I knew he sensed my emotion. He nodded and then glanced back at the tabloid in his hand. 'Says here there's a circus owner in hospital because his elephant sat on him. A hospital spokesman says he was comfortable. The elephant thought so, too.'

I smiled, knowing that nothing need be said between us, and moved to the side of the bed. 'Hamish not here?'

Duncan jerked his head to the toilet door just as I heard the cistern flushing. Hamish appeared, drying his hands on a handful of blue paper towels. 'How come no matter how many of these things you use, your hands are never properly dry?'

Duncan said, 'It's a conspiracy by the paper towel makers to make hospitals buy more.'

Hamish thought about this. 'You think that's true?'

Duncan nodded, his eyes still locked on his newspaper. 'Read it on the internet.'

'Must be true, then,' said Hamish, deadpan.

I glanced at the open door and the corridor beyond then dropped my voice. 'Hamish, I'm bursting to know – what did you do with the guns?'

He smiled. 'Didn't have them when the cops arrived.'

I was puzzled. 'So where were they?'

He shot a look over his shoulder then walked to the door and closed it. He came back to the bed but still spoke softly. 'After you had taken off after that bloke Sykes, I realised that Duncan here wasn't as badly hit as we thought.'

'Bad enough,' said Duncan, still reading. 'Stung like buggery.'

'Away, man! Cowboy up, for God's sake. I've had worse wasp stings. Anyway, I took his gun and my gun and, still keeping them all hidden mind, placed one on the big lad and another two on Fast Freddie's boy. They were both dead so they wouldn't mind, would they? I wiped them all first. Even managed to fish that one out from under the van. Figured any cameras wouldn't be able to see me if I kept behind the vehicles, like.'

'That was quick thinking.'

'I have me moments.'

'But I don't think the cameras were working.'

They both looked as if I'd just told them I liked the third *Matrix* movie.

'I think Sykes disabled them somehow. He's a professional, he'd know how. It explains why he happily exposed himself.' Hamish's mouth twitched, *oo-er missus*.

Duncan lowered his newspaper and looked at me. 'So where is he now?'

I told them about chasing him onto the covered walkway and the conversation. Hamish's face blanched when I got to the part about Jenny, but Duncan's face remained emotionless as he studied my expression.

'So everything has been for nothing?' Hamish asked. 'That bastard still got the girl? And Father Verne?'

'No,' said Duncan.

'No,' I agreed.

Hamish looked from me to his brother. 'What am I missing?'

Duncan smiled. It was barely perceptible but it was there. 'Sykes strikes me as being very precise. His bullets go where he wants them to go. I think he's just as careful with his words.'

Hamish still didn't get it, so I stepped in. 'He said he'd told his employers he'd fulfilled his contract. He didn't say he'd done it. I think Jenny and Father Verne are still alive.'

'So what's his game?'

'Payback,' I said. 'His employers turned on him. They sent hired guns after him. He didn't like that. He seems the type to operate some kind of perverted code and they broke it, at least in his eyes. He told them he'd killed the girl in order to take the heat off but he's still steamed. Someone's going to be punished.'

'Excelsis,' said Duncan.

I nodded. 'Excelsis, right there on the poster. Sponsored by the Excelsis Corporation. I used Eamonn's phone to do a quick web search on the way over.' Hamish's eyebrows shot up at the idea of me doing a web search, but I pressed on before he could say anything smart-arsed. There's only room for one smart-arse in a room and I was very protective of the title. 'Excelsis is a big American Corporation with fingers in every business pie under the sun – media, energy, defence. Pies too, come to that – they own a string of bakeries in the States. If there's a buck being made, they're getting some of it.'

Hamish said, 'Yeah, but Ritt Bobak? He's a Christian, isn't he?'

'Christians have done a lot of nasty things over the centuries,' I said. 'And anyway, he's a conman first.'

'But why would he want Jenny dead?'

'Beats me.'

There was a silence in the hospital room as Duncan and Hamish took in what I told them. Somewhere I could hear a bucket clanking and the soft sweep of a mop on a polished floor. A male nurse pushed a drugs trolley with a squeaky wheel past the doorway. Bright sunlight emerged from behind a cloud, beamed through the room's window then vanished again.

I looked at Duncan and saw his face had become set in stone, his eyes cold and hard. 'Sykes is a professional.'

'Yes,' I said.

He exhaled through gritted teeth. 'You think they're dead already?'

'If they're not, they soon will be. He may keep them alive just now as a bargaining chip, should he need it. We're only alive because he needed us to act as fall guys for the shootings in the car park, to delay the law. While they're dealing with us, they're ignoring him. He's good, really good, thinks things through, which he as much as told me. It hit me while I was sitting in the interview room at Govan – he'd shown himself in that car park, so that meant he'd already disabled the CCTV cameras. The police didn't tell us that. They wouldn't, would they? But it explains why they let us go so easily. As I said, he's good, doesn't leave things to chance. In this case, it worked in our favour.'

Hamish asked, 'So what now?'

'I phoned an old mate of mine at the paper,' I said. 'She said that Ritt Bobak was due to arrive at the SECC this afternoon, prior to his first show tonight. If he's involved in all this – although God knows how – then I think Sykes will go after him.'

'So?' said Hamish. 'Let him. Brother Bobak is a dick anyway.'

Duncan stared down at the bedclothes, his eyes scanning the pile of newsprint. I saw a memory register in his eyes and he began to rifle through the pages.

'Saw something here...' he said, just as he revealed a brightly coloured brochure, glossy A4 size, four pages thick. He held it out to me. 'This was inserted in the paper today.'

It was an expensive flyer for the Bobak Crusade. The front cover showed his wide, apple-pie grin and I quickly turned the page to the centre spread, a series of photographs of Bobak pressing the flesh and meeting foreign dignitaries, carefully posed behind-the-scenes images of him in meetings and conducting his Christian Crusade gatherings in the USA. There was a snatched shot of him at a White House Ball, dancing with his wife – the couple just off-centre, the focus being the President and his wife. The idea was to show that Bobak was in with the political elite. I stared at the photograph, feeling electricity tingle through my fingertips. I couldn't believe it, I really couldn't.

'Jesus,' I said, hoarsely.

'What's up?' Hamish asked.

I didn't answer him at first, couldn't answer him. I was too fearful to sound like a lunatic. The whole idea was outlandish, unbelievable. And yet...

'Let me have your phone, Hamish,' I said, and he handed it over without question. They'd seen me like this before and knew I'd explain all soon enough. I fired up the internet search engine. I was becoming quite expert at this now and beginning to see what the world saw in being online. I punched in Ritt Bobak's name, scanned the information that popped up. He'd been a widower when he met his second wife six years before, his first wife having succumbed to leukaemia. He kept the new Mrs Bobak and his two daughters from his first marriage out of the public eye as much as possible, believing there was too much emphasis on a politician's home life and not enough on his message – I had to agree with him there, but knew he was leaning against an open door, given the way everything had to be reduced to soap opera. However, he'd dug in his heels and so far there were very few photographs of his family in the public domain. In fact, the one at the White House Ball could well be the only public shot in existence. I dropped the phone on the bed and picked up the flyer again, studied the snap.

'Oh my God,' I said. Actually, it came out as a croak because, frankly, I still couldn't believe what I was beginning to believe.

'What?' Duncan asked and took the brochure from my hand. 'What did you see?'

I swallowed, which was easy. It was the thoughts racing through my brain that I found hard to swallow. 'I think I've just worked out what this is all about, why Jenny was so important, why they hired someone like Sykes.'

My voice trailed off and they watched me expectantly. 'Well, you gonna tell us or keep us in suspense?' Hamish said. So I told them. It came out in fits and starts because I was piecing it together on the fly, but at the end it sounded neat and almost plausible. Hamish, though, didn't think so.

'Away, man! I can't believe that!'

I shrugged. 'It all fits, Hamish.'

He frowned and took the brochure out of Duncan's hands to study the pictures on the centre. 'You certain?'

'As certain as I can be. And it would explain why they're so desperate to find and kill Jenny...'

Hamish took this in. Duncan, I knew, was way ahead of me and was already pulling tubes and wires from his arms and chest and struggling out of bed. 'We go see this bloke Bobak,' he said. 'We blow him out of the water. Sykes has got him in his crosshairs, so where Bobak is, we'll find Sykes too. We stop him. We get him to take us to Jenny and Father Verne.'

'Simple as that,' said Hamish with a smile.

'Piece of piss,' said Duncan. 'Now, where the hell are me clothes?'

* * *

The girl was crying but Father Verne had given up trying to comfort her. She was scared, so was he, but there comes a time when you have to let people go with their emotions. Anyway, there was very little he could do while he was trussed up in the back of a van. It was stationary now, which was a blessing, because while in motion the two of them had been bounced around like so much rubbish. The man had paid them no heed, had no interest in their comfort. He was so confident that he had tied them securely that he did not even turn in the seat to check on them. And they were tied securely, Father Verne had been testing his bonds for what seemed like hours and had felt nothing give.

He had picked them up at the hospital. The elaborate ruse with the young girl wearing Jenny's clothes had not fooled him one bit. Father Verne sighed inwardly as he realised they should never have underestimated this man. They had visited the old parishioner, who was succumbing to cancer, the poor soul, and was completely unaware of their presence. But the priest had done what he could, more to console the woman's son and daughter, who stood red-eyed at her bedside. It was as they were leaving the building that Father Verne felt the man materialise at his side and something digging into his ribs.

'Just keep walking, Father, and no-one will get hurt,' the man said. His voice was calm, friendly even, but when Father Verne looked into his eyes, he saw nothing. The man might have been ordering a cup of coffee, for all the emotion he showed. For a moment Father Verne considered tackling him and telling Jenny to run, but the man sensed his thoughts and pressed the barrel of the gun deeper. 'Don't be stupid, Father. I'll shoot you and I'll shoot her before she could get ten feet. And then I'll shoot whoever gets in my way. All those deaths, Father, and all your fault. You want that stain on your soul in the afterlife?'

Father Verne's soul was already stained quite enough, and he knew the man would be as good as his word. He looked at Jenny, who had stopped in her tracks when she realised what was happening.

'Don't run, Jenny,' he said. She didn't run. Father Verne saw her working out the odds and deciding they were against her. She fell into step alongside them, but her face was pale, her eyes already welling up. She had seen a lot in the past few days and it was taking its toll.

'Smart girl,' said the man as he hooked an arm through Father Verne's. 'Now, let's head for the car park, shall we? Your carriage awaits.'

'Where are you taking us?' Father Verne asked.

'Somewhere safe, until all this is over.'

'And then?'

'And then I'll let you go.'

'Just like that?'

The man nodded. 'Just like that.'

Father Verne was a man of God and he believed that most people are basically good. However, he also knew a lie when he heard one.

Chapter Twenty-Four

Ritt Bobak had arrived in Glasgow earlier that morning and had gone directly to his suite in one of the city's swankiest hotels. That much I learned in another phone call to my old mate on the newspaper. She was an old-fashioned hack and I saw her sitting at the other end of the line, probably longing for a cigarette because she smoked like an Arbroath fisherman's hut, her eyes narrowing as she put my two calls together and coming up with a front-page splash. She was sharp and she made me promise I'd tell her everything when it was all over.

'I want it all, Dom,' she'd said. 'I want to know where the bodies are buried.'

I wished she hadn't used that term, but I agreed. If we lived through this it would have to become public knowledge anyway. If we didn't, as Freddie Mercury said, nothing really matters, nothing much at all.

It was the kind of hotel that made me feel distinctly uncomfortable, as if the staff could take one look at me and tell I really did not belong. And if I didn't belong, the Sutherland boys certainly resembled a pair of scruffy fish far away from the wet stuff. The woman behind the reception desk looked as if she had just stepped off the pages of a fashion magazine, even wearing the dark blue jacket the hotel chain demanded. She was already sharp-featured but her fair hair was pulled back so tightly it made her look like an axe-head. She watched us approach the desk with the expression of an avant-garde film director being offered the chance to direct a *Carry On* film. She took in the off-the-rack Marks and Spencers gear I was wearing and the jumble sale chic of the boys and her face froze.

'Can I help you?' she said. Southern English accent. I'd lay odds she could make it as smooth as honey for paying guests but with us it was less than sweet.

'We'd like to see Ritt Bobak,' I said, smiling to show her she didn't faze me one little bit.

The face defrosted long enough for a contemptuous smile to crack across her ruby lips. 'Is he expecting you?' She said, but it sounded to me like, *You don't honestly expect me to let an oik like you get anywhere near him, do you?*

'No,' I replied to both questions. 'But I think he'll want to see me.'

She gave me a look which told me she doubted that very much indeed, but she picked up a white phone anyway. 'And your name?'

'Dominic Queste.'

I saw an eyebrow raise slightly and I knew she thought I'd made it up. 'Dominic Queste,' she repeated.

'Got it in one, hen,' I said in my best Springburn accent. She punched in a number and waited for someone to answer. 'Hello, it's the front desk here. There's a Dominic Queste here asking to see Mr Bobak.'

'Tell them it's about Jenny Deavers,' I said and she repeated it. I saw her cold expression warm to mild surprise and she hung up. 'Someone will show you up presently, Mister Queste.' *Mister* Queste. A bit of respect there. Maybe she'd have my babies after all.

We didn't have long to wait. A big guy standing near the set of double lifts touched his ear and looked in our direction, then spoke into his wrist. Some sort of private security. Or someone who liked to natter to his Timex. He lumbered in our direction like a tank on legs and loomed over me. His hair was high and tight, like a US marine, and his dark suit was filled with solid muscle.

'If you'd follow me, Mister Queste,' he said, his accent still bearing traces of a Bronx boyhood.

'These two gentlemen are with me,' I said and he gave the boys the once over, no doubt sizing up whether he could take them in a fight. Obviously he felt he could because he shook his head. 'Just you, sir.'

I glanced at Duncan, who tightened his mouth in resignation. 'We know where you are, like. If you're not back in thirty minutes, we'll be up there with the cavalry.'

I nodded and followed the poster boy for *Semper Fi* to the lift, thinking a lot could happen to me in thirty minutes. I stopped and turned back to the lads. 'Make it fifteen,' I said and looked pointedly at my escort, but his expression did not change. All those steroids had probably frozen the muscles.

He poked the button and the lift door opened immediately. That never happens for me. We stepped in and I gave the Sutherlands a final look as the doors slid together, leaving me with GI Joe and some bland music piped in on a speaker. He hit the button for the top floor and we ascended in silence. Nature hates a vacuum, though. At least my nature does.

'So,' I said, 'how'd you get into this line of work?'

He didn't answer. He didn't even acknowledge I'd said anything. Maybe he was thinking of Iwo Jima.

'You ex-military?'

Still nothing. I could've been in the lift alone.

'I take it you're armed,' I said, undeterred. 'You ever had to use your weapon?'

He stared ahead, hands clasped in front of him. I knew I was beaten and we completed the journey in silence. When the lift came to a smooth halt and the doors opened, I was met with a carbon copy of my big pal – same cropped hair, same big broad face, same dark suit, same taut expression. I wondered if they were brothers.

'Nice chatting to you,' I said as I stepped from the lift into the hallway. Naturally he did not reply. My new escort was already walking down the hallway as the lift doors closed. I sped up to catch him.

'Any more of you boys back home?' I asked.

He did not answer either. I didn't expect him to. I also didn't expect him to suddenly throw me face first up against the wall, place my arms palm flat on the wallpaper above my head and then kick my legs further apart. However, that's exactly what he did.

'Hey!' I said then felt his hands touching parts of me that I was reserving for the future Mrs Queste, whoever she may be. 'Hey! You could at least buy me a drink first...'

He finished frisking me, then pulled me upright and propelled me bodily to the door of suite number 121. I hung in his grip like a wet rag as he produced a key card from his pocket and thrust it into the lock. He threw open the door and effortlessly tossed me inside the way you'd throw a jacket onto a bed. I fixed my collar where he'd crumpled it up and said, 'Was that as good for you as it was for me?'

He fixed me with a steady eye and said, 'Wait here, sir.'

'No need to call me sir, now that we've been so intimate,' I said, but he'd already closed the door. *Men*, I thought – *get what they want from you then toss you aside.*

I was alone in a sitting room about the size of my entire flat. Another door led off it, but it was closed and I was too polite to have a nosey. A large picture window filled most of one wall and I could see the M8 below, traffic speeding south towards the Kingston Bridge and north to wherever. It was a beautiful day outside. The earlier cloud cover had evaporated, leaving it clear and crisp, and the sun sparkled on the surface of the river. It was a hell of a view, sure enough, but even if I sold both kidneys I'd never be able to afford a single night. The entire room smelled of ill-gotten gains, but I'd be a liar if I didn't admit I could get used to it.

The side door opened and I turned to see a tall man with white hair and a grey suit stride into the room. He was maybe about 70, but his skin was smooth and ruddy and he had a little goatee, white like his hair. If his suit had been white he would have put me in the mood for some fried chicken. He fixed me with a pair of blue eyes that burned brightly with some kind of fervour and walked towards me, his hand stretched out.

'Mister Queste, glad to meet you,' he said, his voice as southern as a mint julep in summertime. 'Lester Butterworth, Director of Special Projects with the Excelsis Corporation.'

Director of Special Projects. It was conveniently vague, I

thought. Special Projects could cover a multitude of sins. Nevertheless, I shook his hand. It was soft and warm and the aroma of some expensive cologne drifted in my direction. I knew it was expensive because it didn't make my eyes water.

He waved his hand towards a couch and two armchairs arranged around a coffee table. 'Please, sir, take a seat. No need to stand on ceremony.'

I sat in an armchair that welcomed me into its embrace like a lover. I wanted to curl up and sleep, but that was out of the question. Butterworth seated himself in an identical armchair opposite me.

'Can I order you anything? Coffee? Tea? A drink, perhaps? Or is it too early for such wickedness?' Southern hospitality, you can't beat it. I told him I was fine and he smiled benevolently, like a favourite uncle offering you a boiled sweet.

'Then do you mind if I smoke?' he asked. I resisted the temptation to say I didn't care if he burst into flames and merely inclined my head. He reached into the inside pocket of his jacket and produced a cigar about the size of Cuba. I'd seen a stogie like that before – in Jessica Oldfield's house on the night she died. So this man was the person Sykes had dropped off that night, leaving Jessica with Tiger.

He fired the cigar up and blew a cloud of smoke towards the ceiling. 'My one vice,' he explained. 'So, sir, what can I do for?'

'Will Mister Bobak not be joining us?'

'The *Reverend* Bobak is otherwise detained, as I'm sure you'll understand. He has a mission to perform in your fair city this very evening. Have no fear, sir, I have his complete confidence.'

I nodded, wondering if the good Rev was simply a monkey and I was now dealing with the organ grinder. 'Jenny Deavers,' I said.

The smile did not falter. 'I am sorry, who?'

'Jenny Deavers. Twenty-years-old, pain in the arse, but you probably say ass. The girl you've been trying to have killed.'

The smile broadened and then developed into a laugh. 'Really, sir, you are very amusing.' He was giving me the full Sydney Greenstreet now. 'Most amusing, sir. Have her killed, you say?' He laughed again. 'I know of no young lady by that name.'

'Then why did you agree to see me?'

He was still smiling, but it looked kind of forced look for a second, before he laughed again. '*Touché*, sir, *touché*.'

'Your man out there all but checked my prostate, so you know I'm not wired or armed. Why bother with subterfuge?'

'We do enjoy our little games, sir, and sometimes they can become something of a habit. However, it is my understanding that the Ms Deavers affair has been settled.'

'Sykes tell you that?'

His brow furrowed. 'I know of no such individual, sir.' His puzzled expression seemed real so I guessed he knew the Terminator under another name.

'Tall guy. Good looking. Moustache. Likes to kill people. Does it very well, too.'

Butterworth's eyes crinkled in a pained fashion as he recognised the description. He stood up, walked to the window and looked down at Glasgow stretched out below us like a carpet lumped by the dirt swept under it. Some of it was his. 'Yes, Mister...Sykes, did you call him?' So he did know him by another name. I love it when I'm right. Butterworth glanced back at me and I nodded. He resumed his study of the city. 'Yes, he did tell me that he had completed his contract.'

'He lied.'

That surprised him. He turned back from the window and studied me. 'Perhaps it's you who is lying, sir.'

'Why would I do that? You're probably going to have me killed anyway.'

He laughed again. 'Have you killed? Oh, please! Why be so melodramatic?'

'Because I know too much.'

'You know nothing, Mister Queste, precisely nothing.' The voice had hardened now. It was less magnolia in blossom and more cross-burning and eye holes cut in bed linen. 'You, sir, are nothing more than an inconvenience. You are not worth killing. An inconvenience, no more, no less. If you had ever reached the dizzy heights of being an irritation, then I might have taken steps.'

'Well, get the talcum out, Lester, because I'm just about to irritate the hell out of you. I know everything.'

The smile returned, along with the honeyed tones. 'Really? Do tell.'

I gave him a smile back. 'You know, this really is a nice room. Set you back a pretty penny?'

'Mister Queste, do not make me ask Paul to step in here. You really do not want Paul to be part of this conversation. When Paul becomes involved in situations, they tend to get bloody.'

I really did not want Paul to step in here so I said, 'I'll tell you what, Lester, why don't you ask Mrs Bobak to join us? I think she would be interested in what I have to say.'

I'm sure he didn't mean to, but as soon as I mentioned Mrs Bobak he glanced at the side door. She was behind that door, probably listening to us. I stood up and moved towards it. He stepped in front of me.

'That room, sir, is not for you.'

I stepped back, made a show of sizing him up. 'You better call Paul in, Lester, because I don't think you're up to the physical stuff. Maybe once, but not any more. But then, maybe you don't want Paul hearing what I have to say. He's hired muscle, but not a hired killer, otherwise why need freelances like Sykes. What do you call him anyway?'

I saw his mind working behind those fierce blue eyes. 'Mister Miller.'

Another bland name. I doubted it was real either. He'd have more names than the phone directory.

'Mrs Bobak, perhaps you'd like to step in here,' I shouted, and we waited. Nothing happened and I was beginning to wonder if I'd guessed wrong, but then the door opened and she stepped into the room. I'd only seen photographs of her until now but the family resemblance was even clearer in the flesh.

'Mrs Bobak...or should I say Ms Deavers?'

She glared at me. I'd seen her daughter do that many times in the short time I'd known her. 'Mrs Bobak will do just fine.' The accent was American, but there was still a trace of Glasgow in the consonants.

'Jenny sends her regards,' I said, and she gave Butterworth a querying glance.

'It seems Mister Miller may have misled us, my dear.'

'Have him dealt with, Lester,' she said.

'He will be, I assure you...'

She jerked her head towards me. 'Kill him too.'

'Not a good idea, Mrs Bobak,' I said as calmly as I could. To be honest, there was something about this woman that unnerved the hell out of me. 'I've got friends downstairs and they know everything I know. If I'm not in the lobby in another five minutes with all my body parts intact, then they will phone the police and tell them the story.'

'You have no proof.'

'You're the proof, Mrs Bobak. You're here. Jenny's alive. She'll identify you.'

She moved her vicious gaze from me to Butterworth. 'Do something, Lester.'

He sighed and sat down. He suddenly looked old. 'What would you have me do, my dear?'

'Offer him money...'

I smiled at Lester, 'Hey, that's a great idea. Please, Lester, offer me money.'

His face lit up. Greed was something he understood. 'How does a quarter of a million sound?'

'Not as good as half a million.'

He nodded. 'Very well, half a million.'

'Ah, you gave in too easily, Lester. Let's make it an even million. You're not very good at haggling, are you?'

He knew then I was playing with him and his face darkened again. God knows I could do with the cash, but I'd been shot at, chased, threatened, battered and generally discommoded. I wasn't in the mood for a pay-off.

'So,' I said, 'was all this because of Reverend Bobak's political ambitions?'

Lester nodded.

I looked at the woman. Her eyes blazed back at me. If I was bread and cheese, I'd have been a toastie. 'And he knows nothing about your past, Mrs Bobak?'

'Go fuck yourself, prick,' she said.

'Not very becoming for a preacher's wife, I'm sure. You can take the girl out of Glasgow, I suppose, but...well, you know the rest. You had all those people killed just because some religious fruit-cake wants to be President?'

Lester stirred then and I saw the fire rise in his eyes again. 'Fruitcake, sir? That man is the best hope our civilisation has of stemming the scourge of secularism, sexual deviance and the rising tide of Islamic fundamentalism. He would lead us away from our sinful ways and regain our Lord's eternal love.'

I gave him a look that I hoped told him the Reverend wasn't the only fruitcake in the shop. 'What's he going to do? Build a wall?'

He caught my look and my tone. 'You can mock me, sir...'

Very kind of him, I thought, but he carried on talking before I could think of something suitably disparaging.

'..but our civilisation is in mortal peril and if we do not return to the path of righteousness we are lost. The way forward is through the Lord and we must make our Government – and the unbelievers across the world - understand that.'

'So Excelsis is on some kind of religious crusade?'

'Excelsis is many things, sir, and the Reverend is just one of many, many projects and enterprises all over the globe.'

'And you're what, at its head?'

He gave me a humble tilt of the head. 'I am just an executive, high ranking to be sure, but just an executive, one of many who report to the CEO.'

'And who is the CEO? Is he here?'

'Our CEO need not concern you, sir. That individual has many, many matters to attend to.'

'So Bobak is your project?'

'That is correct. It is also my honour to help facilitate his onward progression.'

Jesus, I thought. 'And you really think you have a shot at the Oval Office?'

'Why not? All it takes is a message and money, and we have both. Oh, it'll take us a few years, we need to get him into office – Congressional, Senate, maybe a Governor - but that's more or less in the bag, as they say. The Republican Party will back him, get his name on a ticket in the mid-west or in the south, and we'll take it from there. Excelsis has many interests, and we will not hesitate to utilise them to achieve our goals. We will save the world, Mister Queste, you wait and see. We will not flinch, we will not falter, we will not fail.'

'Lester, shut up,' spat Mrs Bobak, and I saw she was watching me intently. 'You're forgetting Mister Queste plans to upset the apple cart.'

There was a nasty look in her eyes that did not fill me with confidence for my immediate future, so I decided to keep her talking. 'And you, Mrs Bobak, you've got your heart so set on being First Lady that you put all this in motion? You'd kill your own daughter, your own sister?'

She smiled. It wasn't a very pleasant smile, and I knew then that old Lester was just a religious idiot but this woman in front of me was the real danger. I decided to let them know what I'd put together, even if only to kill time until Duncan and Hamish either blagged their way into the lift or called in the law.

'Here's the way I see it. I'd been working under the assumption that Jessica's death was an accident, and it was, but old Tiger suffered an attack of premature assassination, didn't he?' I waited for an answer, but neither of them were in the mood to tell me. They didn't even notice my clever wordplay, which was hurtful. 'My guess is that Aunt Jessica was always going to go. She was in on everything from the beginning, wasn't she? Your death in the fire? She knew. She ID'd the body. She hired me to find Jenny, but she had a sudden attack of conscience and was planning to warn me.' I looked at Lester. 'You were there that night, Lester. You heard her end of the conversation with me, you and Sykes, but she wouldn't tell you where we were, would she? So you left Tiger to get what he could out of her. But he wasn't skilled enough, he went too far, killed her. You misjudged him, Lester. Wasn't your only error, was it? In fact, this whole scheme has been pretty cack-handed all the way along, if you ask me.'

I paused again, giving them an opening to defend themselves, but they elected to remain tight-lipped. Couldn't blame them.

'So what was it all about, eh? Power, I suppose. You, Excelsis, want a puppet in the Oval Office and Bobak is the ideal candidate.' Lester began to protest but I waved him away. 'Oh, yes, I know – world going to hell in a handcart, need to return to decent values, Old Glory must lead the way, blah-blah. But see, that's *your* thing, Lester, old man. I'm betting Excelsis is only in this for the bucks, these large corporations not being known for their altruism. Now, I've never met Bobak, but from what I've read he's a fanatic and fanatics are easily manipulated, making him just the job for Excelsis. You think you're in charge, Lester, but really you're a patsy, a pawn – just like the rest of us. Someone who can be sacrificed if things don't work out the way the boys in boardroom hope.'

Lester pulled himself erect. 'I am a valued member of the management team, Mister Queste, and have been loyal to Excelsis for over fifty years.'

'Sure, that and a pound coin will get you a chocolate bar. They'll drop you like a hot rock the minute the temperature rises.' I looked back at the woman, flinched a little at the animal hatred that burned in her eyes. 'And then there's you, Mrs Bobak. You didn't tell anyone about your other life here in Glasgow, did you? It didn't seem to matter much at first, when your husband was just another preacher on the hustle in tents and town halls across the Midwest. But when political opportunity came knocking you realised you could be a liability, so you laid it all out to Lester here, right?'

A look passed between them and I knew I'd not only hit the nail, I'd driven it squarely home. I was proud of myself because although I'd pieced some of it together earlier, I was really filling in the blanks now. It was guesswork, but I was on fire.

'Does your husband know what's been going on? All the lies? All the murders? I'm betting he doesn't. It's a conspiracy and they only work when a few people are involved – you, Lester here, whoever he reports to at Excelsis, eh, Lester? Bet the company's done all sorts of dirty deals over the years. Bribery. Small wars. Revolutions. Murder.'

Lester held my gaze, his face blank. He was good. I could see why he'd kept his place at the Excelsis table all these years. I smiled at him, turned back to Mrs Bobak.

'Who did you kill first, Mrs Bobak? Jenny's father?' She declined to answer. 'Doesn't matter anyway. I'd say anyone who had any contact with you back then had to go. It helped that some of the crooks you'd consorted with had already gone, the rest would be easy meat. Once you got round to them. Jessica was destined for the chop, so was Jenny if you'd got your hands on her. You'd managed to keep your face out of the public arena, thanks to your husband's views on family being protected from the glare of publicity. But that wouldn't last, would it? Sooner or later there would be more photographs like the one I saw.'

Her eyes flashed at that, and I realised she didn't know about it. 'Oh, yeah – a shot of you and Ritt dancing the night away in the White House. It was in a publicity handout. That's what tipped me off about you. It's an irrefutable law of nature, Mrs Bobak – the dead don't boogie.'

She glared in Lester's direction, her mouth a tight line. She didn't look so attractive now. 'Lester.'

Lester looked flustered for the first time. 'It was an oversight, my dear. A PR man found the shot, thought it would be good to include in the brochure. It was issued before I'd seen it.'

'That was sloppy, Lester,' I said before she had the chance to verbally rip him a new one. 'Should never have happened, but as I said – the entire endeavour has been ill-advised from the start. Frankly, it's just plain bonkers.'

'Oh, shut up, Queste,' said Mrs Bobak, her voice weary. 'You really are a smart-arse. They said you were, but I didn't really understand the extent of it till now. Yes, you're right about every-thing, satisfied?'

Lester's face turned red then. 'My dear lady, you shouldn't...'

'Lester, belt up. He's worked it all out, there's only us here, what harm can it do?' She whirled back to me, began to walk across the room. 'Here's something you haven't factored into your little tale, Queste – I love Ritt. I've loved him from the moment we met and I would have been happy with him even if he'd remained a back-road preacher. I admit Excelsis approaching him was a surprise, but I will allow nothing – *nothing* – to get in his way. No, he doesn't know what we've done to protect him, he'd be horrified if he ever found out, for he is a genuinely good man who can be something great. So I shared my little secret with Lester here and he agreed to help me fully erase my past. Jenny's father? Dead. Jessica? Dead. Anyone else who knew me back then? All dead, or soon will be. Accidents do happen. Dead, Queste, dead, dead.'

Her eyes were like little pinpoints of flame but despite that I felt the room chill.

'Dead,' she said again, and this time I swear there was a hint of a smile.

I wrenched my gaze away from her, fearful she'd turn me to stone, turned back to Lester and said, 'And you went along with all this?'

It was the woman who answered. 'Lester has ambitions too, and my husband in the White House was the key. Excelsis is happy to smooth the way. You're right, this kind of thing is not new to them. In their various lines of business, you can't make an omelette without breaking a few heads. And I can be very persuasive when I want to be, can't I, Lester?'

Lester nodded, and I saw his face redden. Even the most self-righteous of men can be led down a path by their genitalia. 'Why, Lester,' I said, 'have you been coveting thy neighbour's wife's ass? That's another commandment you've broken, as well as the "Thou Shalt Not Kill"?'

He continued to flush, but I doubted whether she had actually done the wild thing with him. I suspected he was somewhat smitten with her and she had used that to her advantage. Women have a sixth sense for that sort of thing. And men are weak, after all. He regained his composure and the hardness returned to his voice. 'Casualties of war, Mister Queste,' he said. 'They died for the greater good. They will receive their reward in a better place.'

I looked from his pious face to her dark madness and smiled. 'You know what I think?' I asked them.

'Do tell, Mister Queste,' Mrs Bobak said, her voice coated with sarcasm.

'I think you're both as crazy as a box of frogs.'

Her eyes darkened. She didn't like that. 'And you'd know all about madness wouldn't you, Mister Queste? A little bit of it runs through your veins, doesn't it? Or at least, that's what worries you.' She smiled at the guarded look that I knew had shadowed my face. 'Oh yes, we know all about you. We did our research. Your mother, wasn't it? Depression. Deep, deep, dark depression. That's what your father told you. But you fear it was more than that. Much more, don't you? And it haunts you. She was so disappointed in what her life had become – she wanted to be more than a wife and mother, didn't she? So did I. The only difference is that I faked my death, gave people something like closure. But your mother? She just vanished, didn't she?'

Her words brought the image of my mother back, standing over my bed with a curiously blank expression. It was early, there was only the faintest glow behind my bedroom curtains and she was in her coat, just looking down at me. I was going to say something, but for some reason I couldn't. I was only ten, I didn't know why she was standing over my bed in her coat. I didn't know why she was always so sad. Then she turned and walked out of my room and a few moments later I heard the front door close. That was the last time I saw her.

I forced the memory from my mind and said, 'Depression isn't madness, Mrs Bobak. I have my bouts of melancholy and I fight it but sometimes it wins. I've accepted it's part of me and it'll probably never change. But what about you? Are you saying you're happy to be a wife now, and a mother to another woman's children? What's changed with you?'

She was beside Lester now, her hand sliding along the broad windowsill. She went on, 'Ritt is a somebody, I knew that the first time I met him. And he's going to be even more of a somebody. And I'm going to grow with him. I'll be the First Lady, do you see that? I'll be a somebody, not just some Glasgow girl with a brat in tow. That was someone else, not me, and I'm not letting her get in the way of my life. I won't let you get in the way.'

Her hand was toying with a heavy glass ornament, a bulbous thing shaped like a large mushroom. She moved so suddenly I wasn't aware of it until she smashed the thing against Lester's head, then she dropped it and screamed. Lester staggered, blood oozing from the wound on his scalp, but he managed to stay conscious. She screamed for Paul and pounded on the door, yelling that she needed help. I was so shocked I was frozen to the spot. I heard Paul's voice yelling into his radio that assistance was needed but I didn't move even when he burst in, a gun in his hand and she pointed a shaking finger at me and said, 'Paul – he attacked Mister Butterworth.'

Paul turned the barrel of the gun in my direction but I didn't believe he would shoot, I could see the confusion in his eyes. But then she said his name sharply and I saw his face harden and the gun barrel settle on me.

Oh shit, I thought, as I heard the sound of a silenced pistol going off.

Chapter Twenty-Five

Duncan and Hamish had settled into a set of comfortable settees in the lounge below sipping a hideously expensive cup of coffee when they became aware of two figures standing over them. They wondered if they were getting too old for this game because they had neither seen nor heard Nick Cornwell and Theresa Cohan approach. In their defence, they had focussed their attention on the security man who had re-established his position at the lift door. The Excelsis Corporation may have been capable of buying this entire hotel chain if they had the notion and still have enough on the corporate credit card to finance a war or two but they clearly had not taken full control of all the lifts. If anyone wanted to use the one he was guarding with such zeal, the marine-type simply rode with them, then returned to the ground floor and stood post again. In the time I was upstairs chewing the fat with Lester and the mad Mrs Bobak the lad had been and gone three times. The Sutherland boys took a guess that the other lift had been rigged so that it did not reach the top floor.

Nick stared down at the Sutherland boys with ill-concealed suspicion. 'Bit out of your comfort zone in this place, aren't you?' He said.

Duncan struggled not to show surprise and said, 'We like to slum it now and then, Mister Cornwell.'

Nick grunted and quickly scanned the foyer. 'Where's Queste?'

'Not a clue,' said Duncan, the picture of innocence. 'You know where Dom is, Hamish?'

'I'm not his social secretary,' said Hamish.

Nick sighed. 'DC Cohan saw him come in with you. So where is he?'

Duncan gave Theresa the once over. If she'd been tailing them and he hadn't noticed, she was either very good or he really was getting old. He liked to think she was very good. 'Been following us, bonny lass?'

'On my orders,' said Nick. 'I know you and Queste are up to your neck in all this, so we let him go and kept tabs on him. We knew sooner or later you'd lead us to the people who have turned my town into Dodge City. So I'll ask for the final time – where's Queste?'

Duncan thought about this, his hand absently giving his wound a gentle rub. He felt tired, washed out. He thought perhaps he and Hamish were past it, for this case had not proved to be their shining hour and to cap it all they'd not spotted this bit of a lass following them. He groaned inwardly. He should never have left his hospital bed, but here he was in a posh hotel, sipping a coffee so expensive you needed credit references just to read the menu and now DCI Nick Cornwell was breathing down his neck. He'd promised to bring the cavalry if I'd not reappeared. And here was the cavalry. Duncan looked across the low coffee table at his brother and raised his eyebrows. Hamish, who knew what his brother was thinking, shrugged then nodded his agreement.

'He's upstairs,' said Duncan, 'we think chatting to that bloke Ritt Bobak.'

'Doubtful,' said Nick. 'Reverend Bobak is at the SECC at this moment doing a sound check. We've got some lads there on security, along with his own team.'

'And this'll be a team hired by the Excelsis Corporation, like?'

Nicky looked surprised. 'What do you know about the Excelsis Corporation?'

'We know that they're behind everything that's happened. We know that they've been trying to kill that lass. We know that it's all got something to do with Ritt Bobak's wife, who's not what she seems. And we know that Dom is up there right now talking to God knows who with only his wits to protect him.'

Nick grunted again. 'He's done for, then. What room?'

'We don't know, but the lift went right up to the top floor.'

Nick nodded, looking towards the burly security man. 'Right, let's join the party then. That walking steroid one of their lads?'

'Aye.'

'You two stay here,' said Nick, and strode away with Theresa in tow. The "walking steroid" suddenly tensed as something squawked in his earpiece and whirled round to punch the button. Nick and Theresa quickened their pace to pile in behind him. The guard opened his mouth but was silenced by Nick thrusting his warrant card in his face and saying, 'Don't waste your breath, son.'

'Something's up,' said Hamish as the lift doors closed. Duncan was already hitting my number on speed dial. When I didn't answer he said, 'Take the other lift up as far as it goes, I'll find the stairs. Make sure no-one we know is using them.'

Hamish frowned. He knew who Duncan meant. His brother looked very pale and fragile. 'You up to tackling the stairs?' He didn't risk asking if he was up to dealing with Sykes.

'I'll be fine,' Duncan snapped. 'Now go!' Duncan wheeled away as Hamish called the second lift. He saw a sign for the stairs and followed it down a short corridor, passing a side entrance to the hotel. He had expected to find another security guard here. but the door was unattended. As he stepped into the stairwell he saw why – another burly ex-marine was sprawled at the bottom of the first flight, a bloody hole where his right eye should have been. Another man lay unconscious against the far wall, his white shirt stained with the blood that oozed from a deep gash on his forehead. Duncan had seen the man walk by earlier, only then he had been wearing the hotel's blue jacket.

Sykes, he thought.

* * *

The soft thud of the silenced pistol was followed swiftly by a mist of red rising from the back of Paul's head and he jerked to one side, his gun tumbling to the ground. I knew it was Sykes even before I saw him appear in the door frame, looking very smart in the blue jacket of the hotel staff. Who else in my circle of acquaintances was in the habit of shooting first and saying to hell with any questions later? Mrs Bobak seemed frozen in time, staring at the blood spray on her arms and chest.

My phone rang, sounding hellishly loud in the sudden quiet, but I didn't make any move to answer it. Sykes kept his back to the wall as he quickly scanned the room, finally settling his eyes on me. I had the impression my presence was not unexpected 'Dominic,' he said, as if we'd met in the street, 'what a surprise.'

'Came to stop you, Sykes,' I said. 'Can't let you kill Ritt Bobak.'

'Not planning to,' said Sykes, and suddenly he snapped the pistol up and fired once at Lester Butterworth. A blossom of scarlet grew and died on the fat man's chest, and he went down without a sound. The woman saw this and screamed, a long anguished yell, before she slumped to her knees, sobs vibrating through her body. Talking about killing, having someone else do it, was all in the abstract. But this was real.

'Jesus!' I said, shocked at the suddenness of it all. Then all the tension, all the terror flooded through me and erupted in a cascade of words 'Fuck's sake, Sykes! Haven't you had enough of killing for one week? What are you, some sort of psycho? You got to kill everyone?'

Sykes stood there and took it, no emotion at all registering on his face, but the pistol still held at the ready. 'You're still walking around.'

That was it for me. I waved my hands at him in a dismissive gesture and slumped down on the armchair behind me. 'Oh, go ahead...I'm done in anyway. Be good to get a bit of rest.'

He stared at me thoughtfully and maybe he was actually going to do it – after all, I could identify him – but we'll never know because there was a gunshot and he spun around to his right, his gun flying from his hand, a wound ripping open at his shoulder. I looked over at Mrs Bobak and saw she was now swivelling Paul's gun towards me, so I threw myself from the chair and sprawled onto the floor. I swear I felt the bullet whine past my head and bury itself in the thick upholstery. Obviously she wasn't as upset by the sight of real-life death as I'd thought. She fired again and the bullet lodged in the floor near my leg. I rolled away, not because a greater distance would keep me safe, but just to keep moving.

She pulled the trigger a third time but the shot must have gone wild because I've no idea where it ended up. The main thing was it didn't end up in me. Sykes was on his knees and scrambling to reach his gun, but she saw this and turned to face him, loosed off another round, which also missed. He reached his weapon, wrapped a trembling hand round the butt, swung it up to fire, but she was gone, her back disappearing from view into the hallway. He fired anyway then slumped, the gun sliding to the floor again. He could be hurt after all, I realised, but he was no longer my concern.

I scrambled to my feet and followed the woman into the hallway. A door to the left led to stairs and I presumed this was how Sykes had got past the guard downstairs. I eased it open and peered through the gap, expecting a bullet to head my way any second, but instead I heard her footsteps pounding up the stairs towards the roof. I could hear footsteps echoing from below, they were faint but they were unmistakeably heading our way, and presumed she'd heard them too. I went after her.

When I punched the bar on the exit door and stepped out she was running across the flat surface as if she knew where she was going, though she had nowhere to go. The view from the roof was spectacular but I didn't stop to take it in.

A stiff breeze swept round my body and I realised too late that the door had swung shut, forcing me to treat it to a short but bitter barrage of curse words. I was on a high roof with a crazy woman armed with a gun and would have preferred to have kept my escape route open. My only hope now was to keep as much distance as possible between said crazy woman, aforementioned gun and me. She had shown herself to be no crack shot. Sure, she'd managed to bring Sykes down with her first one and came close to puncturing me twice, but I was not keen on putting her skills to the test again. She had come to a halt at the edge of the building and was looking over a small ledge towards the street below, the gun dangling at her side.

'Mrs Bobak,' I yelled but she didn't move. 'It's over, Mrs Bobak...'

It was like she was playing a really serious game of statues. She had her back to me, but she was looking down at the city as if she hadn't expected to find it there.

'Mrs Bobak,' I said, edging forward, keeping my eye on her gun hand in case it swung up and in my direction. There wasn't much I could do if it did, except throw myself onto the tar paper below my feet and hope for the best, but I still wanted to be prepared. 'Mrs Bobak. Bernie...'

That got to her. I saw her head come up and she slowly turned round, the gun still dangling in a loose grip at her side. She looked very calm. That scared me even more than her mad moments. 'Nobody's called me that in a long time.'

'Bernie, it's over. The police will be here. It's all over.'

She nodded and looked down at the gun, as if she had forgotten it was there. A voice in my head screamed at me to lie down, to make myself into as small a ball as possible and wish she would just go away. I ignored it.

'Why don't you drop the gun, eh? Just let it go?'

She looked back at me, then down again to the gun. She began to raise it.

'Bernie, don't do anything stupid. Just drop it...'

The gun was level with her face now, barrel upwards, as if she was studying it. Jesus, I thought, she's going to use it on herself. I gauged the distance between us, wondering if I could reach her before she pulled the trigger, then thought how stupid that would be because it would be so easy for her to turn it on me. But I couldn't stand there and do nothing, even though the little voice was saying yes, I bloody well could. Then she frowned and threw the gun to the side. I felt some of the tension drain from my body and the little voice fell silent.

'That's good,' I said, keeping my tone level, though I was far from calm. 'Why don't we go back downstairs now, eh? Get out of this breeze. What do you say, Mrs Bobak? Bernie?'

I knew she had heard me, but she did not move. Instead she said, 'What's she like?'

'Who?'

Her voice was dull. 'Jenny. What's she like?'

'She's a good girl,' I lied. What the hell else was I going to say? That her daughter was a tough-minded, self-centred little bitch who had been scarred by lack of familial affection and the 'death' of her mother? You bet I lied. 'She's smart and she's beautiful and you'd be proud of her.'

She nodded, as if she had expected that. She sat down on the ledge. I couldn't blame her – I could have done with a sit down myself. Her hands were on her knees, wrists up and she stared at them, at the blood that stained them both literally and figuratively. I think in that moment she finally understood what she had caused – all the lies, all the scheming, all the killing. She had ended one life years before because she could no longer cope with it. She had created another one and now she couldn't cope with that.

'Tell her...' she began.

'Tell her what, Bernie?'

She raised her eyes slowly at me and I saw the cold fire in them return. 'Tell her nothing,' she said, and then tipped back.

I cried out, I don't know what, and lunged forward, but she was gone. I reached the edge and peered over to see her body was still falling. She didn't make a sound. I turned away before it struck the ground, but I'm certain I heard it slam into the concrete, a liquid thud, like a pile of wet newspapers hitting a hard, stone floor.

I slid to the roof, my back to the ledge and tried not to hear the screams and screeching brakes below. I saw Nick Cornwell and Theresa Cohan heading in my direction, the door behind them held open by his coat laid down in a bundle. Nick would be peeved if it got dirty, I remember thinking. They both looked pale, I didn't know whether from the scene downstairs or because they'd seen Mrs Bobak go off the edge. I guessed it was a mixture of both.

Nick stood beside me and peered at the scene below. 'She threw herself off,' I said, my voice sounding dull and flat.

'Saw that,' he said. 'Who was she?'

'The wife of Ritt Bobak.'

'Shit,' he said.

'She was also Jenny Deavers' mother.'

He paused to take that in. 'Thought she died years ago.'

'Yeah,' I said. 'She did. She came back.'

Nick sighed as he realised it was going to be very complicated. 'You've got a lot of talking to do, Queste. We've got two more bodies in a room downstairs that require some explanation – and this time I want everything, not just what you want me to know.'

I nodded as I began to haul myself to my feet. It was a laborious process and I might not have made it if Theresa hadn't given me a hand. I gave her a weak smile by way of thanks and then something hit me.

'Two bodies?' I said. 'So where the hell is Sykes?'

* * *

Duncan met up with Sykes on the sixth floor. He looked in a bad way, his shirt plastered with blood from his wound, but then Duncan was not feeling too chipper himself. He had finally realised he wasn't Superman. Sykes leaned against the banister and raised his pistol, but Duncan could see he had very little strength. Duncan stepped back and raised both hands.

'Take it easy, like,' he said, his voice echoing from the bare walls and booming down the stairs. 'I'm no threat to you, man.'

Sykes brought the gun level, but winced as pain raced through him from his shoulder. 'Let me pass,' he said.

'I will,' promised Duncan, 'as long as you tell me where they are.'

Sykes smiled. Or he may have been gritting his teeth, Duncan really couldn't be sure. 'Who?'

'Not the time to be playing silly buggers, mate. The police will be all over this place in minutes. You can't shoot everyone.'

'Don't need to shoot everyone, just you,' said Sykes, still struggling to hold the weapon steady.

'I'm not your enemy, friend.'

Sykes coughed. 'You're not my friend either. Friend.'

'All I want to know is where Father Verne and the girl are. Then you can be on your way.'

Sykes glanced back up the stairs and then at the door to the sixth floor, a few feet to Duncan's left. 'They'll get you before you go a few feet,' said Duncan. 'They'll just gun you down, you know that. Like a mad dog.'

'I'm no mad dog.'

'Not the way they see it.'

Sykes thought about it. 'I'll take my chances.'

'And I'm happy for you to do that. But the longer we stand here jawing, the slimmer those chances get. Just tell me where they are, and you can be on your way.'

'Or I can just kill you now and then be on my way, use them as leverage.'

Duncan sighed. 'Maybe, but I don't think you're firing on all cylinders, are you? When you're on top form I'd bet you can shoot a black eye out of a pea, but right now? Don't think so. And all I need to do is delay you a few more minutes and...'

Sykes fired then, the bullet burying itself into the cement about a foot above Duncan's head.

'The next one takes the black eye out of your pea,' warned Sykes.

'You don't need them any more, Sykes. Okay, so you can kill me, but Dom can still identify you and so can my brother. Killing the priest and the girl won't change that. And I don't think you kill needlessly, do you? If you're paid to do it, certainly. If you have to do it, sure. The security man downstairs, he was a threat, so you took him down. But the other bloke, the hotel worker? You just knocked him out. He wasn't a threat, was he? So just tell me where I can find them and you can get outside. Your chances are a hell of a lot better in the open than locked up in this stairwell.'

Duncan could see Sykes was calculating the odds. Everything Duncan had said was true – Sykes was a professional and killed for profit or if he was threatened. We could all identify him, but I don't think that worried him that much. A man like him had many identities and many bolt holes in which to lie low for an indeterminate period of time. Finally, Sykes lowered the gun.

'Black van, out in the parking lot. It's not locked,' he said.

Duncan relaxed a little then and nodded once to show his thanks. He stepped back, flattened against the wall, raised his hands in a show of goodwill.

'You better hurry,' said Duncan. 'You don't have much time...'

Chapter Twenty-Six

I was back in an interview room, this time in the City Centre station on Stewart Street. I had certainly been doing the rounds of Glasgow's cop shops, although each room was interchangeable. Been in one, been in them all. Eamonn sat beside me, Nick Cornwell opposite me, but the questions were being handled by a local CID heavy-hitter whose name I didn't quite catch. I was more relaxed than I had been for days. Duncan had sprung Father Verne and Jenny from their black van prison. Sykes was in the wind somewhere. Police were scouring the city to find him, but I was confident they wouldn't lay a glove on him. Sykes wasn't real. He was a spectre, a shadow, a diabolical bloody fiend. He was long gone.

'So why did Bernie Deavers fake her own death in the first place?' It was the Stewart Street CID guy, struggling to understand it all. Couldn't blame him, I'd pieced it all together bit by bit but I was still kind of winging it, though talking out loud helped.

'She'd got herself into a pile of shit and didn't have a snorkel,' I said. 'Life hadn't turned out the way she wanted. She had a kid she hadn't planned and was dragging her down. She had got herself into some nasty business thanks to her scumbag pals. When you lot got to know about her, she turned grass to save herself, but that only made things worse. So she decided it was time to get out. With the help of one of her boyfriends – Big Tam McCutcheon, the only one she hadn't betrayed – she rigged the fire.'

'Whose body was it that burned?'

'Christ knows,' I said. 'Could be anyone. Her sister Jessica ID'd what was left of the body, but she was in on it. No-one thought twice about it. Why would they? There was nothing suspicious about the fire, it looked like an accident. Big Tam did his job well.'

'So she went to the States.'

'Yeah, courtesy of Big Tam again. He must've really cared about her to go to all that trouble and expense, creating a new identity, passports, papers, birth certificates, what have you. Mind you, it's just as well he died of cancer a couple of years ago, otherwise he might've ended up the same way as the others. We worked out how many yet?'

Nick grunted. '*We* have made some inquiries and it seems there have been another three sudden deaths around the country that lead back to friends of the former Bernice Deavers. All unexplained deaths.'

'So with Aunt Jessica, Jenny's father, those three, that makes five in her immediate circle, plus Tiger, the two in the office, two in the car park and the three in the hotel. Thirteen.' I still wasn't saying anything about the two in Alexandra Park. I shot Nick a glance, but if he spotted my omission he said nothing. He glowered at me a lot though.

'And all because someone wanted her husband to be President,' said the CID bloke.

'Yeah, she met Bobak early on in his crusade, fell arse over tip, but never told him about her past. How could she? She didn't know he would become the media sensation he did – and she certainly didn't know he was in line for the White House. But then Lester Butterworth felt the rapture and he threw the weight of Excelsis behind Bobak. When Bernie realised that her previous life could prove unfortunate, she used her wiles on Butterworth and convinced him to tie off the loose ends. Must've seemed like a good idea at the time. Excelsis had the cash and the know-how.'

'You think it was as simple as that?'

'I don't think we were dealing with stable personalities here. Can't speak for Reverend Bobak because I didn't get to meet the man, but Bernie was a fruitloop short of a full bowl and old Lester wasn't much better. Lester hired the best...'

'This fella Sykes.'

'Or Miller, or whatever his real name is.'

'And you have no idea where he is now?'

'Not a clue. But when things got a little messy – Aunt Jessica, Tiger, and the two in Elite Security – they panicked and wanted him out of the picture too. He didn't cotton none to that so he turned on them.'

I thought about the way he was unsurprised to see me in that hotel room, wondered if he'd banked on me getting there to act as yet another diversion. I couldn't be certain but I wouldn't put it past him to gamble on me finding out about Excelsis. Maybe he knew I'd see the poster. Maybe he was bloody psychic.

The detective fell silent and stared at me for a full minute. I think it was supposed to unnerve me. He was wasting his time because after the week I'd had, I was pretty unnervable. And I didn't give a shit whether or not that was a word.

'Okay,' he said.

'Okay?' I said. 'That it?'

'That's it. Unless you've got something more to tell us.'

'Not that I can think of.'

'Okay, then. You're free to go.'

I looked at Nick. He glowered and grunted.

I like to think he was saying thanks for the help.

* * *

I felt as if I hadn't seen my flat for weeks. All I wanted was to get home, slump in my armchair and watch something mindless on TV. Anything but reality TV. I wasn't feeling *that* bad. Eamonn dropped me off with a warning to stay out of trouble. Yeah, like that would ever happen.

A smooth-looking fellow in a smart suit climbed from a dark four-wheel drive very like the one used by Hattie and Derek and called out my name. Another man alighted from the driver's seat. He was also in a smart suit, but he was a lot taller and looked like the two guards at Bobak's hotel. So they were triplets. I wondered if I should commiserate him on his loss.

I waited until the smaller man came closer. He had a large brown envelope containing something bulky in his hand and a salesman's grin on his face, but I wasn't sure I was interested in what he was selling. 'Mister Queste,' he said, holding out a hand. 'The name's JK Lamont.' He was American and I shook his hand because I didn't want him to think Brits were surly bastards.

'You're from Excelsis, right?'

His smile broadened. 'Let's just say I represent some very powerful interests.'

'Let's just say it's Excelsis. Police Scotland will want to have a word with your bosses pretty soon.'

His smile didn't falter but he did jerk his head a little, telling me that wasn't a concern. 'Could we step inside?'

'No,' I said. Brits could be surly after all.

Still the smile didn't fade. I was beginning to think it was painted on. 'Okay. No problem.' He held out the envelope. 'This is for you, with our compliments.'

I looked at the envelope as if it would go off, but he kept it hanging there. He knew I would take it. He knew my curiosity would get the better of me. He was a top salesman and he knew people. He was right. I took it from him and looked inside. The envelope was stuffed with banknotes, all crisp and clean and if I'd sniffed them, bearing the unmistakeable whiff of blood money.

'It's our way of compensating you for the inconvenience you've been caused over the past few days. You deserve to come out of this with something more than a few bruises and the enmity of local law enforcement.'

I asked, 'Excelsis, right?' Say what you like, I'm dogged.

The smile was beginning to piss me off. 'As I said, powerful interests. Interests who have been very impressed with your behaviour of late, very impressed. They believe that impressive behaviour behoves them to show their gratitude in a tangible form.' He actually said behoves. Colour me impressed.

'They're paying me off?'

'They're showing their gratitude,' he said again. 'Events have been...' he searched for the right word, 'unfortunate.' He'd found the right word. 'My employers regret them very deeply. However, it has brought you to their attention.'

'Is that a good thing?'

'It can be,' he said, and his grin widened, which I hadn't thought possible. The inference that it could be a bad thing was not lost on me. 'It may be that sometime in the future they will have need of your services.'

'What services would that be?'

'Come now, Mister Queste, you have many skills and contacts that may be very useful to my employers someday. They recognise talent when they see it and like to nurture it.'

I raised the envelope. 'And this is what? A retainer?'

'No, whatever arrangement is made in the future will be separate. As I said, this is to recompense you for the inconvenience caused by these recent events.'

'The unfortunate ones?'

That smile again. 'That is correct.'

I looked in the envelope again. There was a lot of money in there. That was Excelsis's answer to everything, lots of money. And as answers go, it's a pretty good one. I tried to estimate how much was in there. Enough, I thought, to get a new car with a CD player that worked and a holder for my coffee cup. That would be pretty nifty. Or I could go on a spending spree, buy a Blu-Ray player, and splurge on a shitload of movies. Get myself to LA, I've always wanted to do the Hollywood thing. All I needed to do was thank old JK here nicely and walk into my flat with this tidy little bundle under my arm. Yep, that's all I needed to do.

I handed back the envelope. 'Not interested,' I said.

He was so surprised, the brilliance of his smile dimmed a notch or two. 'There are no strings attached,' he said.

'JK,' I said, wearily, 'with the likes of Excelsis, there are more strings than the London Philharmonic. Thanks, but no thanks.'

I turned away because as an exit line, I didn't think I'd come up with better. He had one for me, though. 'We have stretched out a hand of friendship, Mister Queste. When our paths cross again, it will not be proffered a second time.'

I faced him, saw the envelope had already been passed to his minion, who stood behind him like a planetary body looking for a sun to eclipse. 'And will our paths cross again, JK?'

His white teeth glinted. 'Count on it, Mister Queste, count on it.'

He turned and climbed back into the four-wheel drive, the bodyguard walking round to the driver's seat. I waited until they pulled away from the kerb and drove down the street before I went inside. I already wished I'd taken the money. Having principles was proving to be fiscally exacting.

* * *

The next day I stood outside the refuge waiting for Jenny to complete her goodbyes to Duncan, Hamish and Father Verne. To her credit, her thanks for their help were fulsome and her apologies for all the trouble to which she had put them sincere. At least, they sounded sincere. She gave them all a hug, which was kind of touching, and then she joined me outside as we waited for the taxi to take her to the station. She was going back down to Saltcoats to stay with her pal Lesley while she decided what to do next. After all, she'd inherited a nice house in the West End. She could stay there, move her pal in too, which I'm sure would delight Lesley, given the level of infatuation I'd seen that night in her flat, or she could sell it, start fresh somewhere else. The world, as they say, was her oxter.

She had taken the news of her mother's second coming and subsequent going well, I thought, but then I didn't really know what was going on inside her head. I should have, I suppose, because we had a certain amount in common. However, I think Jenny Deavers was one person I would never understand. She had even met up with the Reverend Bobak, who turned out to be an okay sort of bloke, despite the super white teeth, the too-perfect tan and the religious mania. Nobody's perfect, I suppose. He insisted in meeting her in order to apologise profusely. Naturally, he was cutting his mission short and had shelved his plans for a political career. I think he was genuinely horrified by all that had been committed in his name.

The black cab rattled towards us on a crest of diesel fumes and I opened the door to throw Jenny's bags into the back. She hesitated before she climbed in, then threw her arms around my neck and gave me a brief hug. Maybe she wasn't as bad as I thought.

'Thanks,' she said, 'for everything.'

'That's okay,' I said.

I held the door open and she climbed in. I was about to close the door when she poked her head back out and looked at me with an appraising eye.

'You know,' she said, 'if you got your hair cut, it would take years off you.'

'I'll keep it in mind,' I said, wondering if she was flirting with me. She was, after all, her mother's daughter. On the other hand, Jenny had nothing to gain by 'persuading' me, so maybe she was being sincere.

I cleared my throat and asked, 'You going to be okay?'

'I'll be fine,' she answered. 'I've got the house, that'll fetch a fair bit of cash.'

So she was going to sell. Maybe it was for the best. She took her hand away and I swung the door. I saw her say something to the driver, telling him to wait a second, and she rolled down the window.

'And in the meantime,' she said, 'I've got fifty grand sitting in a storage unit I've rented.'

I was stunned. 'Fifty grand? Jerome's fifty grand?'

She smiled and rolled the window back up. She waved at me as the taxi pulled away, leaving me open-mouthed. The little bitch, I thought, she had told me she didn't know about the fifty grand, that it had ended up on the bottom of the Thames with the cocaine. I then wondered if the drugs were in that storage unit, too. The lying, deceitful, calculating, self-serving little cow. And I had handed back a fistful of dollars just the day before.

But as the taxi pulled into the road and merged with the city bound traffic, I began to laugh.

Acknowledgements

and Author's Note

Please remember this is a work of fiction. There has never been a shoot-out in Alexandra Park or in the car park of a hotel near the SECC. I made up that particular hotel anyway. I also made up the side street and café in Saltcoats, so don't go looking for Joe. The visiting ship berthed at the Riverside Museum is also a figment of my imagination, although the MV Glenlee is well worth visiting, even though Dominic has never bothered his backside to go.

There are people I must thank, because writers don't pull this kind of thing off without a lot of help and support. This may turn into a Sally Field Oscar speech, so make a cuppa.

There are the people who read this before it became something you could actually hold in your hand and wave about and those who have assisted in some way after the fact. In no particular order can I shout out to Gary and Elizabeth McLaughlin, Karin Stewart, Helena Morrow, Sandy Kilpatrick and Graham Turnbull. Also, I must mention Ben McLaughlin and his sister Toni (I promised this in an earlier book and forgot, so hope this makes up for it.) Also, Eve Broderick – I haven't forgotten about that Young Adult book. And, of course, to Margaret, who kept me fed and watered.

Then there are the crime writers – Caro Ramsay, Alex Gray, Lin Anderson, Theresa Talbot, Michael J. Malone, Neil Broadfoot, Mark Leggatt, Matt Bendoris, Mason Cross. Thank you all for taking the time to make your comments.

Crime writers are incredibly supportive so thanks in general should go to Craig Robertson, Alexandra Sokoloff, James Oswald, TF Muir, Val McDermid, Craig Russell, Quintin Jardine and Chris Brookmyre. And all those others, too many to mention, who share posts on Facebook and Twitter. It's appreciated.

Thanks also to my Crime Factor world tour of parts of Scotland colleagues Gordon Brown and Peter Burnett. And to Clare Cain of Fledgling and Linda MacFadyen of outsideIN events for putting it all together.

To the festival organisers, particularly Dom Hastings, lately of Bloody Scotland, Bob McDevitt, of both Bloody Scotland and Aye Write, and Marjory Marshall of Grantown's Wee Crime Festival, as well as librarians everywhere. You have all made me feel I am part of something larger than a dusty room lined with books and a desk with a laptop.

Of course, thanks also to all booksellers, especially Caron Macpherson, David McCormack and Kenny Bryan.

To all the book reviewers and book bloggers and book clubs and book groups and book readers. We can't do it without you. Special mention must go to Sharon Bolton, Noelle Holton, Marsali Taylor, Colette Lamberth and Gordon McGhie who have supported me above and beyond, as well as the CrimeSquad and Crime Fiction Lover sites. And, of course, Shari Lowe!

To my editor Louise Hutcheson who always keeps me on the right track, Laura Jones, for her expert typesetting and uncanny prescience with a slush pile, and Sara Hunt at Contraband for allowing Dominic to breathe.

Special thanks must go to Iain K. Burns, for his incredible support, and to Stephen Wilkie. He knows why.

If I have forgotten anyone – and I probably have – please accept my heartfelt apologies.

Now read Dominic Queste's second case...

TAG –
YOU'RE DEAD

Maverick investigator Dominic Queste is on the trail of missing butcher Sam Price. But he soon uncovers links to a killer with a taste for games.

What began as a simple favour for his girlfriend quickly descends into a battle for survival against an enemy who has no qualms about turning victims into prime cuts. Amidst a twisted game of cat and mouse, suspicious coppers, vicious crooks and a seemingly random burglary, Queste has to keep his wits about him.

Or he might just find himself on the butcher's block.

Prologue

The mobile phone was cheap and nasty, but that didn't bother me.

It didn't offer internet access or even have a camera. That didn't bother me, either.

It was sitting on the coffee table in my living room and what really bothered me was that it wasn't mine.

I froze, listened for the sound of someone moving in my flat. It's not a big flat. If a fly sneezes at one end, I'll still say 'Bless you' from the other. I heard a car pass in the street. I heard, somewhere, music playing. I think it may have been One Direction. I heard the click of heels as someone climbed the stairs in my tenement building. I heard nothing disturbing. Unless you count One Direction.

My breath had stilled, so I exhaled and then inhaled before I lifted the phone, turned it over in my hand. Someone had come into my home while I was up north and left it behind. A burglar wasn't likely to lay his phone on the table while he rifled my valuables – it wasn't much of a rifle, to be honest, unless you like CDs of film music and DVDs. However, the flat was undisturbed. Maybe not tidy, but the mess I'd left was untouched. Everything was where I'd dropped it.

That meant the phone was left here deliberately.

I thought, who?

I thought, why?

I thought, who?

I know I thought that twice, but I really wanted to know.

And then it bleeped. A text. It wasn't loud but it made me start.

It wasn't my phone but something told me the message was for me:

Hello, Mr Queste

Hello yourself, I almost typed, but then the phone bleeped again. Another text. Four words this time.

You have been selected

No, thank you, I thought, I don't know what you're selling, but I'm not buying. Whatever was coming next wasn't good.

And then it came.

Two words. Capitalised for added emphasis. Not that they needed them.

FOR DEATH

I'll be honest, I felt my skin crawl. I now knew what this was about. I knew this was no prank. I knew that whoever sent these texts was very serious indeed. He had killed before.

Right then, another question swirled in my head.

How the hell do I get myself involved in these things?

Chapter One

I FIND it hard to refuse an attractive woman when she asks for a favour.

I find it damn near impossible when we're both naked.

Let me tell you, that doesn't happen very often these days. Hell, that's never happened often, because even though I'm no Quasimodo, I'm not exactly catnip for the ladies. You can count the number of women I've been intimate with on one hand and still have fingers to spare should you feel the need to make an obscene gesture. In fact, for a long time the closest I came to sweaty bedroom action was changing the duvet. So I was very grateful that Ginty O'Reilly had seen fit to end a dry spell that made Lawrence of Arabia look like *Waterworld*.

I'd met her after her ex-husband, a former boxer nicknamed Tiger, had introduced me to his fist when I found him in the home of a recently murdered woman. Tiger later wound up hanging from the yardarm of a tall ship, but that's another story entirely. Ginty and I seemed to hit it off, though. She was tall and slim and blonde. There's a Raymond Chandler line about a blonde who would make a bishop kick a hole in a stained glass window. If the bishop met Ginty, that stained glass window would have more holes than Marlon Brando's vest. I was punching way above my weight but she didn't seem to notice. Don't get me wrong, she wasn't some high-toned kind of gal from the West End. She was an East End hairdresser who, when pressed, was capable of bleaching a barnet with the kind of industrial language that would shock Quentin Tarantino.

She was also no doe-eyed teenager looking for any kind of permanent arrangement, which was fine with me because I don't think I'm a permanent arrangement sort of guy. For one thing, I like my own space. For another, the work I do calls for some pretty unsociable hours. But more importantly, I have a streak of Celtic melancholy that can emerge when the wind changes direction, and I wanted to shield her from that. Call it what you will – depression, self pity, a dark side – it's not something I wished anyone to see, let alone Ginty. She was one of those people who liked to see the bright side of life, despite her having been round the block a time or two.

So we saw each once or twice a week, if I wasn't working. We went out for lunch, dinner, we went to the movies. We did all the things pals did and a few things pals didn't do, like rolling around in bed. That's what had happened that night. We'd had dinner in Frankie and Benny's at Springfield Quay – our sophistication is the envy of the trendy set – then headed across the car park to the Odeon where we ignored this week's clutch of superhero movies (all that testosterone and rippling muscles makes me feel insecure) in favour of a Melissa McCarthy comedy. Ginty laughed like she was watching something funny. I didn't. Still, the fact that I'd done the manly thing and taken her to a film of her choice earned me brownie points. It's all about the giving with me.

Suffice to say that later we were cuddling in my bed having sated ourselves. John Barry's 'The Beyondness of Things' was on the CD player and the beautiful melodies were both soothing and melancholy at the same time. Some people think Barry was only about Bond music, but the real heart of the composer came through in his gentle moments. It was raining outside for a change and the curtains were drawn. The furniture was real, though. Sorry about that. I may be prone to dark moods but that doesn't stop me taking advantage of a feedline.

The street light outside my bedroom window cast a pale glow through the thin drapes as I lay on the bed with Ginty's head resting on my chest, my fingers stroking her hair, listening to the sinister opening chords of 'The Fictionist' give way to another gently romantic melody. I was happy, which despite my tendency to a smart-arsed quip was not something I was used to. The rain caressing the window, the soothing music and my recent exertions combined to make me contemplate slipping softly into the sleep of the just after.

'Erasmus,' Ginty said. Her voice was low and throaty. It turned me on just to listen to it. But then, I'm a guy. I get turned on when I squeeze a melon. And Erasmus isn't my name, it was simply something I said the first time we met and it stuck. She knew my real name, of course, she just preferred to call me Erasmus.

'Present,' I said.

'Would you do something for me?'

'Well, if it entails dressing up and/or swinging from the light fitting, you'll need to give me fifteen minutes.' I thought about that again. Who was I kidding? What was I? An athlete? 'Maybe half an hour.'

She laughed in a slightly derisive way. 'No, but hold that thought for an hour or two,' she said, rather unnecessarily I decided. 'I need a favour.'

'Go ahead. But don't think I didn't notice that slight on my manhood. I'll think of a snappy comeback, don't you worry. Once my breathing returns to normal.'

She raised her head from my chest and propped her chin on one hand. She wasn't smiling. I loved to see her smile but there was something in those blue eyes that told me this was serious. 'So what's the favour?' I asked.

'It's my cousin, Sam. Sam Price. I think he's in trouble.'

I almost said that trouble was my business but I restrained myself. I could see this wasn't the time for my usual nonsense. 'What kind of trouble?'

She bit her lower lip. Normally that would drive me crazy, but Ginty was right, it would take another hour or two. 'I don't know. All I know is that he's disappeared. He's not turned up for work, he's not seen his family. His sister has a key to his flat and he's not there. She told me it looked like he'd been gone for days.'

'What does he do?'

'He's a butcher, has his own shop on Dumbarton Road, near Partick Cross, but it's been shut for two weeks. He had two assistants and they say he gave them a month's pay and told them not to come in.'

'He sacked them?'

'Not in so many words but they've not seen or heard from him since.'

'Is he married?'

'Divorced.'

'Girlfriend?'

Ginty shook her head. 'Don't think so.'

'Does he have money problems?'

'Not that we know of. The shop is very popular – he was a good butcher, won prizes for his steak pies.'

'Does he gamble? Drink? Take drugs?'

Something registered in her eyes. 'He doesn't take drugs as far as I know. He takes a drink but who doesn't?' I was about to say my mother, who condemned alcohol while shovelling Valium down her throat, but this was no time to depress Ginty. Or me.

'I sense a "but" coming,' I said.

She took a breath. 'Sam was always … ' She looked for the right word and found it: '… dodgy.'

'In what way?'

She hesitated. I could tell this wasn't easy for her. Talking about your family's shortcomings never is. 'He's not crooked exactly but he's not exactly straight either. He's … '

'Dodgy,' I said.

'Yes. He's not into anything heavy, just petty stuff, receiving stolen goods, that sort of thing.'

I understood. To some people I was pretty dodgy, too, but that's because of the company I keep. And some of the things I've done in the past, which don't bear too much scrutiny, even by me.

TAG – You're Dead

'Will you have a nose around? Please, Dom? For me?'

She'd used my real name. This was seriously serious.

'Okay,' I said, but there really had never been any doubt that I'd do it. 'I'll look into it. But you have to know, your dodgy cousin may have dodged into something heavy, which is why he's on the lam.'

A laugh began in her eyes and then made it to her throat.

'What?' I said.

'I can't believe you just said "on the lam". You're such a tough guy. You should be in black and white and wearing a fedora.'

Her laugh finally erupted as I pushed her onto her back and loomed over her. I made a show of leering at her body. Believe me, it was no hardship. Unlike me, she'd kept herself very trim indeed. Again, I wondered what she saw in me. 'Listen, sister, I don't work cheap. You gotta pay the freight.'

She smiled, made a show of patting her chest and stomach, looking for pockets. 'I don't have any loose change on me, right now, Bugsy. Can I pay in kind?'

'Well…' I looked at her nakedness again, licked my lips in an exaggerated fashion. 'You know what I like at times like this.'

She wiggled closer to me, one hand running down my chest to where I was sucking in my gut. 'Oh, I know what you like, right enough,' she said, her voice even throatier than usual.

I leaned in, kissed her. It was a long kiss, all lips and tongues. I pulled away and said, 'So what are you going to do about it?'

She rolled her head back, her long neck inviting me to run my mouth along it but I had something more important in mind. 'Okay,' she said with a slight sigh. 'You want jam or marmalade on your toast?'

Continued in **Tag – You're Dead**

Also from Douglas Skelton

"A defining work by our finest emerging crime fiction talent."
QUINTIN JARDINE

"A breakneck thriller." MASON CROSS

"A natural successor to Ed McBain, Douglas Skelton gives us a
sharp and thrilling ride – a brilliant read." MICHAEL J MALONE

"Skelton really delivers with *The Janus Run* … a story that draws
you in and won't let go till the final page." CRAIG RUSSELL

"Ludlum meets Grisham in this fast-paced, fast-talking New York
City thriller. Fascinating, utterly compelling." DENZIL MEYRICK

"What do you get if you mix a deep-cover agent, a witness-
protected mob member, a psychotic killer and more action than
you can pull a trigger at? *The Janus Run*." GORDON BROWN

"Bullet-ridden, bold, brilliant … utterly unmissable."
NEIL BROADFOOT